IN HER CLOSET

THE LUST DIARIES: BOOK ONE

TASHA L. HARRISON

Tasha L. Harrison/Dirtyscribbler Press

Tashalharrison.com

Publisher's Note: This is a work of fiction. Names, characters, places, and incidents are a product of the author's imagination. Locales and public names are sometimes used for atmospheric purposes. Any resemblance to actual people, living or dead, or to businesses, companies, events, institutions, or locales is completely coincidental.

In Her Closet/ Tasha L. Harrison. -- 2nd ed.

ALSO BY TASHA L. HARRISON

THE TRUTH DUET

AMPERSAND STORIES

IF SHE SAYS YES

Coming soon...

THE ROSE & THE THORN

a small town romance

I'd love to hear from you!

Connect with me at:

Twitter | Instagram | Email

FOLLOW ME ON BOOKBUB!

Visit my website:

TashaLHarrison.com

You were wild once.
Don't let them tame you

—ISADORA DUNCAN

1

I woke with a start, struggling through an alcohol-induced fugue to sit up in a bed that wasn't mine. With dry eyes, sticky with last night's mascara, I took in my surroundings. Polished concrete floors gleamed in the sunlight, filtering in between the heavy curtains that covered a wall of windows. A rectangle of buttery yellow framed a contemporary nude portrait that hung on a soaring wall of exposed brick: a portrait painted by the man sleeping next to me--the talented, Jamaican-born Julian Webster.

He lay on his belly, exposing a broad back that tapered down to a narrow waist and a pretty little ass that the sheets barely covered. A smile spread across my face as I remembered how those powerful arms held me in midair while he lowered me onto his waiting dick. I rubbed my thighs. They were deliciously sore from our romp--yet another night of delicious, guiltless sex. Now, if I could escape without waking him, it would be perfect.

That wasn't going to be easy.

Fit and muscular, Julian looked like he spent as much

time at the gym as he did creating his one-of-a-kind paintings. His arm was thrown across my waist, trapping me in place.

I closed my eyes and channeled my inner ninja.

He took a deep, sonorous breath, and on his next growling exhalation, I shimmied out of his clutches and onto the floor. Not graceful, but at least I was free.

The concrete floor was warm, probably heated. I padded into the living space of the big, open loft as quietly as possible, hunting for my clothes. My panties -- tangled around my left ankles -- were easy enough to find. Shoes and bag were near the front door, but my dress was MIA.

I was pretty drunk when I stumbled into Julian's loft the night before, but not so drunk that I would have arrived naked. I'd worn a short, flirty Diane von Fürstenberg. It was a priceless find that I probably would've never been able to afford if I hadn't found it at my favorite consignment shop. My search for it would have to be quick because Julian's microwave clock said it was 7:15.

"Shit," I hissed under my breath before I grabbed my shoes and bag. I had a little over an hour to get home, change, and head to work.

I continued searching as quietly as I could. The place was huge. Developers had bought up most of the old factories and warehouses near the waterfront and converted them into lofts. I'd never actually been in one until now. The ceilings, which were composed of industrial steel and brick, soared upwards for about twenty feet. There were three main living spaces, and each had its own wall of levered windows, which Julian had covered with heavy drapes to control the light. The living room functioned as his workspace and was crowded with easels, paints, and half-finished portraits. As I admired one of these, I was startled by the sound of someone clearing their throat.

"Good morning."

I bit back a scream and clutched my naked breasts. "Holy fuck!" I cursed, turning around to find Julian leaning against a pillar at the center of the room, naked as the day he was born.

He was tall, much taller than he seemed last night, but that might have been because I was wearing skyscraper heels. The morning sun adorned his copper skin in a way that made him look like an Adonis. Still, those brown eyes gave away his youth and innocence, no matter how big and manly he was physically.

And he was oh-so-big and oh-so-manly.

Why am I rushing off again?

"Good morning," he said again. His voice was soft and deep with an island accent. I remembered that from last night, too. The way it murmured and moaned in my ear, telling me how good I felt to him. He grinned at me with a smile as sweet as plantain, and I had to cross my ankles to keep my knees from falling open.

"I w-w-was l-looking for my dress," I stammered. My eyes fixed on his semi-erect dick. Part of me knew it was counter-productive to stare at his dick when I knew I needed to get to work, but...fuck...it really was lovely.

"I can't say I approve of dat. Kinda like ya in this right 'ere," he answered, his eyes on my breasts.

Hmm...I wasn't the only one feeling a little distracted at the moment.

"I'm sorry..." For him and for me, but mostly for me. "But I've gotta get going. I have to be at work in an hour or so. Have you seen it?"

"Yeah... but things got a lick'il reckless last night."

I loved how Jamaican patois prettied up the English language, making little sound like lick'il and reckless, like something everyone should do at least once. I could listen to him talk all day. Except I didn't have all day.

Julian turned and headed back into the massive bedroom and walked right up to the enormous bed. "I'm sorry, star," he said, picking up a shredded heap of black fabric tangled in the sheets. "Ya dress didn't survive the tussle."

"Oh, no!" I gathered the shredded remnants in my hands. It was ripped straight down the seam. I couldn't wear this home. I wasn't even sure if it could be mended.

"Sorry, star," he said again and brushed my hair off of my shoulder. "Was it ya favorite or something?"

"Not my favorite, but pretty expensive."

"Lemme give ya somethin' so ya can replace it--"

"Nah, it wasn't your fault." I stood up and shook it off. Or at least I tried to. Damn my first and only Diane. And she was gone. "But I do need you to give me a shirt to wear, so I don't have to ride the train home like this."

Julian's eyes dragged up the length of my body. "What if I don't have anything that will fit ya? Will ya stay 'ere? In my bed?" He slipped his hands around my waist. "Surely, you can call off of work for one day..."

He leaned in and kissed me, and I swear I tasted the word yes on his tongue. Yes, I will get back in bed with you. Yes, I will fuck you all morning...

Yes, I will get fired if I didn't get my ass to work on time.

I pushed him away as gently as possible. "Listen, I would really love to, but..."

He placed another soft peck on my lips.

"Wait...what was I saying?"

"Some foolishness about how ya got to work," he mumbled against my mouth.

"Yes...work...work!" I pushed away from him. "Fuck! I really, really have to go."

"Oh," he said and backed away, looking like I'd stolen his bike. Clearly, he saw my need to maintain employment as some sort of rejection. Silly boy.

"Your bathroom?"

"Just over dat way," he said, pointing to his left. "There are towels and washcloths in the cabinet next to the sink."

"Thank you." I stepped around him and made my way toward the door he'd indicated. Once inside, I turned to survey a room that was roughly the size of my entire fucking apartment.

"Jesus," I muttered under my breath.

The cabinet he spoke of was large and hand-painted with a crazy amalgam of beautiful nudes, twisting and turning over each other until their skin, hair, eyes, limbs, and bodies created an abstract landscape. The bottom right corner of the cabinet was signed with his name.

Holy shit. This was Julian Webster's loft. I was in Julian Webster's loft. How the fuck did I, out of all the women that crawled all over him last night, actually end up in Julian Webster's loft?

Last night, Julian was part of a group show at a small, exclusive gallery in Old City. As the lifestyles and entertainment writer for the moderately prestigious Philadelphian, I was charged with attending and writing about what was quickly becoming Philly's most talked-about young artist. Barely twenty-four and a prodigy among his peers, Julian's contemporary nudes echoed a more stylized Gauguin with Klimt's sensual, erotic aesthetic. He was also a broody, reclusive type that made him damn near irresistible and pretty enough to make you stare. There was something to be said for a man brave enough to go completely bald. That smooth skin practically begged for the palm of my hand. He also sported what I liked to call the oops-I'm-sexy-beard; just enough scruff to remind a girl that she was kissing a man, not a boy. Every woman in the room had ogled him last night, but somehow I ended up chatting him up. Later, we wound up at a reggae club called The Dip, where I proceeded to get drunk off Jamaican rum and wine my waistline to some dancehall. After that, we--well, I had to stop thinking about what happened after that. If I started down that path, I would never make it to work on time.

I looked at my reflection in the mirror. The mass of dark brown hair that I had styled so carefully before going out last night was now all over my head. My large, honey-brown eyes were only slightly bloodshot. My lipstick had been kissed off, leaving my lips bare and looking thoroughly abused.

Morning after sexy--nailed it.

When I emerged from the bathroom, I found Julian in the kitchen pouring coffee into a travel mug. His sweet brown eyes lit up when he saw me.

"You drink coffee?"

"I'm pretty sure my blood is 75 percent caffeine."

He laughed. "How do you take it?"

"Black with a little sugar."

He smiled. "A girl after my own heart."

No, sweetie. I don't want your heart. I got what I wanted from you last night.

"Here's the shirt you asked for." He passed me the travel mug of coffee, then he came around the counter and picked up the shirt draped over the bar stool. Like a gentleman, he wrapped it around my shoulders. "I think it's long enough to cover the important bits."

I slipped my arms into the sleeves and stood still while he buttoned it for me. The shirt smelled clean, but like him, too. The scent of his cologne was soaked deep into the threads.

"Thank you," I said when he was done. "Maybe now I won't get arrested."

"Good thing. Still don't think ya will make it very far looking the way ya do. This attire is much better suited for my bedroom."

I pouted. "You know I don't want to say no, but...I have to go."

Here was the part I hated. The part where I had to dash his hopes when he asked to see me again. The part where I had to make up something clever to soothe a hurt ego so I could escape without the scene getting ugly. Luckily, Julian was the intuitive type. He didn't ask for my number. He just slipped his card in the breast pocket while giving me another one of those kisses that made me want to quit all of my jobs and live in his bed.

He walked me to the door, and as I stepped outside, a brisk early morning breeze tunneled through the courtyard. I shivered and wondered if I had enough money on me for a cab.

"I hope to hear from ya soon, Ms. Santiago. Until then, I look forward to reading the column ya write on me."

I kissed his cheek and gave him my best smile. "Good morning, Julian."

"Good morning, Yves."

Out on the street, I discovered I was still in Old City and easily found a bus heading up Market Street. I had just enough time to head home and grab a quick shower. I would be cutting it close, but it could be worse. It could be like the time I got drunk and woke up in Jersey and had to drag myself to work wearing some guy's tuxedo shirt...and nothing else. At least I had my underwear this time. There was nothing worse than sitting bare-assed on a plastic subway seat. Who knew what communicable diseases you could get that way?

On the bus, I sipped Julian's good, strong coffee, snuggled down in his shirt, and pulled out my phone. This bus ride was a gift. I could write my column and email it before I even made it all the way home. Thank God for smartphones. I probably would've been fired by now if it wasn't for the convenience of writing on a Septa bus or train after spending the night in a stranger's bed.

First, I wrote about Julian's work. It was hard to convey the vivid, dynamic impact of his paintings in words, but I tried, hoping the photos Ava, our staff photographer, and my best friend, took last night, would fill in what I left out. Then I wrote of the man himself, his passions and influences. His complete worship of the female figure and all its hills, valleys, and sweet, dark spaces. His boyish, dimpled grin. His calloused but gentle and deft hands. That fit body of his, which he used to its full advantage when he gave a brief demonstration of his technique.

Damn, the man was fine.

"Julian Webster..." I murmured. "Wait until I tell Ava."

I LIVED IN AN APARTMENT IN SOUTH PHILLY ON 8TH STREET between Washington Avenue and the famed South Street. Once upon a time, it was a single-family row house, but somewhere along the line, someone thought it was a grand idea to split the floor plan and make separate dwellings of the first and second floors. Both spaces were about seven hundred square feet. Tiny, but plenty of room for a single girl.

I loved my shitty little apartment, though entering said shitty apartment was always a bit precarious. Maniac, my scrawny, black cat, always tried to escape. Every time I opened the freaking door, she saw it as her opportunity to make a break for it. I guess that's what I get for trying to turn a stray into a house cat. I must have caught her off guard because I was already inside before she made her mad dash for freedom.

"Aha! Thwarted again!" I teased.

Maniac gave me a disinterested, haughty glare and returned to her perch in the living room window without so much as a meow. If I were the sensitive type, I might've taken it personally.

I dropped my bag under the hall table, slipped out of my shoes, and shucked Julian's shirt on my way to the bathroom. My underused apartment looked like the dusty, abandoned rooms of a spinster. I made a mental note to allot some time to clean it this week. It wouldn't be this morning, though.

While the shower heated up, I threw together an outfit and arranged for a cab to arrive in thirty minutes. Just as I was about to toss my phone on the bed, I noticed a voicemail and several emails waiting. I checked the email first. I'd pitched several articles and copywriting jobs at the beginning of last week and hadn't heard back yet. The first two were rejections. Ouch. Rejections weren't personal, but I had yet to grow immune to the sting. The next email was forwarded from the account attached to my anonymous sex blog, The Lust Diaries. Well, as anonymous as someone as low-tech as me could make it. If someone really wanted to find me, it wasn't that hard. This email proved that, I guess.

I started Lust Diaries a year or so ago. It was just a silly little something to do--a place for me to explore my sexuality and write about the men I slept with. Over the last year, it had grown in popularity, gaining more than a couple thousand subscribers--which isn't a lot compared to other sex blogs I follow, but a huge jump in readership, nonetheless. Once in a while, I toyed with the idea of monetizing it somehow, but I wasn't sure how I could make that happen and maintain my anonymity. Writing a sex blog made me a target. I received at least thirty emails a week from men who wanted to dominate me, be my daddy, spank me, and stuff my holes with their life-altering dick. Don't get me wrong, I wasn't opposed to the idea of life-altering dick, but I preferred a drink (or several) and a little conversation before I did the deed. As a result, I routinely deleted messages sent from my blog after only reading the subject line. But the subject on this one read: Regarding publication.

Curious, I opened it.

Good morning, Ms. Santiago,

I stumbled upon your blog last night, and I'm ashamed (and delighted) to say that I've read every entry from the first to last. I love what you have here. I would like to get together to discuss your work and present you with an opportunity to publish with Leaf Press.

Hope to hear from you soon.

. . .

Elijah Weinstein
Creative Nonfiction Editor
Leaf Press

I stood there for a moment, gawking at the message. Part of me wanted to call him immediately, but the logical, realistic part of me was instantly suspicious.

How did he know my name?

It seemed unlikely that the nonfiction editor of Philadelphia's largest publishing house would contact me this way. The blog wasn't connected to the work I did for the newspaper. I made sure of it. The last thing I wanted to do was shame my mother with the graphic telling of my drunken sexcapades, and I most certainly didn't want to jeopardize my job. There were no written rules about this sort of thing, but I imagine it wouldn't be welcomed, especially since most of those drunken escapades happened at or after events I covered for the paper.

My knee-jerk reaction was to delete this email and move on with my day. Yet, for some reason, I stopped short of deleting it and sent a quick response asking for more information, then marked it important. There was a remote possibility that this email could be a legitimate inquiry. I loved writing for The Philadelphian, but it was just a free weekly rag, geared toward young professionals and college students, which gave me credibility and kept the bills paid. Any sort of offer from Leaf Press would be undeniably amazing.

After saving Elijah Weinstein's info and checking a few more emails, I moved on to checking the only voicemail I had from last night.

"Yves..." a disembodied and too-familiar voice breathed from my phone's speaker.

Oh, hell, no. This better not be...

"I know we haven't talked in a while, but you've been on my mind a lot lately. I miss you--"

"What the fuck?" I cursed, deleting the message as aggressively as my phone's touchscreen would allow. Cesar Suarez. My ex-boyfriend. "How did he get this number?"

The answer to that question was obvious. Only one person would give my number to my ex, and that's my mother. This was so fucking irritating. What part of "we are over" didn't she get?

I sighed angrily, realizing that I would have to change my number again, and I had just ordered new business cards for this one. This had to stop. Me and Mamí needed to have a conversation about this--another one. Hopefully, she would hear me this time.

After the quickest shower ever, I grabbed my laptop bag, purse, and keys and went downstairs to wait on my stoop for the cab. The morning was already well on its way to sweltering. It felt good. I loved the summer. Part of me still associated it with those lazy, Italian ice, roller skating, water-sprinkler days of my childhood. Growing up was a huge letdown in that respect. Working at the Philadelphian and Burke's Books, a bookstore near my alma mater, left very little time for lazy summer days--even less now that I'd taken on freelance writing jobs to supplement my minuscule pay.

Down on our shared stoop, my elderly neighbor Mrs. Doris McKinney sat perched on the second step, working on what looked like her second cigarette. I sighed wearily and sat down next to her.

"Morning, Mrs. Mac."

"Mornin', little girl."

She knew I was twenty-five years old, but anyone younger than Mrs. McKinney must seem like an infant. The woman had to be at least seventy. She may have been pretty once, but now she was so heavily wrinkled that she resembled hand-wrung washing. She had a long salt and pepper braid that hung down to her waist, blue eyes slightly clouded with cataracts and a crabby attitude that scared the neighborhood kids. There was a Mr. McKinney, but he died a couple of years ago. Mrs. McKinney hasn't been the same since. She seemed a bit sadder--a bit slower. Her kids tried to make her move to a nursing home, but she put up such a fuss, they decided it was better to just leave her alone. They came by from time to time to check on her--take her to the grocery store, doctor's appointments, and such--but mostly it was just Mrs. McKinney and like ten cats. She kind of smelled like stale cigarettes and dirty kitty litter, but who was I to judge? Especially since Maniac was one of the feral kittens she fed, who had run into my apartment the day I moved in and never left.

"Can I bum a cigarette off you?"

Mrs. McKinney looked at me with her rheumy, blue eyes, and tapped out a cigarette. "If you have a habit, you should be able to support it."

I took it and pinched it between my lips. "I know, I know, but I thought I would try to quit."

"Didn't stick, huh?" She passed me a tattered book of matches.

I grunted, struck the match, and lit the long, thin cigarette. Mrs. McKinney smoked Virginia Slims. They tasted like shit, but they would do in a pinch.

"Late night?"

"Kinda." I gave her a sideways glance -- nosy, old bird.

"Were you out with your pretty boyfriend? The one that drives the shiny, Japanese sports car?" Mrs. McKinney waggled her bushy, grey eyebrows, and smiled mischievously. I couldn't help but laugh.

"No. I quit him."

"Hmm...He didn't stick either, huh?"

"Nope."

"Shame. I kinda liked him."

I frowned. "Really? Why?"

"He was always polite, and he helped me bring my groceries in once."

"Yeah, he was nice. Really good-looking, too." I smiled and took a drag of my cigarette. "He was a shitty lay, though."

"Oh!" Mrs. McKinney cackled with surprised laughter. "Well, good riddance!" she said, her boney shoulders shaking. "How many more do you think it will take?" she asked when she was done laughing at my expense.

"What do you mean?"

"How many more before one sticks?"

"I don't know," I said with a shrug. "I'll let you know when one finally does."

I didn't have the heart to tell her I wasn't really looking to make any of them stick. Falling into the beds of strange men topped my list of favorite pastimes. So much so that in the far back corner of my closet there lived an ever-increasing collection of shirts like the one I'd worn home this morning. A sort of shrine to my decadent nights. Those fabrics held the scent of the hungry strangers who knew me carnally but rarely knew my last name.

I wasn't always the sort of woman who would carelessly seduce a man to an end of my own design. That's not how my mother raised me. "Good little Catholic girls don't," as Luz Santiago always said. I used to feel a little bit of animosity toward her for that, though I knew I shouldn't. She was raised just as her mother was, so she knew nothing else. But there had to be more to life than being a good girl, a good wife, and a good mother. In fact, I've made it my personal business to find out.

My life's mission was to live as carelessly as a man. Eat what I wanted, drink what I wanted, and fuck who I wanted whenever I wanted. I wanted to do what felt good and make no apologies for any of it. In this life, there were only two people to answer to--God and yourself. And since God and I weren't really on speaking terms, that only left me, and I was just fine with how I lived my life. There were very few disasters and even fewer regrets.

My cab rounded the corner a few blocks up. I took a couple more puffs of the cigarette then flicked it into the tin can Mrs. McKinney kept by the steps for exactly that purpose. "Thanks for the cigarette, toots," I said with a wink as the cab screeched to a halt in front of me.

Mrs. McKinney waved me off with a dismissiveness that I knew was put on. She kind of liked me. I kinda liked the old bird, too.

2

The Philadelphian's offices were in what used to be some sort of old mill. Its worn brick facade and the slightly musty smell of the lobby never failed to inspire nostalgia in me. I started out as an intern in my junior year at Temple University, and they hired me right after college. As the entertainment columnist, dining out, attending balls, fundraisers, restaurant openings, and having all-night benders at the local bars were all in my job description. As a regular girl about town, I kept our readers abreast of Philly's hot spots with a few personal experiences thrown in for authenticity. Of my three jobs, it was easily the most fun.

With my column written, I just needed to do a quick check for errors before I emailed it to Louise, my editor. I just had to make it to my desk before she spotted me. Usually, she lurked near the receptionist's desk at the coffee station, so I figured I was home free when I didn't see her.

"Yves!" she barked the moment my ass hit the seat.

No such luck.

"You got my copy for your column?"

"Emailing it now!" I yelled back. It was just a little white lie. By the time asked me again, it would be waiting in her inbox.

"Damn, girl. You look like shit," Ava said as she made her way to my cubicle.

"Thanks," I answered dryly.

"I'm just saying. If you come out of the house like that, you really can't expect me to say something sweet to you. I love you too much for that."

"Well, damn..." I pulled out my compact to check my face and immediately cringed. Last night's rum binge had made itself known in the dark circles around my eyes.

"Let's go. I can't have you in my presence looking like that." She hefted her bag on her shoulder and dragged me out of my seat.

"But my column! I have to email it to Louise--"

"This will take all of five minutes. I just can't allow this,"--she gestured to my face -- "to continue. You gotta do better."

Ava and I had been friends since college, and we started working at the paper together four years ago. She was the resident photojournalist, but she looked and dressed like she ran the health and beauty column. Tall and model thin with flawless dark skin, a Naomi Campbell pout, and wide brown eyes, Ava turned plenty of heads, but it was her personality that won me over. She was straightforward, almost as crass as me, and spoke with the same brutal honesty that was my native language. For a minute there, I thought she might become my sister-in-law, but it didn't work out between her and my brother.

"Hop up on the countertop," Ava demanded.

I hopped up and crossed my feet at the ankles.

"So why do you look like something stuck to the bottom of someone's shoe?" she asked.

"Early morning trek from Old City."

"Yes, but what's with the Pollyanna ponytail?" she asked, twirling it for emphasis.

"It's all I had time for. I barely had time to run home and wash my ass."

Ava leaned in and smelled me. "Mmm hmm, you hit all the hot spots."

We both laughed. It was an ongoing joke between the two of us that I rarely had time for little more than what I jokingly called a "whore's bath," on the mornings after my late-night romps. It wasn't uncommon for me to come in smelling of men's cologne.

She pulled a mammoth-sized makeup case out of her shoulder bag and applied a foundation of mineral makeup with a fluffy brush. Ava had what bordered on an unhealthy addiction to beauty products. I absolutely admit to taking advantage of that addiction whenever possible.

"You've got to take better care of yourself," she murmured.

"Don't I know it?"

" So, who was it last night? Somebody from Julian's show?"

I grinned. "Not just somebody."

Ava frowned, then her eyes widened. "Nuh-uh."

"Yep."

"Julian Webster?"

I nodded.

"And you slept with him?"

I gave her a look that said you-know-better-than-to-ask-me-that-question because the answer was always yes, yes, and yes. I had no impulse control. If I saw something pretty, I wanted it. And that most definitely included swarthy, gorgeous young artists. But Ava knew this about me. I could be completely uncensored with her.

Ava finished my makeup. Afterward, we hung out in the bathroom and giggled like two schoolgirls as I retold my weekend adventures, and she filled me in on hers. We were so immersed in our storytelling, neither of us noticed how much time had passed until Louise appeared at the bathroom door.

"Either of you got my copy?" she interrupted.

I hopped off the countertop. "Gonna work on it right now, boss lady."

"Sure you are. Hey, some guy named Weinstein called from Leaf Press for you."

"What? How the fuck did he know I work here?"

Louise shrugged and passed me a yellow message slip. "Give him a call, will you? He seems to think that I'm your secretary."

"Sorry about that. I'll take care of it."

"I hope you do," she said as she turned to walk away.

Ava smacked my arm. "Someone from Leaf Press contacted you?"

"Yeah, but it was through my sex blog." I whispered as we neared our cubicles. No one but Ava knew about the blog at work, and I intended to keep it that way.

"So?"

"So I'm a little freaked out! How does he know I work here?"

"It's the internet, honey. It's not hard to find someone if you're willing to do the legwork. You're going to call him, right?"

"I have no idea what he wants."

"Well, obviously, he wants you to write something for him."

"But I haven't written a book--"

"What the fuck does that matter? Maybe he wants your editorial advice. Maybe he wants a blurb from you. But you know, it really doesn't matter what he wants, as long as he's paying. Call him now!" she demanded and bullied me back to my desk.

I sat and picked up the receiver of my desk phone, punched in the digits, and waited while the line rang.

"Good morning, this is Leaf Press. How may I direct your call?" the receptionist chirped.

"Uh, yeah, uh...Elijah Weinstein, please," I stammered.

"Hold one moment while I transfer you."

I chewed on my bottom lip nervously as she transferred me to Elijah Weinstein's line. This whole thing suddenly seemed like a much bigger deal. Why was he trying so hard to get in contact with me? Did he seriously want to publish my blog? And if he did, how did I feel about that?

"This is Elijah," he answered.

His voice caught me off guard. This wasn't a voice meant for the daytime, or strangers, or any place but the bedroom.

"Hi, I'm Yves Santiago? You've been trying to reach me?"

"Oh, yes! Yves! I'm so glad you finally called! How are you?"

Wow, excited much? "I'm okay. Though I'm wondering how you found me at this number."

"I have my resources," he answered cryptically.

"Well, you went to all this trouble...how can I help you?"

"I thought I made myself clear. I want to talk to you about publishing a book."

"I don't understand. I haven't written a book."

"Your blog, Ms. Santiago...I want to publish your blog. I think you really have something there. It's sexy and fresh, and I think it would make a brilliant book. Can we get together and talk about this?"

Publish my blog? "Uh, sure."

"Don't sound so nervous. This is a good thing."

"Says the guy who stalked me on the Internet..."

He coughed out a surprised laugh. "I can't deny that. But I promise you, it was for a good reason. How about this evening?"

"Shit! I mean--" Fuck! Did I just curse on the phone with an editor from Leaf Press? "I have to work, but I can call off--"

"No, that's not necessary. What time do you get off?"

"Eight o'clock."

"Well, I could meet you there. If that's okay with you?"

"Okay. Sure, we can do that."

"And where should I meet you?"

"Burke's Books? It's a bookstore near Temple University."

"I'm sure I can find it. So, I'll see you around 8:30, I guess? And maybe we could grab a drink or something?"

"Sounds great. It's a date." Date? I nearly groaned out loud. What else could I do to make a complete ass of myself on this call?

He laughed a bit, and that dark little chuckle immediately set me to wondering if this Elijah Weinstein looked as good as he sounded.

"Yeah," he finally agreed. "It's a date."

~

AFTER I HANDED IN MY ARTICLE AND GOT MY NEXT assignment for the paper, I went to my mother's for dinner. My childhood home was about ten blocks from my apartment. The old neighborhood was a few well-kept row houses with postage-stamp yards and cracked sidewalks under a canopy of trees. Nothing ever changed here. Kids still played on the sidewalks and rode their bikes in the street, just as I had when I was a kid. The residents of the mostly Latino block kept their doors open to welcome in the summer breeze. Through those open doors, I caught snippets of conversations in Spanish and heard the crooning of Hector Lavoe and Celia Cruz, as well as the over-the-top dialogue of telenovelas.

The aroma of dinner greeted me as I climbed the front steps. My mother cooked dinner six out of seven nights a week so that she could see us on a regular basis. I ate here almost every night. It was usually the one balanced meal in my day. My sister made an appearance about three times a week, even though she lived way out in Langhorne. The only person scarcely present at the table was my brother Marcelo. His job as a firefighter across the river in Camden, New Jersey, kept him pretty busy. He ate at the fire station most nights, but he tried to show up when he could. All in all, we were a close-knit family. Sometimes too close.

"Mamí!" I shouted as I walked through the door.

"¡Yves! Estoy en la cocina!" she called back.

I shook my head and laughed. Why did she bother to tell me that? She was always in the kitchen.

"¡Ven aquí! I want to talk to you. Come keep me company."

"Ya voy," I called back, dumping my bag and kicking off my shoes.

An old prom picture caught my eye as I made my way through the living and dining rooms into the kitchen. My sixteen-year-old self grinned at me from the frame, looking fresh and innocent. A lean, eighteen-year-old Cesar held me tight around the waist and smiled like he'd won the NBA championship.

"Incredible," I mumbled to myself.

I'd asked my mother to take that picture down so many times I'd lost count. Just like I'd asked her numerous times not to give him my number. Cesar and I broke up three years ago. Sure, he was never completely out of my life, but I didn't want to be reminded of that every time I visited her.

My mother stood over the stove in the kitchen, tending to pots steaming with smells that made my belly complain at its emptiness.

"Hey, chiquita," she said warmly. She always called me little girl. At five foot four, I was the smallest of her children.

My mother had an enviable natural beauty, though she rarely did anything to play it up. At fifty-three years old, she still had a trim, but curvy figure, and her long dark hair was salted with just a little bit of grey. She and my father had divorced years ago. I wondered, not for the first time, why she never remarried.

I walked over to where she stood and kissed her on the cheek.

"¿Como e'ta?"

"Good, I guess." I peeked into the pots and pans on the stove to see what she was making for dinner, some sort of stewed chicken and beans and rice.

"Get away from my stove."

I grumbled and opened the fridge to rummage for leftovers.

"Yves, we're eating in an hour."

"I can't wait an hour. I'm hungry now," I found a plastic bowl of cold spaghetti and ripped off the lid. After ingesting nothing but cigarettes and coffee all day, cold spaghetti seemed like a seven-course meal.

"So?" my mother implored.

"So, what?"

"How did it go? Did you meet any nice young men at the fundraiser?"

It took me a minute to catch up. I hadn't spoken to her since Friday, the night I accompanied my brother to the yearly firefighter's ball. I considered her question. Did I meet a nice young man? I guess the firefighter I met was nice enough. He told me how beautiful I was all night--even when he had his face between my legs. But that wasn't what my mother wanted to know when she asked if I met any nice young men.

And yes, that's two men in one weekend for anyone keeping count.

I climbed up on the countertop and ate the cold spaghetti with my fingers, purposely ignoring her question.

"Yves, use a fork," she complained and handed me the utensil. "So did you meet someone?" she asked again.

"I met someone."

"What's his name? Does your brother know him?"

I shrugged. "I don't know."

"What do you mean, you don't know? You don't know who he is, or you don't know if Marcelo knows him?"

"I don't know," I repeated.

My mother looked confused for a moment, but when she realized what I was implying, she sucked her teeth. "Chiquita, díos mío," she muttered and then made the sign of the cross. "When are you going to settle down?" she asked.

"I'm not the settling-down type."

"How would you know?" she asked, giving me a meaningful look. "You've never really tried it."

"Hey, since we're talking about settling down and all, I

thought you might want to know that I got a call from Cesar. Did you give him my number?"

"I saw him at the grocery store, and he asked about you. Said he was trying to get in touch, but the number he had was no good. I gave him your new one."

"Why would you do that?"

"Why not?" she asked with a shrug.

"Because I asked you not to."

"Aye, chiquita, that was months ago. I forgot."

Seriously? Was she seriously going to play dumb like she forgot? "Mamí," I began patiently. "Please, stop giving Cesar my number. I have nothing to say to him."

"How would you know? You haven't talked to him in ages--"

"What's to talk about? He's with someone else."

"He finally broke up with that girl. I never liked her. Even when you were friends. She always thought she was la gran caca. What sort of person goes around with the ex of her best friend? Thank God he finally got rid of her. She was no good for him, anyway."

"I would argue that it's probably the other way around--"

My mother turned to me. "And you're such a gem? Belleza se desvanece, chiquita. You would do well to remember that. You're not always going to be this pretty face drawing all the boys."

I rolled my eyes. "Mother, don't talk to me as if I'm so vain. You know I don't believe that--"

"What do you believe then, eh? You're running around with all these different men. What good does that do you?"

"How did this get turned around on me? Stay on topic. I asked you not to give Cesar my number. It's a hassle to keep changing it over and over again."

"Why change it? Just talk to the man! You nearly married him three years ago, Yves. There has to be something there."

"Ma, we are over."

"What's over? Nothing's over. What could he have done that is so impossible to forgive?"

I had to literally bite my tongue to keep from telling her. There were so many things that my mother didn't know about what went on between Cesar and me. Things I would never tell her because it would break her heart. She loved that boy just as much as I did--probably more. My brother and Cesar were best friends when we were growing up. She treated him like a son. He was a part of our family, which didn't make it easy for me to decide not to marry him. I had my reasons, but I'd kept them secret for so long that it seemed wrong to bring it up now if I never brought it up back then. It felt slanderous, like I was trying to bad-mouth him or something, which couldn't be further from the truth. The real truth was that I didn't want to hurt him, even though he had hurt me in so many ways.

I just wanted him out of my life.

"Mamí, look. I don't want to fight, but I need you to hear me when I say I don't want to talk to Cesar."

"Fine," she said and turned her back to me. "If that is how you want to live your life. Fine."

My niece Tatiana bounded into the kitchen, sing-songing her hellos, and ended the uncomfortable conversation. I was glad. These talks seemed to be the only kind I had with my mother lately. All of my choices were wrong or questionable, according to her. My mother had an entirely different idea of the type of woman I should be, and that idea was in stark contrast to the way I lived my life. Her ideals were deeply rooted in her religion, and in her opinion, I should be married to Cesar and working on our third kid by now.

Mercedes came in, cradling her youngest daughter Sacha in her arms. "Hey!" she chirped and kissed me on the cheek.

Three years younger, a shade lighter, and a touch skinnier--despite the two kids--my baby sister looked just like me. She wore her hair straight and cut in a bob where my mane angled toward a kinky, tangled mess. Her style was more cute department store than expensive consignment shop finds like mine, but she was far from a soccer mom.

"What's going on in here?" she asked. Obviously, feeling the leftover tension from me and Mamí's conversation.

"Nothing. Where'd Tatiana go?" I asked. Sacha reached for me with chubby, grabby hands, and I took her from my sister's arms. I could never resist her beautiful little face.

"Already glued to the TV. Do you need a hand, Mamí?" she asked, grabbing an apron.

"Of course. You can finish off the beans and rice."

My sister stepped right in beside Mamí, and I stepped back to observe the two of them. They were like matching bookends. Sometimes I envied the ease of their relationship. The older I got, the less I seemed to have in common with them.

The front door banged open, startling us all. "Yves Alphonsa!" my brother Marcelo's voice bellowed.

"Yeah, we're back here in the kitchen," I called out.

Marcelo's work boots shook the floor as he made his way back to where we were. When he appeared in the doorway, and I saw his face, I was taken aback. Somebody was angry. He looked just like our father when he swelled up like that. We all had Papí's hazel eyes, but only Marcelo had his heavy, thick eyebrows and coarse hair. "Black behind the ears," as my mother called it, but looking the way we do, we just called ourselves Black.

"¿Que paso?" I asked.

"I should be asking you that."

"What do you mean?"

"Robbie Sirrillo dropped by the station house this afternoon. He asked about you."

"Is that name supposed to mean something to me?"

"Uh, yeah. Don't you know Robbie Sirrillo?"

"No..." I responded apprehensively.

"He's the deputy-fucking-fire chief, Yves!"

"And?"

"That's my fucking boss, Yves. You fucked my fucking boss--"

"Marcelo!" my mother cautioned.

"Do you realize how embarrassing it was to have him walk in the station and ask about my sister and if she made it home okay the next morning?"

I chuckled, which only made Marcelo more upset. "Is that why you came storming in here, calling me by my Christian name? You have nothing to worry about, Marcelo. Believe me."

"You have got to be kidding me. This is not a joke. This is my life we're talking about."

"It's not your life; it's your job. And trust me, you don't have to worry about Robbie Sirrillo. He had a very good time. If anything, he will keep you close in hopes of seeing me again. I helped you out, hermano."

"Oh, my God! I can't even talk to you!" Marcelo said before he stormed out of the room.

"Ohh-kay, overreact much?" I muttered. I turned around to find my mother and sister staring at me like I had tempted Christ himself. "What?" I asked defensively.

"You better watch what you do, chiquita. All of this is going to come back on you. Mark my words," my mother warned with a shake of her finger.

I rolled my eyes. "And I guess all of you will be happy to see that finally happen, eh? Selfish, narcissistic Yves finally gets her comeuppance?"

"It's inevitable, Yves. The way you treat people, you're going to end up alone when you least want to be," Mercedes added, in complete agreement with our mother, as usual.

My brother came back into the kitchen. He took the baby out of my arms and gave her to Mercedes. "Come here. We need to talk," he said, shoving me toward the door that led to the tiny backyard.

I have always felt closer to my brother than to my sister. During my early adolescence, Marcelo and I were inseparable. Back then, he probably thought of me as the annoying kid sister, but I always looked up to him. That didn't mean I liked it when he went all patriarchal and scolded me, but considering that I had fucked his boss, I had to hear him out.

"Look, I'm sorry I yelled at you."

"Apology accepted. I'm sorry I slept with your boss or whatever. I didn't know that's who he was."

Marcelo shook his head. "Yves, you're my sister, and I love you, but don't you think this shit is getting out of hand?"

"What shit?"

"Don't get cute with me. You know what shit I'm talking about. All these guys... it's getting out of hand."

I threw up my hands. "Jesus, you, too?"

"I'm just concerned about you, Yves. It's no good for you to be getting around like this. You know how guys talk--"

"Would you say the same thing to me if I had a dick?"

"Don't make it about that--"

"But that's what it's really about, isn't it?"

"Of course not! I just don't understand what's going on with you, Yves. I'm worried about you. I mean, at first, I thought it was just a phase. I figured that when you got over this breakup with--"

"Don't you say his name to me!" I warned.

He paused, and a frown darkened his brow. "¿Qué?"

"First Mamí and now you. You guys just love to invoke his name--"

"Look, the guy is a dirtbag. I'm not saying you guys should get back together. He has a baby with that girl. He made his decision. I'm talking about you, Yves. What's going on with you? Talk to me."

"Nothing!" I said with a shrug. "I'm just having fun."

"You really expect me to believe that all this fucking is about having fun?"

I grinned. "It is when you do it right." å

He rolled his eyes. "I'm serious."

"So am I. There's nothing to worry about. I'm fine."

"You sure?"

"Absolutely."

"Okay."

He pulled me in for a hug. I relaxed into it. Marcelo smelled like Irish Spring and ash. He'd fought a fire before he came home. My brother, the hero.

"If there was something wrong, you would tell me, right?"

"Of course," I said, even though we both knew that I wouldn't.

It was hard to make my family understand that none of this felt wrong to me. The way I'd lived before, losing myself in a guy that felt more wrong than living my life on my own terms. The idea of settling down with one man for the sake of marriage and family seemed silly to me now. Maybe that was selfish, but as far as I was concerned, selfishness was a virtue. Too many selfless people ended up used, unhappy, or just plain victims. The way I saw it, in the end, someone always gets used and discarded, and I would rather be the user than the one who gets used up.

3

"Big crowd tonight," my manager Thompson Burke said as we set up folding chairs around the makeshift stage for the monthly poetry reading at Burke's Books.

"Yeah, looks like that Facebook page I set up is doing its job."

"Okay, okay. You were right," he groused. "It's not something my father would've done, but it did work."

I smiled at my boss's half-assed compliment. "You know, if we get a lot of traffic from that page, we can start posting videos of the readings."

"Don't get ahead of yourself, Yves."

As the largest and oldest bookstore in South Philly, Burke's Books was practically a historical landmark and was one of the few independent bookstores left in the city. It was definitely one of the few that was still family-owned and a favorite haunt of many aspiring novelists, poets, and journalists, including me. Poetry night was popular, and I often read a piece or two, even if I was working. I signed up to read a little something tonight, but found it difficult to pay attention to the poets on stage. Every time the door opened, it drew all of my attention because I hoped that the next person to step through would be Elijah Weinstein.

He told me he would be wearing a charcoal-grey suit and a green tie. I scanned the room, but I didn't see a Jewish guy in a suit and tie. I checked the clock on my cell phone--eight forty-five. Had he changed his mind? It seemed unprofessional to stand me up, but why else would he be so late? It upset me, but how disappointed could I be when it was only a half-realized dream to begin with?

"Calling the poet Yves Santiago."

Well, that was quick. I was tenth on the list, and somehow they had blazed through the first nine poets already. I stood and wiped my sweaty hands on my jeans while making my way across the room. Reading my poetry in front of a crowd still made me nervous, even though I'd been doing it since college.

The stage was little more than a square platform with secondhand couches and folding chairs angled around it. I stepped up to the mic and pulled my phone out of my back pocket, opening the app I'd written my poem on earlier. I didn't need it, but I liked to have it, just in case I lost my way.

"Good evening. I'm Yves Santiago," I said, introducing myself to the room. My voice bounced off the back wall, and I hated the way it sounded when it made its way back to me. Any other time I fancied that it was deep and sultry, but up here, it sounded high and nervous.

"This is more of a ramble than a poem. I call it 'Sleek and Tawny.'"

I cleared my throat, closed my eyes, and took a deep cleansing breath to steady my nerves before I recited the poem from memory:

She's lost all the parts of her that were pretty.
Her shine and nubile beauty wore off long ago.
Rubbed off--rubbed raw by men.
She's nothing sweet anymore.
She's something feral,
something wild.
Sleek and tawny. Un animal.
Something constantly in search of something--
someone to devour.
She sees her prey, and when he passes her way
the scent of him enlivens her.
She pursues him because in this moment, he
is what she needs.
What she hungers for.
That tender morsel she draws across her teeth
hungrily...
But when her passion is spent
she remains discontent
until a hint of some other succulent scent
rattles her cage.

When I opened my eyes, a wave of satisfaction washed over me at seeing the appreciative smiles from the crowd.

"Thank you," I murmured, backing away from the microphone to a chorus of whoops and applause. The instant gratification of reading in front of an audience thrilled me like nothing else. It was the immediacy of knowing that I got it right...that a room full of people understood exactly where I wanted to take them with my words.

A man approached me as I walked back to the cash wrap

to collect my bag and head home -- a damn fine man. Mmm, tasty, I thought as he offered me a smile.

"Yves Santiago?"

"Yes?"

"I'm Elijah Weinstein," he said, thrusting out his hand. "It's a pleasure to meet you."

I could barely keep my mouth closed. This was Elijah Weinstein? If so, he was staggeringly attractive. Belatedly, I realized that he wore the charcoal-grey suit and green tie I'd been searching for all night. The color of his tie complemented his moss-green eyes. He reached for my hand and shook it, holding on far longer than was necessary for a greeting. Our hands swayed between us--a frizzle of friction forming between our palms.

"Nice to meet you," I sighed, trying my best to keep from licking my lips.

"Sorry, I'm late. I got a little lost."

"It's okay. You want to have a seat?" I offered, gesturing to the table a little ways from the stage.

"Of course, thank you."

We sat, and I couldn't help looking him over again. Elijah Weinstein didn't look anything like the man I'd expected. I thought I would be sitting across from a short, balding Jewish guy. The man who sat across from me was a tall, Abercrombie & Fitch model type with wavy, light brown, almost dirty blond hair and one of those goddamn sexy-ass smiles that made me weak--one that spread across his full lips like a secret. And that look on his face--both guarded and inquisitive. Was the curiosity that I saw there about me? I felt a familiar tingle of lusty heat between my thighs.

Tranquilo, Yves. Keep it professional.

"So you look nothing like I thought you would," he admitted as if he'd been reading my thoughts.

"Oh? What were you expecting? Blonde? Buxom? Legs up to my neck?"

A shy smile pulled up the corner of his mouth. "Not quite like that, but mostly I didn't expect you to be so..." he paused for a long moment, searching for the right words. "Exotic," he finished.

"Exotic?"

He blushed. "Shit, I meant--"

"Food is exotic. Animals and destinations are exotic."

"I'm sorry I didn't mean to offend--"

"Oh no, I'm not offended," I interrupted. "But next time, you can just tell me that I'm beautiful."

"Well, you are beautiful."

"I'm flattered that you think so."

"Well, I'm flattered that you're flattered," he said. That shy smile spread across his lips again. The blush in his cheeks deepened and spread down his neck.

He's not going to make this easy.

He cleared his throat. "So you write poetry? I had no idea."

"I like to think that I can write anything, but poetry was my start. Like all writers, I have a notebook somewhere filled with super-angsty, teenage poems."

"Angst? What reasons did you have to feel angst as a teenager?"

I leaned back in my chair, crossed my legs, and smiled. "Don't all teenagers feel angst? I wasn't always this exotic creature you see before you," I answered jokingly. "I had my share of pimples and unrequited love."

"I can hardly believe that. I haven't even been sitting here for ten minutes, and I'm already in love with you."

Was he flirting with me? Naughty, naughty, naughty. I shook my head and laughed to myself. I would eat you alive, Elijah Weinstein. "How about we head out and get those drinks?"

I COULD TELL BY THE LOOKS OF HIM THAT ELIJAH WEINSTEIN frequented trendy bars and nightclubs, so I took him to a place that was completely the opposite, Donnie Darla's on South Street. DD's was probably best described as a dive bar -- my favorite kind of place. I preferred dark, seedy bars and hookah stands to the local club scene. I ordered us the city-wide special--Pabst and a shot of Jim Beam--and we sat down at one of the sticky, wobbly tables for a chat.

We'd talked a little bit on the way over. Elijah was a New Yawker but didn't have much of an accent. He didn't hesitate to tease me about mine, though. He also joked about my height. I'd consciously dressed down for this meeting because I didn't want to get my hopes up, plus I'd had to work before my meeting. Now I wished I had worn the damn stilettos. Without them, I barely cleared the middle of his chest. I guess that would make him over six feet. Perfect height. Not that I considered him potential arm candy, but six-foot-plus left room for my sky-high heels.

He flirted nonstop on the walk over, too. I didn't know how to feel about that. Ahh, please. Who was I kidding? I loved it. But this didn't feel like a meeting. It felt more like a date.

"So, about your blog, what made you decide to write it in third person?"

"Now you want to talk about my blog? Now that you've got me all liquored up?"

He laughed, and it did things to me. Things below the

waist. The boy had a gorgeous mouth on him. A mouth meant for kissing, and I didn't necessarily mean the lips on my face.

"Well, I guess we should get around to it. It's kind of the whole point of our meeting."

"I guess you're right. And to answer your question, it's just the way I've always written."

He nodded with approval. "I love it. I like how it mirrors what you write in your column for the Philadelphian. A dark and light view of the same night."

I smiled, secretly pleased that he understood the concept. "To be honest, the blog was just a silly something I started doing to siphon off the sexed-up bits I always seemed to be writing about the events I attended. I really wish I could include it in my column, but the gatekeeper says no."

"Either way, you've done a brilliant job of it."

"Thank you, but you really don't think it's brilliant, do you? It's just some bullshit blog with a minuscule following."

"Look...I gotta be honest, here. My motives aren't entirely innocent."

"Oh?" I asked with a raise of my brow. "You have a nefarious motive?" I leaned in close and whispered, "Is it dirty? Tell me it's dirty!"

He coughed out a nervous laugh. I'd caught him off guard.

"What? No! Not nefarious or dirty. It's just...I am a huge fan. It was the reason why I had to track you down. This duality that you've created between your blog and your column, translating your love for the city into your love of men...you write about Philly like you're in love with this city. You made me fall in love with it, too. And your sex blog... it has a raw intensity, yet literary quality I haven't seen before."

Whoa, gut shot. Had anyone ever said anything like that about me before? Forget me, had anyone ever said anything like that about my writing? I couldn't think of one instance when I'd felt as proud as I did right now.

"I have another confession to make," he said, staring down into his empty shot glass.

"What's that?"

"I got promoted to creative nonfiction editor at the beginning of the year, and I need a breakout book to cement my position. I've been reading memoirs for months, and honestly, I can't think of a story that I want to hear more than yours."

My face grew hot, and I leaned away from him. "Laying it on a little thick, aren't you?"

He shook his head and smiled. "Is my flattery making you uncomfortable?"

"Just a little bit," I admitted when I meant to lie.

He leaned into the space I'd left between us. "Maybe because you're afraid it's true?" Sometime during the evening, Elijah had loosened his tie and unbuttoned the top button of his shirt. A tiny bit of gold winked at the hollow of his throat--the Star of David on a thin gold chain. Suddenly I was aware of his shoulders. Very aware. They were broad and strong and would be the perfect place to hook my knees.

I cleared my throat. "Maybe."

Elijah rested his elbows on the table. "Tell me why you started writing."

"Well, I always kept a journal when I was a kid, but when I got to high school, I began to take writing more seriously. My teachers noticed that I had a knack for it."

"That's not the real reason you started writing."

"It isn't?"

"Nope."

I leaned in and rested my elbows on the table, too. "Then, what was it?"

"You tell me," he said with a shrug of those amazing shoulders. "What compelled you to set pen to paper and write down your thoughts?"

I didn't need to think hard. The answer sat on the tip of my tongue. A response too pathetic to admit.

"It was a boy, wasn't it?"

Fuck if he didn't nail it. "Yes."

"And it was a boy you weren't supposed to love?"

"Yes," I answered again and left it there, though I could tell he wanted more of an explanation.

"That's the story I want to read."

He had no fucking idea what he was asking of me. "Well, it's not necessarily a story I want to write."

"Is he why you write in third person? To get some distance from it?"

I narrowed my eyes at him. "Are you some kinda psychic or something?"

His lips parted into another smile, and now that raunchy mouth of his drew my attention again...and reminded me how much I wanted to kiss it. That thing really needed an NC-17 rating.

"No. I just pay attention. Like the poem you recited tonight."

"What about it?"

"Is that how you really feel about yourself? That you're some sort of hedonist drawn to the scent of your prey? I don't see you that way at all, but I think that's how you want people to see you." He narrowed his eyes. "I think it's just something you do to keep people at a distance. To keep them from knowing you."

Too close. I felt him right under my skin. I backed away. Actually pushed my chair away from the table a little bit. I needed to create some space. Diffuse this sudden intimacy with a joke or witticism--something to lift the tension.

"Elijah, I--"

His big hand shot out and wrapped around my wrist. I froze. That harmless bit of contact made me sit still and hold my breath. It also made me feel positively tiny and more than a little helpless. My heart pounded right up to my throat and echoed in my ears. It was so loud that I barely heard him when he said, "I know this all feels a little...intense. But I wanted you to see that I have a real interest in you. There's a story there. A story about how you came to be this beautiful, uninhibited woman sitting across from me. I want to know it."

He let go of my hand, and slowly my heart rate returned to normal, and I could breathe again.

"A little intense?" I squeaked.

"I'm sorry. I get that way when I'm passionate about a thing."

"Wait a minute." A sudden sinking fear gripped me. In my excitement about his interest in my writing, I hadn't even considered the fact that he might not be who he said he was. I hadn't even asked him for a business card. "Seriously, how the fuck do you know me?"

"I told you. I found your blog."

"The blog is anonymous--"

"And published on a public blogging platform that is forwarded to your personal email. If you want to keep it private, you should be more careful about how you respond to emails. It wasn't hard to follow the bread crumbs from there."

I wasn't very tech-savvy, and I'd made that mistake more than once. There was no way to know if he was telling me the truth. The fact that he had an answer so readily available made me less and more worried at the same time.

"By the way, that journal you talked about earlier, do you still keep it?"

"Of course. I mean, the blog functions as a journal of sorts now, but yeah. I still have all my old ones. Why?"

Elijah Weinstein smiled, big and bright like a schoolboy. It was so fucking genuine that my wariness fled instantly.

"Perfect. Let me tell you my idea."

We talked well into the night, and when the bar closed, we walked the streets of my neighborhood. He wanted me to write the book in the same vein as my blog--a memoir, of sorts. But he wanted me to start further back to show how I came to be the woman that I am now. It was flattering that he wanted to know these things about me and believed in my writing. In his eyes, I saw an open admiration and honest to God interest--almost as if he was in awe of me. I couldn't remember the last time someone looked at me that way. Hell, I couldn't remember the last time a man looked at me with something other than lust.

Though I definitely saw that in his eyes too.

AT AROUND 3 A.M., WE FINALLY FOUND OUR WAY TO MY BLOCK. All was quiet. Well, all was quiet except for Maniac yowling in my open living room window.

"This is me," I said as I stepped up on the stoop.

"Oh." He looked and sounded genuinely disappointed.

I leaned against the door and stared at him for a good,

long minute. That shy blush crept back into his cheeks, making them ruddy under his deep, brown tan. This blond Jew was a delicious contradiction. Forward and digging around in my head one moment, shy and blushing on my doorstep the next. It also didn't hurt that he was so ridiculously gorgeous. During our chat this evening, my attraction had risen to a nearly irresistible level. It was strange to me. He looked nothing like my usual type. I liked pretty boy thugs. Brawlers. Rough boys. Elijah Weinstein looked like he'd just stepped out of a rugged runway model, and strangely...I liked it. I liked it a-really-fucking-lot. I had to applaud myself for not jumping him hours ago.

"Let me ask you something," he began a bit apprehensively.

"Okay."

"Your blog, what you write in it...is it all true?"

I smiled and slipped my hands into the pockets of my jeans. "That's not the question you really want to ask."

"What do I really want to ask?"

I moved in close enough to look deep into his green eyes and ran my fingers through the silky wave of his dirty blond hair. Fuck, his hair is soft. I fisted it in my hand and yanked him closer. "You want to know if you can come upstairs."

He smiled. "I can't say the thought didn't cross my mind."

That sexy, full mouth of his was close enough to kiss. I waited for him to close the gap, but he didn't. His inaction made it easier to push him away, along with all my devilish thoughts.

"I think we should try to keep this professional," I whispered. Try being the operative word in that sentence. All of my words lacked conviction because my mind was spinning off to thoughts of me ripping off his neat Ralph Lauren suit and kissing his chest.

How very Harlequin romance, I thought with a giggle.

Elijah backed away a little and nodded. "You're right."

Don't give me the eyes.

He looked up at me through the blond fringe of his lashes.

Shit... he's giving me the eyes.

"Well, here's my business card. You will give my proposal some thought, right?"

"Of course. I'll give both of them some thought," I added slyly.

He coughed a short, nervous laugh. "Well, I hope I've given you enough to persuade you to take me up on at least one of them."

"You have," I said, and looked him right in the eye. I wasn't about to cross the line, but if he were to press just a little bit, I wouldn't resist.

"Goodnight, Yves. It was wonderful to finally meet you." He embraced me with his eyes for a long moment that nearly weakened my resolve. Somehow I mustered up the effort to turn away and unlock the door to my apartment.

"I'll be in touch," I said and ducked into the dank hallway of my apartment stairwell.

Once I was inside with the door safely locked behind me, I sighed and leaned against it. A little thrill of excitement rushed through me, and not just from the near kiss that happened with the dead-sexy man I'd left on my stoop.

Holy fuck. A book?

I wanted to call someone and share my news, but no one would answer at this hour. Wow. It was more than a little pathetic that I didn't have anyone I could share the news with.

With no one else to tell, I grabbed my phone and

opened my Twitter app, and tweeted these thoughts in quick succession to my two thousand followers.

> *@SantiSexy: I think something amazing just happened to me.*

> *@SantiSexy: Something so amazing that I hardly believe it's real. I'm afraid to say it out loud.*

WITHIN SECONDS, AN ALERT APPEARED IN MY DIRECT messages...from Elijah.

> *@EWeinstein: It's real. It's happening.*

> *@EWeinstein: Just say it to yourself really quietly until you believe it.*

"I'M GOING TO WRITE A BOOK," I MURMURED. "HOLY FUCK. I'M gonna write a book!"

Wait....

> *@SantiSexy: You follow me on here?!?!?*

> *@EWeinstein: have been for a while. Told you I was a fan.*

Immediately I worried about the things I had tweeted in

the last few days. Oh, my God. Did I tweet about the firefighter? Or Julian?

> *@EWeinstein: I'm especially fond of the "in bed" and "bathtub" tweets...and the attached pics.*

> *@SantiSexy: You have a filthy mind. I dig that about you. ;)*

> *@EWeinstein: You have no idea. I really wanted to kiss you tonight, but you're right. We should keep things professional.*

> *@SantiSexy: grrr....you're a filthy tease.*

> *@EWeinstein: Not usually, but I'll behave from here on out. G'night, Yves.*

DAMN... HAVING AN EDITOR AS FINE AS ELIJAH WEINSTEIN was definitely going to make writing this book a challenge.

"But who fucking cares? I'm gonna write a book!"

I climbed the stairs to my apartment. Maniac padded over to me, mewing and weaving herself in and out of my legs. I didn't spend more than an hour at home today. That probably qualified as neglect. I picked her up and nuzzled my face into her fur.

"Hey, crazy. Guess what? Mama's gonna write a book. What do you think of that?" She mewed and purred. "Yes, I'm slightly amazing. Secretly, quietly amazing." I muttered to my curiously affectionate cat. I dropped her down to empty out my bag. When I went to plug in my phone, it started ringing.

Do Not Answer flashed across the screen.

I dismissed the call, but I noticed that I had messages from the same number.

Fuck.

The messages were from Cesar. I knew that before I even opened the app. Deleting them without listening to them was the best thing to do. But knowing it was the best thing and actually doing it were two different things.

"Fuck it," I muttered again and listened to the messages.

First message: "Yves, it's about seven-forty-five in the morning, and I'm crossing Front and Chestnut, and I swear...I swear I just saw you. Who the fuck am I kidding? I know it was you. Your hair was all crazy and wild like it is when you first wake up. You had on some guy's shirt and that sexy smile that I love. You know the one--the one that you wear when you've got some dirty secret? Like the one you were wearing that day when I met you in Fairmount Park and when you begged me to fuck you. Do you remember? Anyway, I saw you wearing that smile, and it pissed me off. I was jealous. I know that you hate that about me, but I was jealous that someone else made you smile like that. I wish it was me that made you smile like that."

Next message: "Okay, so, seeing you this morning has me a little fucked up right now. I miss you, Yves. I know it was three years ago, but it feels like fucking yesterday."

A long pause filled the line, and I could hear him swallowing back tears. The sound of him breaking down brought a tight lump to my throat and that all-too-familiar ache to my chest.

"I broke up with Gabby. I know that probably doesn't mean much to you. You probably have someone but, fuck,

Yves. I love you. That shit doesn't go away just because I don't say it anymore. I love you. It wasn't supposed to be like this. I wish you would call me. Talk to me...I need to hear your voice."

Next message: "It's like, one in the morning and I'm sitting in my truck praying that this phone will ring and it will be you on the line. I swear if you were to call, I would come over in a heartbeat. I would take you in my arms and never let you go. I would keep every promise I ever made to you. I know you don't want that now. I know I should accept that, but I can't. I just can't. I know I'm fucked up, and I didn't treat you right, but I'm not that man anymore. I wish you would give me a chance to prove it to you, Yves. Please, call me...anytime...te amo."

My finger hovered over the delete button...but I couldn't make myself do it. Instead, I pressed the playback button and went to my closet. Way in the back, next to my cerulean-blue prom dress, I found what I was looking for--a tattered and stained Eagles sweatshirt. I pulled it off the hanger and brought the soft, fleecy fabric to my nose. It had faded over the years, but a hint of it still lingered there. His scent. Cesar's scent. I took off all my clothes, and pulled the sweatshirt on over my head, felt it tickle against my bare skin. I pulled the hood up so that I could feel and smell him all around me.

Alone in my apartment and wearing his clothes, I gave myself permission to forget all the bad shit. I forgot about Gabby, my best friend who got pregnant with his baby right after we broke up. I forgot all the fights, all the yelling. Forgot the way he hurt me with his words and his hands. I forgot all the bad and just sat in the love I couldn't help but feel for him.

Fucking, Cesar.

I hated that my mother gave him my number. I hated that I let him affect me like this in a moment when I should be happy. He probably could sense that. He knew me too well. He knew just what to say. He knew all the ways in and slipped through the cracks when I least expected it.

Why can't he just stay out of my life?

I fell asleep on my couch, cuddling with my cat, surrounded by his scent and the sound of his voice.

4

On the Fourth of July, my old neighborhood hosted an annual block party. It was one of those events that nobody ever missed. Most of the neighborhood kids were all grown up, and some had families of our own now, but we all made an effort to show up.

We blocked off both ends of the street with cars, and the space between them was filled with picnic tables, paddling pools, lawn chairs, and barbecue grills. Hotdogs, burgers, ribs, and corn on the cob were cooked over an open flame and devoured by kids and adults alike. The more patient among us waited for the slow-cooked pork to come out of the smoker. That tender white meat and the grilled yuca were my favorite. Lawn chairs sat ready and waiting for nightfall, angled to watch the fireworks at Penn's Landing. Of all our traditions, I loved and looked forward to this one the most.

Marcelo manning the grill when I arrived. Mercedes sat at our family picnic table with baby Sacha on her knee. My other niece Tatiana played with some kids nearby.

I went to my brother first. "Hey," I chirped at him and

held up my bags filled with the plantains, avocados, and beer they asked me to bring.

"No, Ava?" he asked, looking over my shoulder.

I shook my head, and he grunted in disappointment. Ava and Marcelo broke up a couple of summers ago. Neither of them liked to talk about it, but something told me they were still messing around. Ava denied it, but my brother asked after her every chance he got.

He gestured toward the coolers near our picnic table, and I unloaded them.

Next was Mercedes. I greeted her with a kiss on the cheek as well. "So, what did I miss?"

"Nothing much. The usual squabble over music and whose roast pork is better. We haven't seen you in a week or so. How're you doing?" she asked.

I was bursting to tell them about Elijah's book proposal. Neither of them followed me on any social media. As Mercedes liked to say, they would rather not know all the intimate details of my day, which I could understand.

"Well, I do have a bit of news."

"Oh? News about what?" she asked.

"Well...remember that blog I started a few years ago?"

"The sex one?"

"Yeah, well, I've been approached by a publishing company to make it into a book."

Mercedes stared at me, her eyes stretched wide. "That's a really excellent opportunity and all, but I hope you're not going to do it."

Her response shocked me. I waited a moment to see if she was going to attempt to correct herself or take it back, but she didn't. "Why would you say something like that?"

"Because...the stuff you write on that blog is really explicit."

"So?"

"So you represent more than yourself. If you write some book chronicling your sexcapades, how do you think it will reflect back on us?"

"Are you being serious right now, Mercedes? You expect me to turn down this once-in-a-lifetime opportunity because it might reflect badly on the family?"

"Really, Mercy. It's not about us," Marcelo chimed in.

"How can you say that, Marcelo?" she asked.

"The blog is anonymous. She doesn't mention us in her work--"

"How hard do you think it will be for someone to figure out who she really is? People get outed on the Internet every day. I don't understand how you think this is okay." Mercedes turned to look at our brother. "You're okay with your sister writing a book about all the guys she slept with? You just went off on her a few days ago because she slept with your boss."

"The two things aren't the same."

"You're delusional," Mercedes said. "Mamí isn't going to be okay with this, Yves."

"Hold on, wait." I leaned in close, so I didn't have to raise my voice. "You can't tell Mamí about this. I want to tell her in my own way. Promise me you won't say anything, Mercy."

Her gaze flicked from me to Marcelo and then back again. "Okay, I won't say anything tonight, but you have to tell her, Yves."

"I will, but please, let me do it. Okay?"

"Okay." Mercedes thrust baby Sacha into my arms. "I'm gonna go play with Tatiana for a bit. You're okay, right?"

"Yeah, sure," I said, bouncing the baby in my arms.

What the fuck was that? I couldn't think of a single thing that Mercedes could do that wouldn't make me proud. The fact that she reacted this way hurt. We weren't very close, but at the very least, I expected her to be happy for me. This would be hard for me to forget. Her reaction made me second-guess my decision. Was this a good idea?

"Do you feel the same way?" I asked my brother. "I haven't written or signed anything yet. I could always say no."

"What? No. Don't pass on this opportunity for us, Yves. And for the record? I think it's awesome that you're writing a book. I always knew you would be a talented writer. It's just amazing to see it finally happening."

I smiled, relieved, and genuinely flattered by his compliment. "Thank you so much for saying that."

"You're welcome." He lined up burgers and dogs on the hot grill, squinting when the smoke billowed back into his face. "It might take a while for Mamí and Mercy to warm up to the idea."

"I doubt if Mamí ever will."

"Well, you can't blame her for that, Yves. You're her daughter. It's going to be hard for her to know this stuff about you. Hell, I don't want to know it."

I nodded. "It would be nice for her to be proud of me for once, though."

"Well, if that's what you want, you better settle down with a nice guy and give her some grandchildren."

"Fuck that," I cursed.

"Yves!" Marcelo scolded, gesturing at the baby in my lap.

I cringed. Oops.

"Is Cesar still calling you?"

I rolled my eyes. "Yes. He left three messages on my phone a couple of nights ago."

Marcelo looked at me with hazel-brown eyes identical to

mine. "Maybe you should talk to him when he comes around tonight."

"I have talked to him, Marcelo."

My brother frowned. "You know you haven't talked to him. Not really. Just sit down and have an adult conversation. Even if it's just to tell him how much he hurt you."

My brother was right. I knew Cesar would be here tonight. No matter how much I denied it, part of me still loved him. I just didn't think talking it out would help.

LATER THAT EVENING, I SAT ON THE STEPS WITH MY TWO beautiful nieces, eating some of my mother's homemade ice cream. I held Sacha on my lap, feeding her the creamy goodness from my own spoon. When it melted in her mouth, she pursed her lips and hummed a delighted, "mmm... " that made me laugh. While I held her, my thoughts drifted to a dream of a child I might have had. I wondered if I would have been as good a mother as Mercedes.

"You're pretty good at that," a voice called out from the street.

Cesar.

I would recognize that voice even if I was surrounded by a din of noise. I glanced up at him as I wiped Sacha's mouth and felt that familiar weakness--that chaos of emotion he always stirred in me. Fear and longing twisted in my belly when his dark, penetrating eyes met mine. I was fourteen all over again, and my fourteen-year-old self still wanted him.

Hours spent in the sun working construction had darkened his skin to a russet brown that reminded me of autumn leaves and lightened his hair to a reddish-blond. Even though he stood a few feet away, I knew how he would smell--sweet like sawdust and cheap baby powder deodorant. And his hands...long, blunt fingers, knuckles crisscrossed with pale scar tissue from breaks, cuts, and too many fistfights. Me and Cesar's hands were well acquainted, but I was especially familiar with his right one. That hand had given me pleasure, fed me, and worked long hours to provide for both of us. But I was more closely acquainted with the fear and pain that it could inflict. He held his daughter, Yasmin, in his arms. A miniature of him with dark hair and the same wide, dark eyes. Did she fear his hands, too? I hope she didn't.

"You look like an old pro."

"So do you," I said, pointing at the two of them. He smiled as he looked at his daughter, and it hit me like lightening.

"Yeah, well, I get a lot of practice." He set the little girl down on her feet, and she immediately took off. "Don't go far, monkey!" he called out after her.

"Okay, Daddy!" she called back.

I felt a sharp stab of pain in the place where my heart used to be. Daddy. Another woman's child calls him Daddy. Would that ever stop hurting?

"She's beautiful. How old is she now?"

"She's almost four."

"Oh...right." Stupid mistake. I knew exactly how old she was. I could nail down the month of her conception if I thought about it long enough. Gabby had turned up pregnant with her right after Cesar, and I broke up.

"Cesar! Hey!" Mercedes and my mother burst out of the door behind us and fell on Cesar, showering him with kisses.

"You look good. Doesn't he look good, chiquita?" my mother asked as she squeezed him until he groaned.

"He looks great," I said.

Mercedes looked at Cesar and me, observing the awkward distance between us. "Come on, Mamí. Let's take the girls to get in Jacinta's pool, huh? Let these two talk," Mercedes suggested.

I watched my mother and sister walk away, casting hopeful glances at Cesar and me. Marcelo caught my eye from where he stood across the street. I gave him a little nod to let him know that everything was okay.

"You look beautiful," he said once they were a safe distance away.

"Thanks."

Cesar leaned against the picnic table and slipped his hands into the pockets of his jeans. He was one of those men who would maintain his boyish charm forever. Something about the way his dark brown eyes sparkled or the hint of insecurity in the way he hung his head reminded me of the boy I fell in love with.

"I know you may not believe this, but I don't want to be angry with you anymore, Cesar." I raked my hair out of my face and pulled it over my shoulder. "It's just so hard."

"I know," he said. We both were quiet for a long time as we watched a group of girls dancing in the middle of the street. There was too much history between us to engage in meaningless small talk.

"You want to take a walk?" he asked.

I looked up at him. "Okay." I stood up and brushed off the back of my sundress.

We walked quietly for a while, heading in the general direction of the river. A strange energy passed between us, and when I looked at him, I realized it was because he was nervous. Had Cesar ever been nervous around me before? If he had, I couldn't remember it. Cocky, dominating and full of machismo, yes, but never nervous.

"I've been dreaming of this conversation and all the things I would say to you. Now that you're here, I'm drawing a complete blank," he said with a nervous laugh. "How have you been?"

"Pretty fucking amazing, actually."

He laughed. "Still got that caca mouth, I see."

"Yes, sorry to disappoint you. I'm still that girl."

"Yves...I don't want to argue."

"Sorry," I murmured. "How's Gabby?"

"Okay, I guess. We broke up."

"Yeah, you mentioned that in your message."

"I tried to make it work for the baby, but..."

"Right."

We'd turned onto a quiet block. Long shadows stretched in the waning sunlight, and in the distance, streetlights fizzed and popped to life.

"I've been reading your newspaper articles," he volunteered.

"Really? That's a surprise."

"You're surprised that I read?" he countered sarcastically.

"No. You were just so...resistant to the idea of me taking that job."

"That was just me being jealous and selfish."

"So, what do you think?" I had no idea what would make me ask that -- even less of an idea why I cared what he thought.

"I like it. I mean, you must meet a lot of people. You're seeing a side of the city that I may never get to see."

"You mean that I meet a lot of men. Is this your way of asking if I'm seeing anybody?"

"Are you?"

I shrugged. "I'm seeing lots of somebodies."

"Yves...All this sleeping around. That's not you."

Sudden hysterical laughter consumed me. Was he serious? He'd called me everything but a child of God when we were together. Now sleeping around wasn't me? "This is definitely a surprise coming from you. I thought I was always a whore in your eyes."

"You're not a whore, Yves. I never thought you were. Not then, and not now. That was just me being insecure. You're so beautiful...I never thought I deserved you."

The laughter died in me like someone had shut off a switch. Here we go. He was as slick as a used car salesman. Don't fall for it.

"So, you got my messages?" His voice was soft -- a little more of that boyish insecurity creeping in.

"Of course, I got your messages, Cesar. I listened to every one of them."

"I meant every word."

"I don't doubt it. You always did. You meant all the other words, too. The ones that weren't so pretty, but they were just as heartfelt."

"How long are you going to hold that against me?"

"I don't know? Until the end of forever, maybe? Until I heal? Until I don't hear them echoing in my head and resonating in every bone in my body?"

"Yves, please...I never meant to hurt you. I know you don't believe that, but I didn't. I'm so sorry about everything."

He was right. I didn't believe him. This apology sounded no different from the hundreds of others.

"I took a job in Mount Airy the other day. I went by that house we almost bought. A couple lives there now. They're young. About our age...they have a little boy, too."

I drew up short. My throat tightened with the tears, and I struggled to hold them back, but I could barely breathe.

"They looked so happy, Yves," he continued. "I can't help but wonder if we would've been happy there, too. Me, you, and baby CJ. God, if there is anything I could take back, it would be that."

No matter how hard I tried, I couldn't stop the tears from coming after he said that.

"Yves, don't cry, baby. I didn't mean to make you cry."

He reached for me, tried to comfort me, but I batted his hand away.

"Why would you bring that up? Of all the things to say...you bring up the baby. The baby you didn't want! The baby that--" I bit my tongue against the memory. Nuh-uh. Not going there. I never touched that raw place inside of me. The place that would never heal. I held up my hands in surrender. "This was a bad idea."

"Yves, wait--"

"Wait for what, Cesar? What am I waiting for? For my memory to be erased?"

"No, but I can't help feeling like there's so many things left unsaid between us--"

"What else is there to say, huh? That I'm mentally, emotionally, and physically scarred from our relationship?"

"No, like there's something between us still. Enough to want to try again."

I stared at him in disbelief. "You can't be serious."

"I am."

"Did you think your relationship with Gabby was the only thing keeping us apart? What woman in her right mind would want to try again with you after what you did to me?"

"Your memory of me is not the man I am now. I've changed. Gabby and Yasmin have changed me."

"Oh, you could change for them, but not for me? Not for me and my baby?"

"I needed to go through all of that with you so I could change."

"Whoa..."

He should have just hit me. Those words were just as hard and mean as his fists had been. They implied that I deserved what he did to me. My tears, hot with anger, burned my cheeks.

"You needed to? Is that what you just said to me? I'm glad it was such an eye-opening experience for you. I wish I could say it was the same for me."

"That's not what I meant," he stammered. "Yves, listen, I can't change what happened. I can only prove to you that I'm different now. I could love you the way you deserve."

"Sorry, Cesar, but I don't think I can survive you loving me again." I turned to walk away.

"Wait." This time he grabbed me and pulled me into his arms. "I won't give up on you, Yves. I won't. I love you, and at one time, you loved me. I think I can make you love me again."

"No!" I tried to wiggle free of his embrace, but his arms were like iron locked around my waist. He lifted me off of my feet and buried his face in my neck. Fear stole across my skin, covering me in cold gooseflesh. This felt too familiar. Too much like how he used to feel.

"Please, let me go, Cesar," I whimpered. I looked up and down the block, frantically searching for someone, anyone, who could help me. The street was deserted. Fireworks cracked and boomed in the distance. No one would even hear me if I screamed. "Please." I squeezed my eyes closed and tensed for whatever might happen next, but to my surprise, he set me down on my feet.

"Why are you shaking? I'm not going to hurt you."

I opened my eyes and looked at him. I couldn't read the expression on his face. His eyes were brimming with tears. I couldn't figure out why. He usually didn't cry until after he hit me.

"Yves...I'm not going to hurt you." He reached for me, and I flinched instinctively. He let his hand drop without touching me.

"Why do you always do this?" I asked him this question, but it should be a question for me. Why do I let him get so close? I already knew that he would hurt me. He couldn't help himself.

Everything in me said run.

This same feeling swept over me when I stared at myself in my mother's antique mirror, my reflection obscured by her lace bridal veil. Something in me, that part of me that wanted to survive him, said run. So I did. That same voice whispered to me now.

I listened.

5

I couldn't go straight home. Cesar might be there waiting for might me, and I didn't want to be caught alone at my apartment with him. Our little discussion left me weak and vulnerable, and I didn't think I would have enough fight in me to send him away. See, that's the thing they don't tell you about breakups. Sometimes it's easier said than done — even when staying together could get you hurt or worse.

I just kind of wandered with nowhere to go and wandering always seemed to land me at Donnie Darla's. I ordered the citywide special, found a table, and moored myself up in my sadness.

My mother was probably worried. I'd left without saying goodbye. When I dug out my phone, I predictably found several voicemails from her and a few frantic texts from Marcelo and Mercedes. I responded to them as a group to let them know that I was okay and opened up my Twitter app.

I scrolled through my timeline, hoping to find some

mindless chatter to get lost in, but then found myself tweeting:

@SantiSexy: why can't the past stay in the past?

Like the other night, I got an immediate response from Elijah in my DMs.

@EWeinstein: maybe because you haven't really dealt with it?

@SantiSexy: get out of here with your logic. Are you twitter stalking me?

@EWeinstein: always.

@SantiSexy: what are you doing right now?

@EWeinstein: depends. What are you doing right now?

@SantiSexy: I'm at Donnie Darla's. That place we went to the other night. You wanna join me?

@EWeinstein: be there in twenty.

While I waited, I decided to do a bit of Twitter stalking of him now. Elijah followed a lot to writers, agents, and editors, so most of his timeline was industry-driven. Not very interesting. But his likes...the tweets he regularly liked made me curious. He'd favorited a few blog posts from other sex writers. Posts about dominance and submission and ambiguously, consensual acts.

"Mr. Weinstein," I murmured. "Very naughty indeed."

Exactly twenty minutes later, Elijah walked through the door. Checkered, button-down shirt. Straight-legged blue jeans. Soft leather loafers with no socks. His jaw sported a bit of five o'clock scruff and that gorgeous mop of his flopped carelessly into his dark green eyes. God, he was such a pretty boy. He looked like he'd just stepped out of an advertisement in Esquire magazine. Nothing like Cesar with his calloused hands, paint-splotched jeans, and dirty work boots.

But why was I comparing the two?

And could this be the same man who liked a blog post about a man forcing a woman to go down on him?

My mind resisted the thought.

But also... I kinda wanted to act out the scene from that blog post of a fellow sex blogger with him.

He smiled and waved at me as he approached, but that smile slowly slid off his face when he looked into my eyes.

"Yves," he sat down across from me and cupped my cheek in his hand. His thumb gently caressed my cheek. "What's wrong?"

"Do I look that bad?" I joked.

"You look like you've been crying." He surveyed the tabletop. "Citywide, special?"

"Yeah."

"Hold that thought," he said, and went to the bar to order another round of drinks. He propped one foot up on the bottom rung of a barstool while he waited.

Elijah was dressed like a model, but the way those jeans molded to his ass and that shirt stretched across the breadth of his shoulders hinted at an amazing body. I was suddenly contemplating the importance of keeping this relationship professional. I mean, we were both adults, right? We could feed this undeniable attraction between us without letting it affect our professional relationship, couldn't we?

He returned to the table with a full pitcher of Pabst and two shots of Jim Beam in his hands. "So," he said as he sat down. "Tell me what's troubling you."

I shrugged. Words and emotions crowded my mind, but all I wanted was for them to go away.

"Come on. You wouldn't be in here crying in your Pabst if you didn't know what was bothering you."

"Fuck you," I sneered. "Don't make me sound so pathetic. I'm not crying in my beer. I finished up the crying on the walk over here."

He smiled, unfazed by my foul language. "Seriously... maybe there's something I can do to help."

Oh, I know exactly what he can do to help. He could take me into the bathroom and fuck me until the doors rattled on the stalls. But I knew that was just a quick and dirty fix. When the endorphins wore off, I would feel just as low, so I decided to try something different.

"That story you said you wanted to hear..." I licked my lips. "Do you still want to hear it if it doesn't have a happy ending?"

"Of course. Happy endings aren't required. Some of the best romances are really tragedies."

"Okay, well — "

"Wait." He downed his shot of Jim Beam and followed it with a few deep swallows of Pabst. "Okay, I'm ready."

I didn't know where to start. I could just give him the abbreviated version, but he might not understand if I didn't start at the beginning.

"You were right. It was a boy, and I wasn't supposed to love him. He was my brother's best friend. My mother loves him like a son. I wasn't supposed to love him—not like that—but I did."

Elijah leaned forward and rested his elbows on the table. He gave me that same focused attention that he had given me the other night. "And he felt the same about you?"

I shook my head. "Not at first. I kind of had a reputation when I was a kid. I've always been sort of...fast...was what his mother used to call it. I filled out before the other girls. The boys noticed, and I can't lie, I liked the attention. I liked kissing boys—a lot. Word got around, and my brother hated it. He and Cesar were always scolding me about it. Of course, it didn't deter me one bit. Eventually, I did it just to get his attention."

"Did it?"

"Yes, but not the way I expected. He got really pissed off at me. Seemed like if I was anywhere in the dark with a boy, he would just appear and drag me out by my hair—"

"Literally?"

I shrugged. "Sometimes." I took a swig of my beer and pondered the next thought. For some reason, it was hard to admit. "We would get into these huge arguments, and he would just bundle me up like I was nothing and carry me out. And for some reason, I kinda liked that."

Elijah grunted, but I didn't know him well enough to interpret what that sound meant. I forged on anyway.

"One night, I kind of accused him of secretly wanting me. That made him more pissed off than ever. He gave me every excuse in the book for why he couldn't want me, but he never denied it. I knew I had him."

For just a moment, I allowed myself to remember that time fondly. It was probably the first time I realized the power of my sexuality. That I could make Cesar—a full-grown man who was bigger and stronger than me—weak was a heady, intoxicating realization.

"I focused all my attention on him after that. I would corner him and unleash all of my fourteen-year-old seduction on him," I said dryly.

"You were fourteen?" he asked.

"I was, and I know what you're thinking. It's not as scandalous as it sounds. He was only four years older than me. And I was relentless," I said with a laugh, remembering how I amateur attempts at seduction. "One day, he just grabbed me by my hair and kissed me."

Like always, my body lit up at the memory. My mother and Mercedes were in the kitchen cooking dinner. Cesar and Marcelo were upstairs in his room playing video games or whatever. I was on the couch watching music videos with the volume down low so Mamí wouldn't come in and change the channel when Cesar came down to get a drink from the kitchen.

He'd stopped at the bottom of the stairs and stared at me. I don't remember what I said. I might have smiled or crossed my skinny legs lewdly, but the next thing I knew, he was on me. His hands were in my hair, pulling just a little too hard, and his mouth was crushing mine.

The moment he grabbed me, a spike of fear lanced through my body. I now knew that I was afraid of what that kiss made me feel. It wasn't kissing just to kiss. This kiss was meant to lead somewhere, and I wasn't entirely sure I wanted to go there.

"I'd never felt anything that intense before."

"Hm. You wanted to turn him on, but you didn't know what to do when it actually worked," Elijah summarized.

"Exactly," I said with a laugh and a nod. "He knew what to do, though."

"I'm sure he did."

"We tried to keep it a secret for a long while, but you know how that goes. My brother was so angry with me when he found out." I shook my head. "He and Cesar got into an actual fistfight. I felt so guilty. Like I was breaking up the family. I especially felt bad for Cesar because I knew that if he couldn't come to our house, there was no way for him to escape his father."

"His father was abusive?"

I nodded.

"Physically? Verbally?"

"Emotionally...all the above."

Elijah went quiet and thoughtful for a moment. I knew where his thoughts were headed. I steeled myself for the question.

"Was Cesar...did he ever—"

"Yes," I answered, simple and straightforward. "But I don't want to talk about that."

He said nothing, but after a moment, he swung his chair around the table next to mine and pulled me close. "I don't know how a man could ever do that to you," he growled through clenched teeth. "If you were mine, there is nothing you could say or do that would make me treat you like that."

I laughed mirthlessly. "I don't know. My mouth gets me into trouble. I'm impulsive to the point of being reckless. Sometimes I wonder if there's something wrong with me. Like there's something written on my skin that says that it's okay for someone to treat me the way he did. That it's okay to hurt me."

He leaned back and looked at me. Really looked at me. "He's a damaged man, but that is no excuse for what he did to you. His pathology didn't give him permission to hurt you. And nothing you did gave him permission to hurt you, either."

I wanted to believe him, but he really didn't know me. Rebellious, confrontational, disobedient—I'd earned my bad girl label long before I reached puberty. My mother often sent me from the room when I was younger, declaring that my mere presence gave her a headache. And that was long before Cesar ever told me I was too much for one man to handle. At the time, I thought it was a compliment.

Elijah pulled the rest of the story—well, most of it—out of me. I kept some parts to myself because there were some things that I didn't like to remember or say out loud. I told him about Cesar cheating with a woman who used to be my best friend. I told him how she became pregnant right after we broke up and how part of me wondered if she'd been pregnant before we split. When I laid it all out like that, it sounded like the plot of a fucking telenovela. Elijah listened intently and curled his arm around my shoulders when I cried again.

"My family...they all think I should give him another chance."

"Do they know what he did to you?"

I shook my head. "Not really. My brother knows we argued, but he doesn't know that Cesar put his hands on me. He would probably kill him if he did. I couldn't tell my mother and sister. My mother would be heartbroken. During all those breakups, they were the ones who told me to go back. I know this is hard to understand. It really doesn't make much sense when I say it out loud, but... I can't have them blaming themselves for what happened to me."

"You've seen this guy recently?"

"Today at a block party. He kept saying he was a different man now. That he'd changed."

"How do you feel? Do you believe he's changed?"

I thought about it for a moment and shook my head no.

"Then that's the feeling you should go with. That's the only feeling you should trust."

"My feelings are far from trustworthy right now."

He frowned. "Do some of those feelings center around a certain book I asked you to write?"

I nodded.

"Interesting," he murmured. "You seemed like you were all in the last time we talked. Why this change of heart?"

"Lots of reasons...but mostly just two. Family and this thing with Cesar."

"Hm. You're worried about what your family might think of you writing something like this?"

"I mean, of course, I'm worried. I told my brother and sister, and my sister said she didn't want me to write it. My mother is a devout Catholic. She has issues with me being so promiscuous, to begin with. I can't even imagine how she will react to this, but considering my sister's reaction, I know it will be anything but good."

"So, don't tell them." He shrugged. "The blog is published anonymously, and you can publish the book anonymously. They never have to know."

"Yeah, I thought of that, but here's the thing...do I want to hide this wonderful, amazing thing from them? I mean, they're my family. Don't I want them to share in my happiness of being chosen to write a book for the oldest and most respected publishing company in Philly?"

"Look, I'm probably the last person to offer family advice, but if you're feeling so proud of being 'chosen,' as you put it, do you want to turn it down because you're afraid of how it will affect them?"

"No. I'd regret it forever if I did."

He smiled. "So again...that's the feeling you should trust."

Just like the other night, we closed down DD's. Elijah walked me home, and once again, I found myself standing on my stoop, looking into his eyes. In the light of my porch lamp, I noticed that they weren't just green. There were flecks of golden brown in there and a ring of blue around his dilated pupils. Hmmm... that was a sign of attraction. That made me wonder how my pupils looked at the moment.

"Thanks so much for listening to me tonight."

"No problem."

I took a moment to mull over the fact that I had just told this man things about my past that I had never told anyone. I usually didn't trust people this way, but there was something about him that broke through my defenses and made me feel...safe. That made absolutely no sense at all. I couldn't figure out why I had done this thing.

"Did you want to come up? I've got some old Chinese food, a Netflix subscription, and cold beer. You could tell me about the first time you fell in love and had your heartbroken. Then we would be even."

He laughed and shook his head. "I think I'll take a rain check."

I nodded and smiled halfheartedly. "I understand. The exotic Latina is not so sexy now that she has all this relationship baggage."

"That's not it at all," he countered quickly. "I just don't want you to think I'm taking advantage of you." He stepped up onto the stoop and brought his lips close enough to kiss. "I think you're very sexy, Yves. And intelligent and talented and beautiful. But we want very different things, and I don't want to start something that would probably end badly."

"What do you mean? I kinda think you want to be naked with me." Admitting that made me feel vulnerable for some reason, which was unlike me. "Am I wrong?"

He smiled. "No, you're not wrong, but I'm not going to be one of your conquests."

"Wow," I said breathlessly. Rejected because I was "a sure thing." That was a first. How did a girl respond to that?

"Don't be offended. I'm just at a place in my life where I'm not really into casual sex."

"But you've been flirting with me since the moment we met."

"You're right. I'm attracted to you. I never denied that. But I want more than sex from you. I know that sex is something you give easily." He stepped a little closer. "I want to know you. Not just the way you taste when you come. I wanna know all the ways to make you smile and cry. I wanna know what scares you the most and what makes you feel loved. I don't think you're ready to give me that or if you ever will be. What I'm interested in is between your ears, Yves. Not your legs."

He wasn't touching me. In fact, his hands were in his pockets, but those words insinuated themselves into my mind and right in between my legs. Part of what he said was really insulting, and I knew I should feel some kinda way about that, but really I just wanted him. Fiercely.

Elijah must have seen it in my eyes because just as I was about to launch myself at him, he backed up and said a polite, "Good night, Yves."

Stunned and left swaying on my stoop, I stood there and

watched him walk down the block with a casual ease that taunted the wanton throb he had created in me. He turned around when he reached the nearest cross street. I felt embarrassed to be so dumbstruck that I couldn't move my stupid feet, but I forgot about that when he smiled and waved. God, that mouth and the things I would make him do with it. Unfortunately, it was the mouth of a man who had some fanciful idea that sex was better with some sort of commitment.

"Well, I'll just have to prove him wrong, won't I?"

FAIRYTALE PRINCES AND DREAMS COME TRUE

JULY 6, 2013

When she started this thing, she didn't think anything would come of it. She thought maybe a few people would read it. Maybe they'd get something from her experiences -- some lesson she'd missed. Maybe they would become more brave and claim their sexuality in the way she had.

But none of what he offered was in her realm of consideration.

She didn't believe in fairy tales -- romantic or otherwise -- but he seemed like he'd just stepped out of one. Tall, lean, and blond, he looked like a prince in his charcoal-grey suit. With a shy grin and an intense green-eyed stare, he granted wishes that she didn't even know she had made.

Was this her fairytale? Was he her prince?

His passion for her writing was intoxicating. She couldn't remember the last time someone believed in her, and that alone was enough to make her want to say yes to everything that came out of his mouth. He wanted to know her story and believed that others would too. No one had ever believed in her like this. She didn't realize how much she wanted that. That she needed it more than anything.

And...

...he had a gorgeous mouth. A mouth that she'd daydreamed about while he sat across from her saying sensible things. She wanted to fuck him--wants to fuck him. She was sure he felt the same.

But...

Instead of fucking him, she was going to write a book.

Level heads won the day.

Still...she wondered about the things that gorgeous mouth of his could do.

6

Someone once told me that charm was getting a person to say yes before you had even asked. The person who said that must have been talking about someone like my father. At fifty-six years old, my father's lean physique and charismatic smile drew more than a few appreciative stares from women half his age when we walked into the restaurant. Their eyes lingered over his lean frame, and their lips returned his smile. I had always suspected he was the type of man who could command a room, but it was something else entirely to see him in action.

"Hi, I have a reservation for two under Yves Santiago," I said as we approached the hostess stand.

The brown-eyed hostess smiled prettily. "Yes, right this way."

We were at a new Thai place called Näo's. It was on my list of new places to try and review for my column. It had been a while since I spent any quality time with my dad, and this seemed like a place he would like.

"If I'd known you were going to bring me to a place this nice, I would have worn a nicer shirt and a tie," he said modestly as he smoothed his hand over the buttons of his shirt.

"Your shirt's fine, Papí. Not that it matters. I'm pretty sure the server has every grey hair on your head counted and memorized by now."

"Is that so?" he asked, twisting around in his seat to get a second look at the server who was not so subtly leaning over the bar and giving him a generous peek at her cleavage. "Humph, didn't even notice," he said, turning around to face me again. "I guess I'm just too enamored with my lovely daughter. She's the most beautiful woman in the room, didn't you know?" He touched my cheek with the curl of his fingers, and I blushed. I couldn't help it. No matter how old I was, I would always be a daddy's girl.

My memories of my father were few...good memories, even fewer. But somehow, I always thought of him as the father from my childhood. The father preserved under glass with me smiling next to him in the frame. Pictures of me as a honey-eyed girl with scabby knees and missing teeth, who stared into her father's face as if he hung the moon.

We didn't have a great relationship. When my parents divorced fifteen years ago, he intended to live his own life, which meant he didn't have much contact with us kids. My brother was twelve years old when my father left--old enough to know what was really going on--and was still bitter about it. Mercedes barely remembered anything about him, except what she heard from us. I was the only one of the three who made any effort at all to get to know him. I think I sympathized with him more than I wanted to admit. The way he treated my mother was unforgivable, and the aftermath was no cakewalk. I loved Papí, and of course, I wished they were still together, but I understood why he had to getaway.

"How are your sister and brother?"

"They're doing great. Marcelo is trying to get promoted. Mercedes is doing well. Her husband is finally back from his last deployment, and Sacha and Tatiana are getting big and so beautiful."

"And your mother? How is she?"

"She seems all right. Same as always. Going to mass. Working at that produce shop down in the Italian market."

"Is she seeing anyone?"

"Did you forget who we were talking about?"

My father nodded knowingly. "I will never understand why that woman punishes herself that way. She deserves to be loved."

The daddy's girl in me wanted to ask, "why can't you love her, Papí?" but I held my tongue.

"And what about you, querida? What have you been up to? Are you seeing anyone special?"

I laughed. "Papí, you know me."

"Almost as well as I know myself," he said with a grin. "So lots of someones, but no one special."

For some reason, Elijah popped into my head before I said, "That would be pretty accurate."

The server reappeared, her ample breasts nearly spilled out of her V-neck shirt as she leaned in to place our drinks on the table.

"Are you ready to order?" she asked, turning to my father as if I didn't exist.

"Yves?" my father gestured toward me to remind the busty lady of my presence. She turned back to me reluctantly.

"Miss?" she inquired.

"Yes, um...I think I'm going to have the Thai Curry Lobster?"

"Okay. And the coconut Rice is okay?"

"Perfect." I handed her my menu.

"Great," she said with a polite nod and turned back to my father. "And have you decided, sir?"

"Yes, I'll have the Teriyaki Filet Mignon with Wasabi Potatoes."

"Excellent choice. It's one of my favorites," she said. "If you need anything, anything at all...just let me know."

"And what's your name again?"

"Karla. My name is Karla."

"Okay, Karla," my father said, offering up one of his killer smiles.

I shook my head as the server walked away, adding an extra twitch to her hips.

"What?" my father asked innocently.

"That poor woman...she has no idea who she's playing with."

"But that's what makes it so fun, isn't it?" he said, waggling his eyebrows.

For the next hour and a half, my father and I played catch up over drinks and good food. He told me about the new woman he was dating and filled me in on the minor successes of his contracting business. We spent a good amount of time marveling at our sameness, which seemed to go beyond our looks.

"You are so much like me. It's uncanny," he remarked.

"You know that creating a child is the ultimate form of narcissism. I mean, what could be more self-centered than creating someone who will look like you, walk like you, talk like you?"

He shrugged and leaned in. "That's very true," he said

with a nod of his head. "And on the surface, we are nearly identical. We have the same nose, eyes, hair. Your left eye even has the same flaw in it as my left does, eh?"

"Oh, yeah. The birthmark. I totally forgot that you had that, too."

"Yep, same eye and in nearly the same position." He widened his eyes, and when I looked into them, I saw the flaw along with my own reflection.

"Do you know why I named you Yves?"

I shook my head, no. "Why?"

"Well, Yves Ramon is not only my name. It was my father's name also. I was the last of four sons. He could have named anyone of them Yves Ramon, but he didn't. He said giving someone your name is important. It means you see some of you in that person. Not just features like eyes, nose, mouth, but spirit. I saw that in you, Yves. Even when your mother was pregnant with you, you had it. Of all my children, you are the most like me. From the way you look all the way down to the way you love. You are just like me."

"Spirit..." I echoed. I didn't know if this was such a good thing. There were some things about my papí that I loved, but there were others that I had tried all my life to avoid becoming.

"Your mother told me about your blog and this book you're writing."

My belly flipped nervously. I hadn't told my mother, so obviously, my sister couldn't keep her damn mouth shut. And now my father knew about it? "Oh?"

He nodded. "I read some of it. You write well, querida. Very entertaining."

"Thank you, Papí," I said apprehensively. Why did I hear a "but" lurking in there?

"Now I'm going to say something, and I want you to

listen," he said seriously. "I've never been the sort of man who can find what he needs in one woman. I could never be satisfied by that. I suspect it may be the same for you, but it doesn't have to be. You're young. Don't let life pass you by, Yves. Find someone you can love. Someone who can love you."

"Papí--"

"Listen to me, querida." He leaned forward on his elbows and looked right into my eyes. "In the end, having someone who loves you unequivocally, unconditionally is the only thing that matters. All this other stuff means nothing. So have your fun, but don't become too cynical."

"Sorry, Papí, but it may be too late."

"Why? Because of Cesar? It's not too late for you and him, querida. I saw him a few days ago."

I bristled. "What?"

"I'm working a job in Marlton, and he's doing the hardwood floors. He asked about you."

"Of course he did," I said dryly. Here we go. I picked up my glass and took a deep swallow of wine, steeling myself for whatever came next.

"He says that you two spoke recently, and it didn't go well. He still loves you, Yves--"

"I'm not going to talk about this with you, Papí. Cesar and I are through. Leave it at that."

"Okay," he said with a nod. "But give what I said some thought."

"I will" was my answer. But I couldn't help thinking that I'd just had dinner with a man who, no matter how much we favored each other, knew absolutely nothing about me.

We ended the night early. Papí had to drive back across the bridge to Jersey, and I didn't want him to be on the road too late. He gave me a warm kiss and a hug outside the doors of the restaurant.

"Are you sure you don't want me to drive you home?"

"No, I'm just going to grab a cup of coffee or something."

"Okay. Next time, don't let so much time pass without calling me."

"I won't. And you should call Mercy. You have grand-babies. You need to get to know them."

"Of course, of course," he said with a nod, though I knew he wouldn't call my sister. He planted a big, wet kiss on my cheek. "Te amo, querida."

"Te amo."

"Be careful. Call me to let me know you made it in all right."

"I will if I don't forget."

"Don't forget."

I watched my father jog across the street to his pickup truck with the name of his contracting company, Santiago Building, and Construction painted on the side. He pulled off, tooting his horn as a final goodbye.

A weird funk settled over me after he was gone. To be honest, it had been with me since my last encounter with Cesar...a strange melancholy that I just couldn't shake. The conversation with my father about finding love before it was too late didn't help things. His thoughts on who and when I should love were not the words I needed or wanted to hear. I wanted him to hug me and tell me that whatever decision I made would be all right, not to encourage me to get back with Cesar.

It wasn't as if I was hurting over it or mourning our relationship. I just felt...meh. Like I needed to do something--or needed someone--to get the feel of him off of me. In my experience, the best way to get over a man was to get under another one. I wasn't about to let that mission be deterred by a bad mood.

But before I did any of that, I needed a pack of cigarettes. With a sigh, I turned and headed toward a corner store half a block up.

"Newport Light 100s, please. The box, not the soft pack," I said, stepping up to the register.

The pimple-faced boy behind the cash wrap tossed the box onto the countertop. "Matches?"

I nodded.

"Anything else?"

I looked around, grabbed a pack of Altoids, and tossed them on the countertop next to the cigarettes.

"Ohh-kay," the boy intoned and began to ring me up. "That'll be eleven dollars and thirty cents."

"Goddamn," I muttered under my breath as I fished a twenty out of my wallet.

"I know. It's enough to make you want to quit."

"I tried that once. It didn't work out," I mumbled as he handed me my change.

I stepped out into the street, packing the cigarettes against my palm as I walked up the block. At the corner, I attempted to light my cigarette using the matches the cashier gave me. The evening was warm but windy, and my match immediately flickered out. I turned my back into the wind, cupped my hand around the flame, and attempted to light it again.

"Shit," I cursed as the match fluttered and flickered out again. Suddenly, another hand curled around mine and blocked out the wind.

"Try it now," said a familiar voice.

Sheltered from the wind by his hand, the newly struck match remained lit, and my cigarette glowed to life. I took a long, deep drag before I looked up at him--a weak attempt at steeling myself against his sweet, boyish charms.

It didn't work.

Julian wore a page-boy cap pulled down low over his brow and tipped at a rakish angle which made him look like a dashing, nineteen-fifties gangster. His long legs were covered in soft, slim-fitting, grey linen slacks that hung low on his hips. The white tee he wore fell just a little above it--just short enough to reveal a hint of his sculpted hip bones. Yes, he looked perfectly dashing, and he knew it. He gave me a slow, sensual smile. One that would steal my heart away if I were the type to fall for that sort of thing.

I exhaled slowly, blowing smoke into his face. "Is this a chance encounter, or should I be worried about my safety?"

He laughed, swiped the cigarette from my fingers, and took a long drag. "Purely chance. Had a meeting with a bunch of painters, poets, and misanthropes after an event at the University of the Arts. I was just heading home. Came out 'ere and saw ya beautiful self-standing on the sidewalk." He curled his large, calloused hand around my forearm and slid it down to my hand. "Likkle woman like you shouldn't walk home alone," he muttered.

"Walk me home then."

Julian led me across the street, and once we were safely on the other side, he slowed to a pace that I could keep up with without prancing.

"So, you're definitely not stalking me?"

"Stalking?" he shook his head, smiling. "Stalking is such an ugly word. I prefer to call it courting."

"You can only court a girl if she's willing and interested."

"Beautiful star, you are definitely willing and definitely interested," he said with a grin.

I let go of his hand and crossed my arms over my chest. "Julian, I don't know if I made this clear to you before, but I'm not looking for anything serious."

He uncrossed my arms and took my hand again. "Ya made that pretty clear when ya didn't call. I'm not 'ere to pressure you into nothin'. Just glad to see ya. Is that a crime?"

He brought my hand to his lips and kissed it, his breath tickling over my knuckles.

"Come on," he coaxed with a gentle tug on my arm.

"Where are we going?"

"Back to your place," he said with a matter-of-fact confidence. "I'm walking ya home, remember?"

"You know where I live?"

"No." He looked at me. His eyes sparkled mischievously. "But ya 'bout to show me." He curled my hand against his chest. Hmm....that broad expanse of muscle. That single sensual gesture brought desire surging to the surface. Maybe this was the man I needed to get out of this post-Cesar funk.

"I tried everything in my power to get in touch with ya since that night."

I smiled shyly, feeling my cheeks warm a bit. It seemed that I was also susceptible to flattery. "Really?"

"Yes," he said, narrowing his eyes at me. He confessed, "I might have called the paper a few times looking for ya. And I might have thought about sending some flowers."

"Flowers are nice," I said.

"Coming on too strong?"

"I mean, sort of, but then it's sort of...romantic, too, I guess. But it is a little crazy after just a one-night stand."

A smile spread across his face, those boyish dimples deepening. "You ever hear dat phrase no one loves as passionately as a madman?"

"Are you mad?"

He laughed out loud then, tossing his head back. "I can't even answer that."

"Why?"

"Because the first thought that comes to mind is so ridiculous that it will change this moment into something outta one of those romantic comedies women are always watching."

I stopped walking and pulled him to my side. The wind kicked up, swirling my hair all around my head. "Just say it. Say what you were going to say."

Julian laughed and bit his lip, struggling to maintain the cool facade he had adopted for the night. "Lawd! I can't believe I'm about to say this!" His cheeks flushed just red enough for me to see it in the waning evening light. "Okay," he said resolutely, then took my face in both his hands. "I'm mad about ya, Yves. I know it was a one-night stand, but I wanna see if there is something more here."

Even though I knew what he was going to say, his words still affected me. They made my stomach flutter. They made me want to kiss him hard and long until both of us were breathless. "But Julian...you barely know me."

"Gimme da chance."

"I'm not good for a guy like you. I've slept with a lot of men." I admitted hesitantly. He was the last person I needed to explain myself to, but I felt like he should know. "Guess how many."

"Nah matter--"

"Whatever the number in your head is...double it. Maybe then you'll come close."

"So what?"

"I blog about it, and I've been approached by a pretty prominent publishing company to make it into a book. The whole world would know."

"I don't care."

I laughed and shook my head. "You can't be serious."

"I'm serious."

"How the fuck did this happen?" I murmured, staring up into his eyes. His earnestness was overwhelming. I hadn't led Julian on. He knew I wasn't looking for anything serious; I made sure he understood that, but somehow I still felt responsible for his feelings. "Listen...Julian, I'm--"

"Don't," he said and pressed forward to still my lips with the tips of his fingers. "Don't ya dare say ya sorry because I'm not sorry."

"You really are mentally ill, aren't you?"

He pushed my hair away from my face and touched my cheek. "I don't know. Maybe. Maybe ya make me crazy. Too-tool-bay ovah ya, star."

I tipped my head to the side, confused. He'd lapsed into patois, and I didn't understand what he was saying. Julian leaned in closer, crowding me against the brick facade of the building.

"Ya sparked something in me. Something I haven't felt in a long time. It makes me want ta keep ya."

"Who says I want to be kept?"

"I think ya lie to yaself. Ya lie to yaself for so long, ya believe it."

Julian flicked the cigarette away and stared down at me. His hand found my hip and pulled me against him. My blood heated at his closeness. I felt him--the pulse and promise of him--straining behind the fly of his slacks, and instantly I wanted it. Wanted to have his mouth on me. Wanted the impassioned, feverish way he kissed. Wanted him inside of me.

His hand cupped the side of my face, and his thumb stroked my bottom lip. I eagerly anticipated his kiss. His dick twitched where it pressed against my pubic bone. There was an answering twitch deep inside of me that blurred the edges for a moment.

"I know ya think I'm telling myself some nansi-story, thinking we gwon be together. And maybe ya right, but instead of pushing me away...why don't we make this into something? Maybe I'll bring you back to my place. Or maybe we can go back to yours, and you could read me one of your dirty stories. I love to hear the things that come out of your filthy little mouth."

And then he was kissing my filthy little mouth. His soft lips teased mine for a moment before his tongue delved in. I knew I was being far too pliant. This boy was falling for me. I needed to put a stop to this. I dug deep, but only surfaced with enough willpower to make a weak sound of protest. Julian ignored it. He slipped his arm around my waist and gave me all of him in the soul-shaking kiss. His mouth was sweet, but it had none of the shyness that I remembered from the last time. I couldn't decide if it was oxygen deprivation or the barely checked passion behind his kiss that made my knees go wobbly and made my hips press forward to meet the hard warmth of his dick.

"See? Look how good we are together."

"Wait," I murmured and tried to push him away.

"I've been waitin'." His island accent bled through and made his next words even more passionate. "Lawd, woman. Ya tryin' ta make me beg?"

"No, I just--"

He kissed me again, hijacking all responsible thoughts. "Fuck it," I muttered and slid my hands around the back of his neck, giving in to his sweet seduction.

"How far away is ya place?"

7

When I decided to embrace my sexuality, I came up with a pretty extensive set of rules to keep my heart and body safe. One of those rules was to never bring one-night stands back to my place. No one needed to know where I lived. Nothing ruined your day like coming home to a sad little boy sitting on your front steps. I was already feeding one stray. I didn't need another one.

These thoughts briefly crossed my mind as Julian's big frame filled my tiny entryway. How did I keep forgetting how big he was? His broad shoulders dwarfed my door, and it almost seemed that he had to stoop slightly to keep from banging his head on the ceiling.

"Who is this, then?" he asked with a concerned smile. My traitorous cat weaved between his legs, completely ignoring me.

"This dirty little pussy is Maniac."

"Didn't take ya for a cat person."

I shrugged. "I don't know if I am, really." I bent over and grabbed Maniac from between his legs. "Come 'ere," I growled at her. The cat gave me a little hiss as I curled her into my arms. "See, she doesn't like me much."

"I see that." He reached out with one big hand to scratch behind her ears. Maniac nuzzled into his palm and purred. "So dis is home, eh?" He leaned into my kitchen and looked down the hall behind me. That was when I realized how my place must look to him--to anyone, for that matter. Could he smell the litter box? Had I emptied it today? A pile of shoes had collected under my hall table, which looked ready to sag under the weight of unopened mail. I wasn't positive that my sheets were clean or if there were panties on my bathroom floor. My apartment was a shit box. Especially compared to that beautiful loft of his.

"Yeah, sorry if it's a bit messy. I'm not terribly domestic."

His mouth slanted into a smile, and he leaned into me. "Don't care 'bout da mess. Just happy to be 'ere with you."

I pushed up onto my tiptoes, and he met me halfway for another kiss. "I'm just gonna feed Maniac. Make yourself at home," I said, gesturing down the short hall.

Julian slipped out of a soft, leather hip bag that I just noticed he was carrying and dropped it beside mine on the floor before he made his way to my living room. I rushed through the task of feeding my emotionally handicapped cat and plucked two beers from the fridge.

When I entered the living room, I found him sitting on my couch in the dark. The light from the window cast his face in deep shadow.

"Ya light is done."

"Oh, shit. I meant to grab some light bulbs on the way home."

"Nah, big deal. We can light the candles."

Groups of candles sat on nearly every flat surface in my living room. Not just any sort of candles, but candles with

Catholic saints painted on them, Santa Barbara specifically. I did it out of habit when I was younger--light a candle, say a prayer. Now I lit them out of nostalgia more than anything else.

"Are you a religious person?" he asked after lighting the third one.

"I used to be." I found my candle lighter and helped him. "My mother is a Catholic, which means that I am too."

"But not anymore?"

I shrugged. "I don't know. I'm not really sure what I believe anymore. I guess I'm sort of an agnostic."

"So why all the Saint Barbara candles?"

"Santa Barbara is my patron saint. She protects me against evil."

"And ya run 'pon a lot of evil in ya everyday life? I think this sumthin' I should know a'fore I start spending a lot of time wit' ya."

"The only demons that live in these walls are the ones that live inside me."

"In that case, light up da darkness," he joked.

With the room lit in warm, flickering candlelight, he examined the pictures on my wall.

"Sweet sixteen?" He pointed at a picture of me in a ruffled, satin dress with teased hair and bad makeup.

"Quinceñera."

He nodded with a chuckle and then came to a complete stop at a picture of me dressed as Frida Kahlo. "Is this you?"

"Yeah, when I was in college, I organized this Frida Kahlo memorial thing where everyone in my oil painting class did a self-portrait. I was the only one who wore a costume. I was a little obsessed with Frida at the time."

"Ya paint a portrait?"

"Yes, but it wasn't any good. I'm not an artist. It was my

first year, and I was still searching for a vehicle of expression."

"Frida Kahlo," he said with a knowing nod. "Her paintings are full of so much pain."

"They are. I guess that's why I sympathized with her so much. The way she lost her baby...her crazy relationship with Diego." I shrugged and turned to light more candles.

"I knew dat bout ya."

"Knew what?"

"That someone hurt ya way down in a place that take a long time to heal."

"Is it that obvious?"

"Nah, obvious, but I see it."

"I see." I grabbed the two beers from where they were resting and sweating on my plastic IKEA table and handed him one.

"Nah like talking about yaself, eh?"

"Why would you think that? Didn't I just tell you that I write a blog where I spill everything about my sexual exploits? I think you have the wrong girl."

"If that's true, why do I feel like I don't know anything about ya?"

I shrugged, biting back a nasty retort. What makes him think he has a right to know me? I brought my bottle of Rolling Rock to my lips and took a long swallow.

"Tell me 'bout the man who hurt ya."

"What's to tell? Once upon a time, I loved a bad man, and now I don't. The end."

"No. That's not the end. W'happen? What him do to make ya so hard?"

I flinched. Was that the way I seemed to him? "I'm not hard."

He chuckled. "Ya hard. Flinty, I think they call it. Ya don't want no man next to ya unless ya decide the terms."

"Hey, fuck you!" I snapped reflexively.

"Hold on. I think ya hearing me wrong--"

"No, I think I'm hearing you just fine. If you think I'm so hard and flinty, why are you here?"

"Ya won know why?"

"Yes, why?"

"This."

He leaped at me, pinning me with his body and assaulting me with his mouth. Whatever soreness I felt from his insult melted away when the softness of his lips pressed against mine. His arms and body trapped me against the arm of the couch while his lips and tongue bullied and invaded me. It was another taste of the aggression he had given me on the sidewalk, and I liked it.

"This is why," he whispered hotly while grinding his thinly covered dick between my thighs. "I thought about ya every day since that night. Can't think on nothing else. Ya fill up my mind."

Jesus. This man could say anything, and I'd give in.

"Ya bad fah me. Know true?"

I curled my hand around the back of his smooth-shaven head and nodded. I couldn't lie. I was bad for him. Wrong. No good. But God, it felt good to be with him. I pushed my hands under his shirt and molded them over the broad slab of muscle on his back and shoulders.

"Now I feel foolish for having told ya that. Especially since ya made it plain that all you want is my dick."

I smiled against his mouth. "And you said you didn't know anything about me," I purred, reaching into his pants. He wore loose-fitting boxers. I loved that. Easy access.

"I know that much."

"Can you blame me, though? It really is gorgeous."

"Gorgeous?" he echoed, except when he said it, it sounded like gaw-juss.

"Yessss...."

He let out a breathy moan as my hand closed around him.

"Well, likkle storytellah," he said. He pushed off me and sat back on the couch. His fly was undone, and his dick peeked just a smidge beyond the band of his boxers. "Why don't ya tell me what makes it dat way, and I leave off all dis serious talk."

Hmm... I guess he was pretty damn perceptive. He could see that all this talk of feelings made me uncomfortable, and he found a way to turn it around without making things awkward. Clever boy.

I didn't bother to hide the smirk that twisted my mouth as I came to stand in front of him. My dress was rucked up around my waist. I didn't bother straightening it either because it gave me room to drop down to a kneel between his knees.

He grabbed my hands when I reached for his waistband. "Hold on."

"What? What's wrong?"

"Take off ya dress. I wanna see ya."

"Okay." I stood again, but this time I pushed my dress down over my hips. I looked down at him as I unzipped it. In the dim, flickering light, his brown eyes were completely focused on me. Seeing this pretty boy, so gone on me, made me want him all the more.

God, why couldn't this be enough? Why can't I be satisfied with the look he gets when I peel off my dress to reveal my mismatched underwear? I knew the reason, but I didn't want to admit it.

He reached for me. His big, rough hands skimmed the curve of my hips, and he placed a kiss just below my belly button.

"What you said was true."

"What was true?"

"That I'm hard. That what he did to me made me hard. I don't want to be that way."

Julian held me a bit further away and looked into my eyes. "Nah mean to make ya feel bad. I just want ya, star. But when I try fah get close, I feel this...wall up inside ya. That's all I mean 'bout ya being hard." He threaded his fingers into my hair. "I just want to feel close to ya."

I shifted around so that I straddled him. "I want to want you close to me."

He laughed, and his big hands came down around my waist. He made me feel positively tiny. "I guess dat be a start, eh?"

"I guess."

"Come 'ere," he coaxed, tipping his chin up at me, his voice soft.

I scooted closer, and his hands cupped my ass, drawing me closer still.

"Tell da likkle story--"

"About your big dick?"

Julian grinned, and I slid off his lap and onto the floor. I grasped the waist of his pants and boxers, and he lifted just enough to allow me to shimmy them off his ass and down to his ankles. I grasped his beautiful dick in my hands, inhaled his scent, and got high on the smell of him.

"Gee-zuz," he cursed. He pushed my hair away from my face and gathered it in his hands. "Ya so beautiful. Ya speak to mah heart."

With my tongue extended and his dick in my hand, I

drew up short. I looked up at him--chest heaving, mouth open, body rigid with expectation. I wanted to please him, but it was a selfish kind of wanting. I wanted to please him because I knew he would shower me with thankful praise...but I didn't want anything more. That was hard to admit.

I stood up. Julian's brow creased in a frown.

"What wrong, star?"

His hand skated up the back of my naked thigh, cupped the round of my ass, and pulled me closer. I wanted him. God, I wanted him. But not at the risk of his heart.

"I can't do this, Julian. I can't do this to you."

"What ya talking 'bout, star? I want ya to do this -- need ya to. Please."

"Julian, I don't feel what you do. I don't think I ever will feel that for you. I can't do this, no matter how much I want to, because I know it means more to you than it does to me. I just want you to shower me with your pretty words...but I don't feel it the same way. Do you understand?"

His hand slid down the backs of my thighs, cupped my knees. "Yves, please, believe me, this nah nothin' heavy. Do I want it to be? A' course, but we just having fun right now. No one's getting hurt."

I smoothed my hand along the crown of his head. "I want to believe you," I murmured. "But it's only because I want to fuck you."

His face... I'd never seen a man look more vulnerable than he did at that moment. I backed away from him, and he let me. My body immediately missed his warmth.

Julian stood, pulling up his slacks and boxers. Looming over me with his sad eyes, I was nearly rendered helpless.

"Ya gwon send me away like this?"

I looked away from his sad eyes. "I think it's best."

"Ya think this'll make me angry wit' ya? That I won't keep trying?"

I laughed and looked up at him. "I hope not. I hope you'll keep trying and that one day, I'll be ready for you--all of you. But right now... I'm just not."

"Ya honest. I appreciate dat." His hands came down on my hips, pulled me close. "I wish it made me want ya less."

I smiled and kissed him gently. "I wish you didn't have such a gaw-juss dick to tempt me with."

He laughed and held me closer. "Will be here when ya ready."

"I know," I murmured, wishing I was ready right now. But knowing that I wasn't made me pull out of his embrace. He rustled around for his shirt and went out to my hallway to retrieve his bag. At the door, he paused and turned around with a great, heavy sigh and gave me another soul-shaking kiss.

"Goodnight, Yves Santiago," he murmured against my lips.

"Goodnight, Julian Webster."

SHE CAN'T STOP DREAMING OF HIS MOUTH

JULY 28, 2013

She had a man in her house last night. A big, beautiful man with a big, beautiful dick and a pretty way of saying things that should have made her knees fall apart.

She didn't fuck him.

He was sweet and capitulating in all the right ways, but still...she didn't fuck him.

She didn't fuck him because she can't stop dreaming of his mouth.

She hasn't posted here in weeks. She could make all the predictable excuses--life is crazy, she worked too much, and, hey, she's writing a book, so it's almost a given that something would fall by the wayside, right?

She can tell you all of those things, gentle reader, but it wouldn't be the whole truth, and we strive to be truthful here...don't we?

The truth is...she hasn't posted here in weeks because she hasn't had sex in weeks. It wasn't for lack of opportunity. Plenty of beautiful men approached her--the man who left her apartment wanting last night was only one of them. And don't worry, her libido is exactly where it always is--in hyper drive. But--and this is going to be pretty unbelievable considering what she writes--the whole truth of it was that...

...she just didn't want to.

She didn't want to, because she couldn't stop dreaming of his mouth.

Just writing those words...his mouth... God, it set her mind wandering.

She has spent long hours daydreaming of his kisses. Kisses on her mouth, her collarbone, the insides of her thighs...

She came numerous times, thinking of his kisses between her thighs.

Was this some sort of puritanical reverse psychology? Some Jedi mind trick he's working on her?

If she could stop thinking about his mouth and all the things she wanted to make him do with it, she might care, but fuck...she just wants that mouth all over her and him under her.

He hasn't even kissed her (yet), but every time she's near him, she wants to fist her hands in that dirty blond hair of his and kiss his pretty bitch of a mouth.

Okay, maybe not just his mouth.

(But really...it is his mouth).

He has this way about him. A quiet way, but intense, too. Maybe it's his eyes or maybe just him, but when he focuses that intensity on her, it makes all of her sit up and beg. His sweet words of encouragement and the completely honest way he speaks to her makes her wonder if he sounds the same when he uses that same mouth to whisper filth in her ear. How would those lips feel as he kissed her while fucking her?

Damn, she came right back around to his mouth again, didn't she?

It's just so perfect.

His mouth...

His mouth.

She can't stop dreaming of his mouth.

8

Life tried to prove to me on a daily basis that I wasn't really a grown-up and that I did not have my shit together. The proof in that was my necessity to work my fifty-eleven jobs (read three-ish) and the bills that piled up whenever I decided to take a day off. So as much as I wanted to call off from work and wallow in my foul mood, I had to clock in at Burke's Books.

To my chagrin and delight, the Facebook page I set up for the store was drawing more poets for the open mic night, which meant more customers and more sales. But it also meant that I spent a lot of unpaid hours operating the page, responding to messages, and organizing events for the store. Thankfully, Thompson was understanding and didn't bitch when I kept my laptop behind the cash wrap. It gave me an opportunity to work on some freelance projects when it got slow. In the midst of putting the finishing touches on my current article for the Philadelphian, I received an iMessage from my sister.

MerSayDeez: *I'm in the city without the kids today!*
Want to get together for a drink or something?

Me: *Sorry. I'm working at the bookstore. I have a coffee break in thirty minutes. Wanna come share it with me?*

MerSayDeez: *Yes! See you in 30.*

I loved my sister. I really did. But something about this nonchalant, spontaneous text set my alarm bells to ringing.

Exactly thirty minutes after our brief exchange, Mercedes walked through the doors of Burke's Books. She looked perfect. Her hair was smooth and glossy, skimming her narrow shoulders. Her knit top matched perfectly with her modest, A-line skirt. She made me feel like a slob standing next to her in my holey jeans, trendy T-shirt, and wedge sandals. But at least the hug she greeted me with felt genuine.

"Wow!" she exclaimed. "This place doesn't change, huh?"

I rolled my eyes. "Not much, but I have managed to bring the store into the twenty-first century in spite of the resistance from management."

Thompson scoffed at my snarky comment.

"Whatever the case, I'm glad to see that it's still here. I have some very fond memories of this place from college."

"Me, too. And that's my only mission, really. To make sure Burke's Books gets enough business to remain a landmark institution for the students of Temple University and the surrounding neighborhoods," I pontificated while affecting an air of importance.

"Well, it seems to be thriving! I'd say you're doing your job."

"Don't inflate her ego," Thompson warned.

"My ego is already so big it can't be measured, Tommy Boy. Mind if I cut out for a coffee break to chat with my sister?"

"Please, go. There isn't room for me, you, and your ego behind this cash wrap."

"Miss me!" I sing-songed before following my sister to the other end of the store.

The coffee shop at Burke's Books was one of my favorites, but I was probably biased. They used real ceramic mugs, mismatched, and donated by the university's art department and local potters. The shop had a bar and a few tables marked up with the graffiti carvings of students. The chairs were wobbly, and the Naugahyde seats were split with the upholstery stuffing bursting. It had a homey, diner-like feel. I loved it.

Mercedes and I bought coffee and settled in at a small table next to the windows. I had a cup of my favorite brew, caramel macchiato, with two extra shots of espresso to wake me up, but what I really wanted was a cigarette. My stomach churned with nervous energy. What was this about?

"Is everything okay? What are you doing here?" I asked, unwilling to wait out the meaningless banter to get to the reason why she was here.

"Yes, everything's fine. The girls are fine. I'm fine. Everything's fine," Mercedes responded.

It set me at ease, but it also lets me know what she wanted to talk to me about.

"Look, I know me, and you aren't as close as you and Marcelo," she began at a hurried pace. "But I'm worried about you, sissy."

Ugh. Not this. Anything but this. "I'm fine, Mercy. Nothing to worry about."

"So why do I feel like there is something going on with you?" she asked as she emptied sugar packets into an already sweet brew of cappuccino. Just watching her take a sip of it made my teeth hurt.

"I have no idea. Maybe you're infected with the same misdirected concern that plagues your mother."

"Come on, Yves. I'm voicing genuine concern here. Stop derailing the conversation with sarcasm."

"I'm not being sarcastic. I'm being honest. Nothing is wrong with me."

Mercedes sighed. "After you told me about the book deal or whatever, I went back to your blog and read it again. All of it."

"Thank you for the page views. Every bit helps."

"Goddamit, Yves! I'm trying to have a conversation with you!"

"What do you want me to say, Mercedes? I have no idea what you're getting at. You read my blog, and now you're convinced there is something wrong with me. Classic. Do you know how many emails I get a day from people saying that I sleep with so many men because I have a hole in my soul?"

"Do you?"

I shook my head and laughed mirthlessly. "You're unbelievable." I stood up. "And you call me heartless." I didn't give her a chance to protest. I just left her sitting there with her sugary coffee and that stupid look of incredulity on her face.

A haze of anger blanketed me as I navigated the rest of my shift. By the time it ended, I had worked myself into a nice froth. Who was she to judge me? I could understand this ridicule from my mother, but Mercedes? She should understand me and be supportive, not judgmental. Where was the fucking support I needed from my family when I was venturing out into the world with all of my sensitive bits exposed?

I left Burke's with every intention of drinking and fucking away my anger. South Street and my usual haunts were in my sights when my phone rang. When I saw who it was, I couldn't help but smile.

"Mr. Weinstein, your timing is impeccable."

"Really? You were waiting for my call?"

"No, but I was about to do something terribly reckless if you hadn't."

"How reckless?"

"Oh, I dunno. Getting dog shit drunk, dancing, and fucking a stranger kinda reckless."

"Well, I'm glad I saved you from that. One-night stands can be so disappointing."

"Tell me about it."

"Where are you heading?"

"Donnie Darla's, of course."

"I'll meet you there in twenty."

Halfway into a bottle of Jack Daniels and shaking my ass off to Marvin Gaye's, "Keep on Dancing," Elijah showed up. I may have been a bit drunk and more than a bit horny, but when he came at me, he looked like a gorgeous, avenging angel. He scooped me up in his arms and danced with me. Not the grind-your-dick-on-my-ass-while-simulating-sex sort of dancing, but real steps and swing outs and turns. Kinda like the Latin dances that I knew, but rarely ever got to dance in public. After a particularly intricate swing out, he turned me and pulled me close, chest to chest, his breath on my face.

"You're a little drunk, aren't you?"

"More than a little. But I'm loving the way your hands feel on me."

He rolled his eyes. "Yeah, you're drunk. I probably should get you home."

"Yes!" I agreed enthusiastically. "Take me home."

"I'm gonna go get my car. Meet me outside in ten minutes."

Seven minutes later, Elijah's Benz G class, with its tinted windows and black rims, slowed to a stop in front of the bar with its hazard lights blinking.

"Holy fuck," I muttered to myself. An assistant editing job paid for this?

He stepped out and walked around the front end of the expensive SUV. "Come on, sweetness. Let's get you home."

"Sweetness? Are we assigning terms of endearment? I haven't chosen one for you yet. And I'm sorry, but I'm having trouble coming up with one now. All that comes to mind is that you're beautiful."

He smiled and beckoned to me. "You're really fucking drunk."

"You're fucking beautiful!" I shouted, probably too loudly. Drunk, yes. Yves was drunk. Much more drunk than I thought. I wobbled in my shoes as I made my way to him, and if I wasn't so fucking drunk, I might be embarrassed. Right now, I could only focus on making it across the acre of cement between me and Elijah's car. I'd wobbled on my feet for the third time when he grabbed me by the elbow.

"I've got you," he said reassuringly.

I stepped into his personal space; his sandalwood and musk smell invaded my senses. "Take me home," I purred.

"Right this way," he said and opened the car door gallantly, tucked me into the cool leather seats, and shut the door.

. . .

WHEN I SAID, "TAKE ME HOME," IT SEEMED OBVIOUS TO ME that I meant his home--his bed. I groaned with disappointment when he pulled up in front of my place.

"Seriously?" I muttered under my breath, reaching for the door handle. I couldn't believe this was happening again. Yet another night of almost kissing on my stoop followed by restless tossing and turning and eventual masturbation. How fucking disappointing.

"Is it okay if I leave my truck here? I don't want to get a ticket," he asked.

My mouth refused to make words as I processed his question. He was staying? My mind quickly ran through all the filthy activities we could engage in once we crossed my threshold. "I think it's safe to park here until tomorrow around nine. That's when the street sweepers come through."

"Okay." He killed the engine, jumped out, and walked around the front end to open my door.

"You're coming up," I said while stepping onto the curb.

"Is that okay?"

"Yes! It's more than okay!" I raced to the door, fumbled with my keys until I found the right one, and hustled him inside before he could change his mind.

I might have stumbled up more than half the stairs. I have no regrets.

"You want something to drink?" I asked once we finally made it to my kitchen. "Water? Juice? Beer?"

"I'll take a beer," he said and bent down to scoop up Maniac. The cat nuzzled into Elijah and purred. Why did my cat love all humans more than she loved me? But I have to say...her affection for him made me smile. I couldn't put much credence in that, though. She'd done the same thing with Julian last night.

"I didn't take you for a cat lady."

"What the fuck? You're the second person to say that. Is there some cat-lady prerequisite I'm missing?"

He smiled. "No...you just seem too carefree and impetuous to have a living being to care for."

"Heh...well, I'm not that good at it."

He held Maniac up in the palm of his hand and inspected her. "She's a little skinny, but it looks like you're doing all right." She mewed, and he curled her against his chest again.

"Yeah, well, she ran into my apartment when I moved in, and I didn't have the heart to put her out. Sometimes I think I keep her around because it's nice to have something to come home to, you know?"

Where the hell did that come from? Was I trying to sound lonely and pathetic?

Embarrassed, I turned away from his confused expression and grabbed two bottles of beer from the fridge. "Thanks for coming out with me," I said as I opened his.

He smiled and took the open bottle from me. "No problem. You seem like you needed to have some fun."

"I did." I leaned against the doorjamb and opened my beer. "I'm sorry that I'm so drunk. I don't know what happened."

"The citywide special tends to do that to a person." He sipped his beer and gestured down the hallway. "Let's go sit down."

"Okay."

I followed him down the short hallway into my living room and turned on the lamp.

Elijah set Maniac down, ushered me over to my couch, and sat down next to me.

"I hope you don't get this drunk when you're out alone. Anything could happen to you," he said as he removed my wedge heels and began to massage my feet. A smart remark about being a grown-ass woman died on my tongue and was replaced by a completely involuntary, guttural moan.

"Good?" he asked when it was clear he knew the answer.

"Fuck, yes. How'd you know I needed that?"

"Are you kidding? You stumbled up those stairs like a newborn baby calf."

I laughed with him, lazily twirling my hair around my finger.

"I don't know why women torture themselves wearing shoes like that. They look great, and when you walk, it makes every muscle in your legs tense and quiver deliciously. I definitely appreciate the visual, but the torture of it seems so unnecessary. I can think of much better ways to torture you."

"Really?"

He smirked. "Yes. Really."

I moaned again as he massaged the arch of my foot. He was hitting all the right spots and looked more than a little pleased with himself for it. At that moment, I realized that there was no awkwardness between us. Being with Elijah was easy. I didn't think about it at all. I just enjoyed my time with him. I had to be careful not to get used to this.

"So let's talk about your aversion to casual sex," I began.

"Ohh-kay," he stammered. "What do you want to know?"

"Well, for starters, how strict is this rule?"

"What do you mean?"

"I mean, what is your definition of sex? Is it the Bill Clinton definition or the Mormon definition?"

"Well, first off, it's not a rule. It's just what I think is best for me right now. And as far as strictness goes...no intercourse."

"No intercourse?"

"Nope."

"None?"

"None."

"Damn," I cursed under my breath. "I really wanted to fuck you tonight."

He laughed. "Was that your mission?"

"Yes. And I fear I've failed miserably before I even left the base. But...can I ask you something?"

"Ask me anything," he said invitingly.

I paused for a long moment, trying to gather my thoughts. The fact that my brain was swimming in bourbon and cheap beer didn't help things. "How or why did you decide to become celibate?"

He smiled. "I never said I was celibate."

"Well, you kind of are celibate if you aren't having casual sex."

"No. It just means I want to have sex with people I trust. People I feel safe with and who feel safe with me. I haven't found someone that I feel safe with in a long while."

"Safe," I echoed thoughtfully. Why would he use that word? "Did someone...did someone hurt you?" I asked, my voice soft and careful. In my experience, most men didn't like to talk about their feelings. They especially didn't like it when women went digging around in them.

"Once," he answered. Short and succinct. It was clear he wouldn't discuss it further.

Liquor erases proper boundaries, so I dug around a bit more, anyway. "And she's the reason you don't have casual sex anymore?"

"That and other reasons."

"So, you're saving yourself for marriage?"

He chuckled and gave me a sideways glance. "No, Yves. I'm not waiting for my bride."

"So you're saying that if the right girl came along, you would give it up?"

"For the right woman? Yes."

"Well, I hope that the right woman is me."

Elijah chuckled again and moved on to the next foot, rubbing the pad of his thumb into the arch, coaxing out that moan. He smiled, licking the corner of his mouth mischievously. "I like that."

"What?"

"When you moan like that, it sounds like I'm making love to you."

I frowned. "I don't make love. You can fuck me, screw me, or even lay me, but you can't make love to me."

Elijah looked genuinely distressed. "Why not?"

"I just don't want to feel that way again."

"And what way is that?"

"Hopeless, helpless, vulnerable."

"That's what making love feels like to you?" he asked.

I nodded, slightly distracted by the weight of his green-eyed gaze. He was studying me. I felt like a bug trapped under a glass.

"Well," he kissed the instep of my foot. The press of those full lips on that thin neglected skin made places further north ache for the same treatment. "What if I want to make love to you?"

"I won't be made love to," I repeated.

"We'll see," he said with a smile.

"Really? If you're feeling so confident, why don't you try it right now?"

The bourbon made me bold. All that talk of his abstinence had only served as foreplay to my drunken brain. I swung my leg over him and straddled his lap. His hands clamped around my waist to push me away, but it was a minute too late. My mouth was already on his, and oh...it was as magical as I'd dreamed. That obscenely sexy pout with its too-full lips was made for my kiss. I traced my tongue along the seam of his lips and coaxed it to open for me. He gave a soft moan, and I took advantage of it--covered his mouth with mine and slid my tongue inside. Dios....Never should've done that. That sound, the taste of him--malty with beer and bourbon--the rough, tender flesh of his tongue surrendering to mine. His hands tightened, fingertips pressing deep into my hips.

"Yves," he breathed over my lips, tongue lapping out for another taste.

If I was questioning if I was "that woman" before, I wasn't now. He wanted me just as much--if not more--than I wanted him. I could feel that want growing against my parted thighs. With fingers spread wide, I pushed my hands into his thick, silky hair, grabbed it in fistfuls, and drew him deeper into the kiss. One of his hands slid up to the middle of my back, pulling me closer. This time I was the one who gave the drunken moan.

"Yves," he said again.

"Yes, Elijah?"

"You're not respecting my boundaries." The hand on my back splayed, cradled me. The other drifted lower to cup my ass. Clearly, he wasn't as concerned about his boundaries as he wanted me to believe.

"Just tell me, no, and I'll stop."

He growled in response and kissed me again. The hand in the middle of my back pushed into my hair. He grabbed a handful and yanked, separating our mouths. I gasped as his mouth found purchase on my neck, sucking and then nipping lightly. My pussy clenched every time I felt the edge of his teeth on my skin. He tipped me back a little further, and the room spun.

"Whoa..." I slurred, holding him tighter.

He pulled away and took a good, long look at me.

"What?"

"You're drunk," he said evenly. "We shouldn't do this."

"Don't worry about it. I totally want this. You don't have to be a gentleman. In fact, the less of a gentleman you are, the better it'll be."

Something about that statement rubbed him wrong because he stood up abruptly and set me on my feet. I swayed drunkenly and looked up at him.

"I'm gonna go."

"Don't," I said and sank to my knees.

Elijah froze. My hands were on his thighs, and they felt as solid as stone under my palms. I looked up into his eyes. Apprehension conflicted with the clearly evident desire there. I reached for the waistband of his jeans, curled my fingers over the thick leather belt. His hands grasped mine, stilling them.

"Don't," I said again. But even to my own ears, it sounded like begging. A strange feeling welled in me. Maybe it was because I was already on my knees, or maybe it was the bourbon, but when I looked up at him, his hair falling over his forehead to hide his eyes, his mouth slack and wanting, I felt...worshipful.

"Get up," he said, his voice tremulous.

Getting up was the last thing I wanted to do. I wanted to unbuckle his belt. Get him out of his jeans and into my mouth. The whole scene unfolded in my mind like it had already happened -- his fist wound in my hair, forcing my open mouth onto his dick -- me gagging to accommodate him, tears blurring my vision. But the moment my hand closed over the buckle, he hauled me to my feet.

"You're drunk, Yves. Go to bed. I'll call you in the morning."

THE KISS OF KISSES

AUG 2, 2013

Four quarter-sized bruises on her hip.
Faint love bites on the column of her neck.
Swollen, abused lips.

She would probably think it was a dream if she didn't see the evidence on her skin.

They finally kissed. (Finally!)

And it was the kiss of kisses.

Part of her was reluctant to write this here because she knew he would read it, but the rest of her wanted him to know. Fuck it...he should know. That kiss and what it did to her...he should know.

He probably thought she was too drunk to remember.

She remembered all of it.

The catch of his breath before she claimed his mouth. His fingers digging into her hips until they bit through the denim of her jeans to leave those four quarter-sized marks. The taste of him...the feel of his tongue. His hard want pressing against the seam of her. The big feeling that surged up between them. Bigger than her body. Bigger than his.

Then she was on her knees with her hands on his thighs. Her mind ran away from her at that moment. The image was so vivid that it felt more like a memory than a daydream. She felt the weight of him in her hand and felt that rigid, silky flesh push past her lips. Tasted the sweet musk of him as he filled her throat, triggering tears so that when she looked up at him, he seemed ethereal and made her feel like she was meant to be on her knees at his feet.

That feeling was so strange, but familiar too.

Four quarter-sized marks on her hip.
Faint love bites along the column of her neck.
Swollen abused lips...

She liked seeing his marks on her. She wanted more.

9

"So tell me about your film. I read somewhere that some are considering this to be your Annie Hall. How do you feel about being compared to the likes of Woody Allen?"

The shy young director beamed. Ava stood a few feet away, snapping candid photos. "Well, I'm flattered, of course. I'm honored that someone out there considers my work equivalent to someone so well-known and respected. But honestly, I'm more concerned with my impact on media by presenting a film that stars people of color in roles that they rarely ever get. We are starved for roles and stories that depict people of color outside of the stereotypes that Hollywood seems determined to perpetuate."

"Definitely. You can count me among those eager to see something other than men dressed as old women and sexed-up ghetto girls. How is your film different?"

As a relatively new event in the already-packed festival season, Phillystar Film Festival was quickly becoming a popular event among local creatives, Ava and I, among them. Ava tagged along to get photos for the paper...well, that and to gawk at all the young, ambitious, creative men who hide in plain sight every other weekend of the year. For me, just being around all these artists and submerging myself in their energy helped me gain a little distance from my relationship issues. With so many events happening, it was easy to lose myself in work.

"So..." the young director said as I ended my interview. "We're having a little get-together tonight at a bar not too far from here. I'd love it if you came."

I turned to look at him. He had a smile that shone brightly against smooth, dark skin. Casual confidence clung to his muscular frame like the soft, grey T-shirt he wore. I could go to this party. I could get drunk. I could end the night in whatever hotel he was staying in and stagger home in the early morning. I could do all of that, but none of it sounded appealing.

"I'm sorry...I just have so much work to do. I gotta get this article in by morning and...you know how it is."

He nodded and reached into his back pocket. With practiced accuracy, he plucked a business card from his money clip and handed it to me. "I'm going to be in the city for the next couple of days. Hit me up if you get a free evening."

I took the card from him and stared at it.

"No pressure or nothing. Just thought the two of us might have more than a little in common."

"You'd be right, but can I be honest?" I asked.

His smile faltered and that open fascination that had been in his eyes just a moment ago disappeared. "Sure," he said.

"I'd really love to, but I'm kind of a mess right now. That's the honest truth."

He nodded and shoved his hands in his pockets. "Okay, Ms. Santiago. It was lovely speaking with you."

"Thanks. I enjoyed interviewing you, and I can't wait to view your film."

The young director nodded again and backed away, melting into the crowd. I shoved my phone into my back pocket and turned to Ava. "That's six interviews. Do you think you have enough photos to fill out the article?"

She gaped at me. "What the fuck was that?"

"What? I just didn't feel like going to an after-party."

"What the fuck do you mean? We always go to the after-party. We come to this thing for all the after-parties. I mean, yeah, we come to see the new and talented filmmakers in Philly, but mostly we come here to get invites to after-parties where we get drunk and fuck pretty, young directors who say we have a face for film. What the fuck is going on with you, Yves?"

I rolled my eyes. "Chase him down and get an invite if you want to go to the party. I'm sure he could care less which one of us shows up."

"Yves!" she squeaked. "Who the fuck are you right now?"

I rounded on her. "Look, I've got shit going on. I'm trying to finish writing this book. I've got articles due...I just don't have time to get drunk and fuck a stranger."

Ava shouldered her camera and leaned in so no one else would hear her. "This is me, Yves. Something else is going on. Talk to me. I'm your friend."

Guilt twisted my gut, but I wasn't ready to talk about any of this shit. "I know..."

"Is it your book? We can grab a bottle of vodka and head back to your place to brainstorm. I'm here for you."

"I know you are, Ava. And I really appreciate that. I just need to be alone right now. It's not about you. I promise it isn't."

Ava's eyes searched my face. She didn't believe me, but I

knew she would respect my wishes. "Okay. But call me if you decide you need to talk," she said finally.

"I will. And...FYI that guy over by the step and repeat has been staring at you since we got here. You might want to give him some play."

Her head whipped around, and she scanned the crowd. When her eyes settled on the man of interest, she smiled. "Yeah, text me when you get home safe."

I smirked as I watched my friend twitch her already short skirt up another half inch and fluff her hair. "Yeah, you do the same."

MY MIND WANDERED ON THE WAY BACK TO MY APARTMENT. Ava was right. I wasn't myself. But it was hard not to feel weighed down with everything that was going on. The calls and heartfelt voicemails from Cesar had doubled since the Fourth of July. This, in turn, spurred more confusion in my already-muddled mind. He told me he didn't love Gabby. He said that he would take care of his kids, but what he really wanted was a second chance at a life with me.

I was stretched taut in four different directions, like the points of a compass. One was in search of myself and the woman I thought I could or should be. Another pulled me back into the past in search of the life that I dreamed of with Cesar--which could only be a condition akin to Stockholm syndrome. Then there was Julian. Strong, sweet Julian. He was the kind of guy a girl settled down with. The kinda guy you had babies for and happily absorbed yourself into. I wanted to want him, but it was a dream of something I thought I should have. The third and strongest pull was toward something, seemingly solid and promising, with Elijah. I couldn't even imagine what had me thinking in that vein, especially after his I-don't-do-casual-sex speech on my steps and flippant dismissal of my drunken sexual overture. It was clear he wasn't interested in going there with me. And to be honest, as fucked up as I was about Cesar, I had no business going there with him. Besides, it sounded so trite. White man rides in on his horse and saves the little Latina from her sad, sorry life. That sounded way too West Side Story, and I was no charming and fair Maria. I couldn't help thinking that it was destined to end almost as badly as the play did.

But that didn't stop me from daydreaming about him.

His dark green eyes. His pale blond eyelashes. That lopsided smile and his surreal confidence. That Star of David suspended on a thin gold chain around his neck that made his shoulders seem even more sexy and irresistible. The man stayed on my mind more often than I'd like to admit...

But that might be classic procrastination.

At this point, I would probably do anything to avoid being locked in a staring contest with my laptop. With only my cigarettes and Maniac to keep me company, my shitty little apartment felt just as empty as the bright, white screen. Coupled with my lack of productivity, it felt more like a prison than the seven hundred square feet I usually called home.

Nearly thirty days had passed since Elijah came to me with his informal book proposal, and I had little more than fifteen thousand words. Yes, all the material was on my blog, but compiling those posts into a book exposed the gaps in my "plot." Giving the book real structure meant I would need to dig into those things I didn't want to talk about, the hurts I wanted to avoid.

I didn't have a deadline. Elijah didn't plan on

approaching his boss until I had most of it done. Still, I felt like I was on the fast track to disappointing the one person who truly believed in me, and it vexed me, to say the very least. Not to mention that it had me consulting the thesaurus and the dictionary far more than I usually did, and my usual street talk was now peppered with words I didn't normally use.

This whole process was a lot more difficult than I thought it would be. Writing the emotional bits forced me to tell the truth in a way that was uncomfortable for me. It revealed too much of myself, and I wasn't happy with what I'd already uncovered.

I pushed away from my writing desk and paced behind my chair a little. The still-blank screen mocked me in my peripheral vision. Just as I was about to collapse onto the couch and resign myself to being a loser, the phone rang. I picked it up reluctantly, praying that it wasn't another call from Cesar. I breathed a sigh of relief when I saw my mother's number on the screen.

"Yeah, Ma, what's up?"

"What took you so long to answer?"

"I was working,"

"Well, that's good. How's it going?"

I frowned. "What's going on? You sound weird."

"Oh, nothing. I just started dinner, but Mercedes and the girls are still out of town, and Marcelo is working."

My mother was about as subtle as a hammer. She knew before she started cooking that she would be eating dinner alone. Marcelo was always working, and Mercedes and the girls were at the beach in Seaside Heights and wouldn't be back until the end of the weekend. Her only reason for cooking dinner was to lure me over so that we could talk. I kinda knew what she wanted to discuss, too.

"I'll be there in an hour," I told her and hung up the phone.

On the bus ride and short walk over, I decided that if my mother brought up Cesar again, I would tell her about what happened between us. It was past time for her to know the truth. At the very least, she would finally stop holding him up on a pedestal. Knowing my mother, she would demand to know what I had done to make him behave that way. Instead of being disgusted by the things he said and did to me, why and what for would be the questions of the day. As if it had to be something about me that would make him into someone other than the man she knew. And honestly, after seeing him with his daughter, I was beginning to wonder the same thing myself.

A blast of cold air greeted me when I stepped inside my mother's house, and I was thankful for it. Air conditioning was somewhat of a luxury for me since I barely made enough to pay my rent and dress in last year's designs. I only turned on the AC at night so that I could sleep comfortably. The rest of the time, I made do with fans and minimal clothing.

"¡Mami!" I called out as I dropped my bag on the couch.

"¡Yves, Estoy in la cocina!"

"You're always in the kitchen, Ma!" I called back, fanning my armpits as I crossed the living room. "Sometimes, I wonder if it's where you were born," I mumbled to myself as I passed that stupid prom picture again. I stopped and took a moment to snatch the picture off the wall before I went into the kitchen. "Mamí, why do you keep this picture up even though I've asked you countless times to take it down?"

"¿Que?" she asked as she turned to see what I was talking about. I held up the picture so she could see it. "Oh, I keep it up because it's a beautiful picture of my beautiful daughter."

Great. That's an argument ender if there ever was one.

"Besides, it's not as if you and Cesar didn't have any good times. You do want to remember the good times, don't you?"

"Sure..." If she says one more thing, I'm going to tell her, I swore to myself. But she grew quiet, as if she had sensed my agitation.

"So, what's for dinner?" I peeked into the pots. She smacked the back of my hand. "Oww!" I yowled, rubbing the place where her fingertips met my skin.

"Stay out of the pots. Make yourself useful by setting the table."

"But it's just the two of us--"

"Yves!" she exclaimed, holding up one finger that said, I-am-your-mother-do-as-I-say. I rolled my eyes and grumbled but did as I was told.

"So your sister told me about this blog and the book you're writing. How's that coming?"

A sarcastic laugh escaped before I could rein it in. I already knew that she knew, and I should've expected to be ambushed after the conversation I had with Mercy, but this approach caught me off guard. "Do you really want to know?"

"Of course, I want to know! I'm very hurt that you didn't share that news with me. I'm even more hurt that you've been writing this blog for almost two years, and you never told me."

I rolled my eyes again. "Okay, Mother," I said. There was no point arguing about it now. I knew my mother well enough to know that she wouldn't like me writing a blog about my sexual exploits, much less publishing a book about it.

"Okay, maybe you're right, Yves. I was a little shocked by the things I read. To do it is one thing, but to write about it and post it on the Internet? I don't know how to feel about that. You can understand that, right?"

"Sure."

My mother sucked her teeth. "You're upset. I don't think you should hold my reaction against me."

I shrugged. "I don't, Ma. Your reaction was textbook Luz Santiago. That's why I didn't tell you in the first place."

"I just don't want to believe you're that type of girl."

"What type of girl, Ma?" I asked, turning to her.

"The type that sleeps around."

"As opposed to the type that abandons all her hopes and dreams to get married?"

"Is that what you really think of me? That I gave up my hopes and dreams to marry your father?"

"No, I--I didn't mean you. I meant any girl who marries young without going to college or finding out who she really is before losing herself in a man."

"So you mean me," she said firmly. "I didn't give up a single hope or dream to marry your father. He was my dream. I couldn't wait to be his wife, and when you kids came, I loved being a mother. Even to you, though, you challenge me far more than your brother and sister."

"But how can you say that when you were divorced before you turned twenty-five?"

"So what? It ended badly, so what? I don't regret a minute of it. I loved your father, and every moment was worth it because I got you and Marcelo and Mercedes out of it."

"And that's enough to make you happy?"

"Chiquita...absolutely." She kissed me on the cheek.

Belatedly, I realized how insulting that could be to my mother. Or even my sister, who prided herself on being a stay-at-home mom. I didn't believe that staying at home to take of your children was an ignoble thing. I just didn't like the idea that it was the default rather than a choice. But in my stance against this, I had been dismissive of her positive influence on my life. My face burned with shame.

"I'm sorry, Mamí. I didn't mean to make you feel like I didn't respect you and appreciate all that you've done for me."

"I understand. It's just not the way you want to live your life. I get it. But you might also want to consider that it might not be as much of a sacrifice if you settled down with the right man."

I nodded, knowing that she meant Cesar. She didn't push the topic any further, though, and I was relieved.

After I set the table, my mother and I sat down to a quiet dinner. I didn't realize how hungry I was until my mother set a plate of beans and rice, marinated pork, and fresh green salad in front of me. When I scraped my fork across my plate, she heaped on another helping. I was halfway through my second helping when the doorbell rang.

"Who could that be?" I asked.

For as long as I could remember, everyone on the block ate dinner at the same time. A visitor during dinner was highly irregular.

My mother jumped to her feet. "I'll get it. Finish eating."

When she left, I piled another helping of pork on my plate. I really needed to learn how to cook. Maybe I could get Mamí to teach me a few easy things to get me started.

A few moments later, she reappeared. "Look what I found on the stoop," she said, stepping aside. Cesar walked in behind her, his face split in a ridiculous grin. The fork full of rice and beans I was in the process of swallowing wadded in my throat.

"Hey, Yves," he said softly.

I knew I should respond with some sort of greeting, but I could barely swallow, let alone force enough air over my windpipe to speak. He sat down at the table across from me.

"I made you something, Cesar." My mother retrieved a plate of crispy, fried plantain from the microwave and served it to him with a dipping sauce that was made from mayo, ketchup, and mashed garlic cloves. But that wasn't what was significant about this dish. The significance lay in the fact that my mother knew it was Cesar's favorite and had made it ahead of time. She knew he would stop by. This whole thing was a setup.

Well, fuck me running.

I glared at my mother as she set the plate of plantain in front of him. My own mother, a fucking traitor. Now that special moment we shared in the kitchen seemed completely contrived.

"Don't look at me like that, chiquita. You wouldn't have shown up if I didn't trick you into it. The two of you need to talk."

I sighed and held my head in my hands. "I don't understand why you keep doing this, Mamí."

My mother patted my shoulder and left Cesar and me alone in the kitchen.

"Listen, I would have never agreed to this if I knew she was going to trick you into being here--"

"You called my mother?"

"I didn't call her. She called me. She told me that you wanted to talk."

I looked him in the eye. "So you're telling me you're a victim, too?"

"It would appear that I am."

We sat quietly for a moment. Neither of us knew what to do next.

"I'll go if you want," he said finally.

"No," I sat back and tucked my hair behind my ears. "She went to so much trouble to get us here. We should at least make an effort to settle this once and for all."

He smiled warily. "Settle it," he echoed softly. "To me, there is only way this can be settled, Yves."

"And I'm sure it's in complete opposition to how I think it should be settled." I snagged one of the plantain chips, dipped it in the sauce, and munched on it quietly while I organized my thoughts.

"Still eat like a horse, I see."

"What are you talking about? I don't eat a lot. Look at this figure. Do you think I could eat a lot and still look like this?"

"I know it looks like you had at least two helpings of whatever your mom made for dinner, and now you're eating the plantain she made for me."

"Whatever. You act like you know me or something," I mumbled sarcastically.

"I do know you. I know you backwards and forwards."

"And inside out," I said with a laugh, finishing the inside joke we'd had for years. "We have known each other a long time," I agreed as I stared at him, leaning my chin on my hand. He reached across the table and touched my other hand, interlocking his fingers with mine. This was familiar, but it was a good familiar. "Cesar?"

"Yes," he whispered.

"I think I'm ready to really talk."

10

As I opened the door to my apartment, it crossed my mind that I was breaking the rules again. The last encounter between Cesar and me involved the cops, and I had no reason to believe that things would be different now. The odds were seventy to twenty in favor of regretting this for the rest of my days. And yet, here he was, crossing my threshold.

"Shit!" I hissed as Maniac slipped between my legs. I was so distracted by thoughts and general anxiety that I forgot to block the door to prevent her escape. When I turned around, I was relieved to see that Cesar already had her by the scruff of the neck.

"Maniac." He curled her into the crook of his arm and rubbed her belly. "Still living up to your name, huh?" he muttered to the cat. Maniac wriggled out of his hands; hissing and spitting, she ran into my bedroom.

I let out a sigh of relief. Chasing my stupid cat was not on my list of things to do. I was thankful he'd grabbed her before she managed to slip out the door.

"You want a beer?" I asked when I reached the top of the stairs.

"No, thanks," he said.

"Are you sure?" I walked into the kitchen and opened the fridge to get myself one. "I've got some Rolling Rock," I told him, knowing that it was his favorite cheap beer next to forty ounces of Old English.

"Nah, I don't drink anymore."

"Yeah, right." I grabbed two beers out of the fridge and handed him one. He didn't take it. "You're serious? You really don't drink anymore?"

"Nope."

"Since when?"

He shrugged and leaned on the door frame in that nonchalant way I used to love. "Since I ended up on probation after I got a DUI."

"When did all this happen?"

"Not too long after our last breakup, so about three years ago, I guess."

"Wow, I didn't know that." I stared at him in disbelief.

"Yep, it took a while, but I've been sober almost two years now. I'm also in therapy and anger management. All of which I needed years ago, but better late than never, I guess. I wish it had been sooner rather than later, but..."

I nodded and put both of the beers back in the fridge.

"You can have a beer, Yves. It won't bother me."

"I don't want to drink if you're not going to. I think it's really great that you're not drinking anymore, and I want to respect that. Thing is, I don't really have anything else in here to drink but water and like a corner of orange juice."

He laughed. "Same 'ole Yves."

I smiled, but the statement made me feel sad. "Some things about me have changed."

"I know. A lot of things about you have changed. It makes me happy to know some things haven't."

"Let's go in the living room so we can talk," I said and showed him into my austere space. Most of my furniture was secondhand, acquired at thrift shops and consignment stores. But what room lacked in modernity was made up in color.

"Your place is a lot nicer than it was the last time I was here," he said as he sat down on the couch. He seemed to be all knees and elbows on the couch that fit me comfortably. "It's nice. It suits you," he said as he looked around.

"Thank you." I tucked myself into the corner of the couch next to him. An awkward silence wedged into the space between us. I didn't know where or how to start this conversation. "Am I a masochist or just plain stupid? I can't figure out which," I muttered, mostly to myself.

He shrugged, looking confused.

"I took down our prom picture today. You know the one that's been hanging on the wall since I was in eleventh grade?"

"I know the one. Why'd you do that?"

"It feels like I can't go anywhere or do anything without being reminded of you and us. When I took it down, I asked Mamí why she kept it up, even though I've asked her hundreds of times to take it down. She gave me a patented Luz Santiago response--'It's a beautiful picture of my beautiful daughter.'"

Cesar smiled a little, but he still looked uncomfortable.

"Then she asks me, 'don't you want to remember the good times, chiquita?'"

"I do," he said, his voice soft and hopeful.

"I do, too, but it's hard for me. The good times are so few, and the bad times overshadow them far too easily."

Cesar sighed and covered his face with his hands.

"I know you don't want to talk about this, but you had your chance to say what you wanted to say. I need to say my piece."

"You just want to beat me up for all the mistakes I made back then--"

"I don't want to beat you up. I just want you to understand how much you hurt me."

"I do understand how much I hurt you."

"No, you don't, Cesar." I shook my head. "If you did, you wouldn't be here right now. You would never bother talking to me, not even in passing because you'd know you have no right to." I watched his jaw flex as he clenched his teeth. It was a tell, one I'd seen often. Even now, it made every muscle in my body tense. "Do you remember the first time you told me you loved me?"

"Of course I do. It was right before the first time we made love."

I nodded quietly and looked at him. "You told me you would never hurt me. And then you made me come so hard I thought I pissed the bed."

He chuckled and relaxed a bit. "You were mortified. You swore I'd broken something inside of you. I had to talk you out of going to the emergency room."

I wanted to laugh with him, but I couldn't because another memory followed that one. "The first time you hit me was a week later. Do you remember that?"

He didn't answer. The tension crept back into his neck and shoulders.

"I knew you before I even had breasts," I began haltingly. How can these memories still be so painful after all this time? "You say you know me, backwards and forwards and inside out, and that's true. But I know you too, Cesar. I've known you all my life, and I've loved you just as long. Maybe that's why I made so many excuses for you back then. I know how fucked up your home life was. I know that your Papí beat you and your Mamí, and you saw some horrible shit when you were growing up. And when you cried, I was the one who held you. I was the one who kept your secrets."

"I know."

"I was the only one who was there for you."

"I know."

"You slammed me into a wall--"

"Yves--"

"I was five months pregnant with our son. Five months pregnant." My body was quaking with anger and resentment. "You slammed me into a wall...you slammed me so fucking hard, and then you left me, Cesar. I had to get myself to the hospital. I rode in a fucking yellow cab with my baby bleeding out of me. I lay on that fucking hospital bed while they scraped what was left of my son out of me. And even then, I protected you. I told them lies. I made them believe that I fell. Until this day, my mother doesn't know what you did to me. What did I do to deserve that, Cesar?"

"Nothing," he whispered. "You never deserved to be treated that way."

"You keep talking about him like I lost him. Like it was some spontaneous miscarriage. Do you realize how that makes me feel?"

"I..." He shrugged. "I don't mean to diminish what you went through, what I did to you. It's just, I have a hard time reconciling the idea in my mind. That I..." he floundered, searching for words to describe what he had done.

"That you hit me so hard that it killed our baby," I finished for him.

He cringed. I was glad. Hurtful words were the least of what he deserved. It was only a nth of what I felt when I thought about our son.

"I didn't--I never--" Cesar stammered. He paused for a moment to get his thoughts together. "I never wanted to hurt you. I loved you. I still do. But when things felt like they were getting out of control or I felt too much pressure from you or just life in general, I lashed out. Unfortunately, you were the one who was there--"

"I was always there for you. The only one."

"I know. And I hurt you the most. You being pregnant with CJ terrified me. It transformed you. You were like a lion for him, Yves. And I felt apart from you. I don't know how else to explain it. That night I was so angry with you for accusing me of turning into my father that I just lost it."

"Even after all that, like an asshole, I wanted to forgive you. Even now, I feel guilty for how alone you must have felt."

He slid off the couch and knelt at my feet. I could barely make out his face through my tears.

"Yves, I..." He struggled with his words and wiped my cheeks as he looked at me. "I won't make excuses, Yves. There is no excuse for what I did to you."

"How could I still love you after all of that?"

"I don't know," he answered honestly.

"You fucked me up, Cesar. You fucked me up bad. You left a hole inside of me that I don't think can ever be filled. And I keep fucking all these guys--I keep fucking all these guys, and I can't feel anything."

He stopped my mouth with his kisses. I tried to resist, but I felt myself giving in. I felt myself wanting to forget.

"No!" I pushed him away, but deep inside of me, I felt a hungry growl that made me grab him back. I wanted to hurt him. I wanted to fuck him and hurt him all at once. Before I even realized what I was doing, I drew my hand back and slapped him. Every hurt that he had ever made me feel was in that slap. All the biting words, all the bruises, all the ways he made me feel inferior, unworthy, and just plain not good enough. I put it all into that slap across his cheekbone.

I knew I had slapped him hard because my hand was stinging, and his jaw was twitching from the hit. But it wasn't enough. I slapped him again and again, and I kept slapping him until tears sprang to his eyes.

Cesar didn't fight back when I hit him, but he didn't crumble either. He took the beating like he deserved it, which only made me want to hurt him more. When I finally grew tired, and my blows lost their steam, he kissed me again. Slow kisses. Sweet kisses. Kisses that made me remember what it was like to be his. Then he undressed me with quiet reverence, like he didn't want to rush or miss one second. He blessed me all over with his mouth.

"God, I've missed the taste of you," he whispered. His mouth was soft, warm, and attentive. He covered each beauty mark along my neck and the left side of my face with his lips. He once told me that they looked like pepper flakes. "This is your spicy side," he used to say. "And the other side is the sweet." I wondered if he could taste the bitterness now.

He whispered to me as we made love. He whispered apologies and promises. He kissed me, touched me, and aroused me in all the familiar ways with his hands, tongue, and finally, his dick deep inside of me. It was brutal and tender, and all I could do was cry. I cried because I knew this would be the last time. I could never forgive him. I could never forget. Making love to him this time made me feel like something used up and empty, and he knew it. He knew it was his fault.

When it was over, Cesar held me and cried quietly into my hair. He could feel it, too. He knew what went wrong couldn't be fixed or undone. He knew that I would always flinch from his touch. That whenever I looked at him, I would always think of our unborn son, and nothing he could ever say or do would change that or make it right.

Cesar gathered himself up and dressed silently. What was left to say? With so many years and so many words between us, we had exhausted both the English and Spanish languages with all the different ways to apologize and all the different ways to express forgiveness. All that was left was to say goodbye. He turned to me at the door anyway, his mouth full of those empty words. I shook my head to let him know that he shouldn't bother. He nodded, and then a slow, sad smile spread across his face.

"The one who got away," he murmured. "It's one of those stupid things you hear old men say as they sip cheap whiskey in bars. It sounds so cliché, but it's true. You'll be my one, Yves. I chased you away. I guess I'll just have to live with that regret."

SOMOS LO QUE HAY

AUGUST 12, 2013

Her sexuality defined her before she really knew what it was. Flat-chested and scabby kneed, she wrestled with boys to prove that she was tough. Tough seemed like the best thing to be where she came from. The meanest, toughest boys had the biggest groups of friends. Everywhere they went, people knew and respected them. When they walked down the sidewalk, people gave way. She had no idea that this was no way for a "lady" to behave. She just wanted to be included. To be deemed worthy. To be one of them.

Being tough was more important than being pretty or smart or funny. No one fucked with you if you were tough. No one tugged on your pigtails or dunked you in the city pool when they knew you would pin them to the ground and punch them until they said uncle or someone broke it up.

She wished she could be ashamed of how she felt in those moments, but she wasn't.

The grappling, the sweating, the cursing, the feel of two

bodies struggling with all their might excited her. She loved the struggle. She loved the helplessness of being pinned down almost as much as she loved to be the one on top. It never occurred to her to be concerned about the way their bodies aligned or where their hands landed because she wasn't a girl. She was tough. She was one of them.

Puberty hit overnight, and the surge of hormones brought about a change in her body that she neither wanted nor understood. Suddenly, she was a girl again. Too delicate to be hurt, pinned, or wrestled with. Doors opened for her, and people gave way for a different reason. It didn't take her long to realize that there was something more powerful than being tough among those rough boys.

Now their hands landed on her body in different ways. They weren't just shoving her to the ground. They were smashing her against the wall to keep her fighting limbs still enough to kiss her. With their narrow hips pressed right up between her legs and their weight pinning her down, she felt the same sort of exhilaration...the same soaring freedom. Because no matter who was on top, she always won in the end.

Part of her wondered if all that tussling in her youth made her think it was okay when he started hitting her. That's love...right? This was how it felt to have someone care about her...right?

But maybe she was just making excuses again...finding ways to justify his brutality and make sense of this weird kink in her psyche because nothing had changed. She still loved the struggle. She still wanted to be pinned down. And he still beat on her while whispering his I love yous.

Nothing changed. She was the same, and so was he.

Somos lo que hay.

We are what we are....

11

I hated waking up to a ringing phone. I really, really did. It was almost always someone I didn't want to talk to, talking about something I didn't want to talk about. When I picked up the line, my first inclination was to immediately start hurling expletives. Anyone who knew me knew I didn't roll over until at least noon. If you called before that, you really couldn't expect me to be anything other than hostile.

"What?" I barked into the line.

"Do you always answer the phone like that, or is this a special privilege you reserve only for me?"

"That all depends. Who the fuck is this and what the fuck do you want?"

"Whoa...it's Elijah. Did I catch you at a bad time?"

"Oh..." I muttered, feeling small and vicious. "I'm sorry, Elijah."

"Do you want me to call you back?"

"No." I sat up in bed and ran my fingers through my tangled hair. "What's up?"

He laughed. "That's something I should ask you, don't you think?"

"What do you mean?"

"I haven't seen or heard from you in a few days, and I open the Friday edition of Philadelphia Inquirer to the lifestyle section and find an article about Julian Webster's latest exhibit--"

"Julian Webster? Yeah, I wrote an article about him and the other artists in the Philadelphian a month or so ago. Is that what are you talking about?"

"No...you really don't know anything about this?"

"Know anything about what?"

"The paintings."

"What paintings?"

Elijah sighed. It sounded bemused. "Julian Webster is apparently painting a whole series of you, Yves."

"No way--"

"Yes, way. The exhibit is going to be at a small gallery in Old City called Desirable Objects. Google it."

I crawled out of bed and stumbled to my writing desk and laptop. When I typed Julian Webster's name into the search bar, over two thousand results popped up. All the links on the first page mentioned me. I clicked on the first one and the web page opened, broadcasting Julian's planned exhibit accompanied by a detailed sketch of me--naked.

"Oh, fuck," I moaned in disbelief. "That little shit!" A strange mixture of pride and horror twisted in my belly. Julian had told me he wouldn't quit trying to woo me, but I didn't expect anything like this.

Elijah laughed. "I can't believe you didn't know about this. He never said anything to you?"

"No, not a word."

"Well, I say you give the guy another chance. These sketches are really amazing."

"Oh, God! The sketches are in the newspaper?"

"Yup, accompanied by a rather long article proclaiming you as his muse."

"Above or below the fold?"

"Above and below the fold."

"Oh, fuck...My mother is going to see this! Isn't this against the law or something?"

"No...not really. You could sue him for defamation of character, but don't take this the wrong way, I don't think it'll hold up in court," he added with a chuckle. "What did you do to this guy?"

"I fucked him once. I nearly did it again, but he was starting to have feelings for me, so I realized pretty quickly that would be a mistake."

"Wow. You bedded this guy once, and he's painting a series of portraits of you? I might be a little scared," he joked.

"You should be," I countered, snidely.

"Do you realize that there will be portraits of you hanging in some wealthy woman's living room?"

"I'd rather not think about it. This whole thing seems so bizarre."

"Well, we couldn't have asked for better publicity for your book. How's that coming, anyway?"

"Slow," I admitted. "Would you be willing to read what I have and give me your honest opinion?"

"Of course, that's what I'm here for."

"What are you doing later on tonight?"

"I have plans," he replied simply.

"Really? What kind of plans? Maybe I could tag along?"

"I don't think that would be appropriate."

"Oh, really?" I said with a nod. "Do you have a date with some other ridiculously talented author?"

He let out a surprised laugh. "Not that I have to tell you this, but no. My parents are in town. I'm meeting them for dinner."

"Hmm...Not good enough to meet the folks, huh?"

"Do you want to meet my folks?"

"Nah, I'm good. I just like knowing that you think I'm worthy of it."

"Are you sure? Cause you're talking kinda slow--"

"I'm sure."

He laughed again. I kinda liked the sound of it. I would like it even more if it wasn't at my expense.

"You'll probably be busy with Julian Webster, anyway."

"Or someone else. Who knows? It's early yet."

"Come on, Yves. It's just the two of us here. You can admit that you want to see me."

"You wish," was my sarcastic reply, but deep down I did feel a little...something? Maybe I did want to see him just a little. If only to do a better job of seducing him than I did the other night. But he didn't need to know all of that.

"Why don't you come over on Sunday for brunch around eleven-thirty? My parents will still be here so you can meet them then. After they leave, we can talk about your book. How's that sound?"

"Sure," I agreed, a satisfied smile spreading across my face.

"Okay, I'll see you tomorrow then."

THE NEXT DAY I STOOD OUTSIDE OF ELIJAH'S CONDO, WITH champagne and orange juice in hand for mid-morning mimosas, and tried to figure out why I ever agreed to this. Why would I need to meet his parents? I never meet the parents. In fact, a suggestion that I should meet the parents usually made me strap on my Nikes and start running in the opposite direction. The only parents I had ever met were Cesar's and, needless to say, that didn't go over well. But somehow, I worked myself into a nervous anticipation over meeting these two people, as if this meeting bore some significance.

Elijah opened the door and slowly took me in from head to toe. Standing in front of him when he looked at me like that felt like being undressed without taking a thing off. He was dressed casually in a T-shirt and soft, well-worn jeans. His feet were bare. I couldn't explain it, but somehow seeing his naked feet seemed strangely intimate.

"Sorry I kept you waiting out here so long. I was helping my mother in the kitchen."

"No problem," I answered nonchalantly, though I was feeling anything but nonchalant. My body was reacting in a way I didn't understand. My pulse thundered in my ears, and my palms were sweaty. I had the urge to run. These clues from my body signaled the fight-or-flight instinct, and paired with the overwhelming desire to jump his bones, it left me feeling completely confused.

"What's in the bag?" he asked, taking it from my hands.

"Champagne and orange juice for mimosas."

His smile widened knowingly. "Yeah, you and my mother are about to become fast friends," he said with a nod. "Mom? Dad?" he called out as we neared the kitchen.

His mother appeared first, an apron tied around her waist and a smile identical to Elijah's on her face. He got his blond hair and green eyes from her. His father followed close behind. He was tall and lean like Elijah. He had dark hair, dark eyes, and a serious face.

"Mom, Dad, this is my girlfriend Yves."

My chin hit my chest, and I whipped my head around to meet Elijah's eyes. He only smiled.

What is he playing at, introducing me like that?

"Yves, these are my parents, Helen and Josiah."

"N-n-nice to meet you," I stammered, extending my hand to his mother first.

"My word, Elijah...is this the young woman in those sketches in the Philadelphia Inquirer?"

Okay, this was horrifying. If I could turn myself inside out right now, I would. I lasered Elijah with another glare that was again met by a smug and amused smile.

"The very same," he answered.

I clenched my fists and looked down at my feet, trying to figure out a way to leave gracefully without embarrassing myself further.

"Did you pose for the artist, Yves?" Helen asked.

"Uh...no, not exactly." My cheeks grew hot with anger and embarrassment.

"Oh, but he seems to know you so intimately. You must have dated for some time."

"You could say that."

Please change the subject!

"Well, those portraits--though they were beautiful--did you little justice. You are breathtaking! With all that beautiful hair; this gorgeous, healthy complexion; and those startling light brown eyes--it's no wonder you inspired that Julian Webster. She reminds me of that song...how's it go, Joe?"

"The girl from Ipanema."

"Yes, that's exactly it!"

I laughed. That was not the response I expected.

"She's definitely beautiful," Josiah said with a wink.

"I don't know about all that, but thank you for saying so," I replied meekly.

We sat down to brunch. Helen downed several mimosas and was soon very loose and pliable. Josiah, however, questioned me like the inquisition.

"So what's your nationality, Yves?"

"I'm Dominican, sir."

"Please, call me Joe," he corrected. "And you are American born?"

"Dad--" Elijah interrupted and then cautioned him wordlessly. They exchanged a look that I couldn't interpret.

"Yes."

"Really?"

I nodded.

Josiah sat back and folded his arms across his chest. "And what do you think of the current state of immigration in our country?"

"What the fuck, Dad?"

I laughed at how quickly Elijah came to my defense. "It's okay, Elijah. I'm a big girl." I leaned forward onto the table, resting on my elbows. "I suppose you want to know my thoughts on immigration because I am obviously from a family of immigrants?" I asked with a raise of my brow.

His father nodded, unfazed.

"You don't have to answer this question, Yves--"

I shushed Elijah with a wave of my hand. "Well, to be perfectly honest, Joe, if I were to say that I have a problem with immigrants, I would be a hypocrite--as would you. If our families weren't able to emigrate to the US, we would not be here enjoying the wonderful freedoms of this great country. On the other hand, I do recognize that border security is a problem. I think that the immigration laws that are in place should be enforced."

"And what about the people who are here and have been here for years. Should they be deported?"

"No. They've been contributing to this economy for however long they've been in the country. Becoming a citizen should always be the goal and they should demonstrate a desire to do so." I leaned back in my chair and mirrored his relaxed pose. "Does that answer your question?"

Josiah glared at me for a long moment and nodded his head. "Indeed, it does."

After brunch and a considerable amount of coffee and conversation, the Weinsteins called a car and prepared to leave. They had a four o'clock flight back to NYC and Elijah seemed relieved to see them go.

"It really was a pleasure meeting you, Yves. When I come down next time, we'll have to do a girls day."

"I would like that," I said as I accepted Helen's airy kiss on the cheek.

"Yves." Josiah extended his hand in a businesslike manner. "I enjoyed your company. We should do it again the next time Helen and I visit."

"Sure." I was nearly positive that this man didn't like me and I couldn't imagine why he would want to spend another moment in my presence. Elijah's mother turned to him before they climbed into the town car and pulled him into a hug. She mumbled something in his ear to which he answered: "I'll try." Then she slipped into the car next to her husband.

Elijah slipped his hand around my waist and pulled me in close as he waved them off. "Well, you were a hit," he murmured.

"And what was this? Some sort of audition?" I asked as we turned to head back inside.

"Sort of."

I eyed him quizzically as I followed him into the elevator. "So what's with introducing me as your girlfriend?"

He shrugged. "My parents are always riding me about settling down. I figured this would shut them up for a while."

"I can totally sympathize with that. My mother's the same way. Every conversation I have with her lately begins and ends with, when are you going to get married?"

He punched the button for the elevator and stood with his hands in his pockets. A tiny smile pulled up the corner of his mouth. "So you're one of those."

"One of what?"

"One of those girls who say they don't want to be married, but have entries in their diary planning out their wedding."

"It's a journal, not a diary, and I plead the fifth."

He laughed again and trailed his fingers down the length of my bare arm. Goosebumps lit my skin in their wake.

"So...what are you going to tell them when I'm not here the next time they come down?" I asked. The elevator doors opened on his floor and he stepped out.

"Are you going somewhere?"

"No."

He glanced at me over his shoulder. "So I won't have to tell them anything."

I frowned. Was there some sort of hidden meaning in his words? I tried to dissect that meaning as we walked toward the door to his place in silence.

"Did you bring your pages?" he asked once we were inside.

"Yeah." I found my bag, dug them out, and handed them over.

"It doesn't feel like much."

"I told you it was slow going."

He nodded, flopped down onto the couch, and kicked his naked feet up.

"You're gonna read it now?"

"That's why you brought it over, right?"

"Well, yeah, but I didn't think you would read it while I was here."

He tossed me the remote. "This shouldn't take me long."

I flipped through the stations for a moment and settled on Volver on HBO. I watched for a little while, but I found it difficult to focus on the story line because out of the corner of my eye, I saw Elijah's eyes dashing back and forth across my pages. His brow furrowed as he continued to read. The furrow became deeper and deeper until a scowl darkened his face.

"Is something wrong?"

He held up his index finger for silence. So I shut my mouth, but I could no longer keep still. I stood up and paced.

"Yves?"

"Yes?"

"Pacing the floor isn't going to make me read this any faster. It's only going to annoy me," he said as he flipped another page upside down on the couch beside him.

"Sorry," I mumbled, standing still. "Can I smoke?"

"No."

I raked my fingers through my hair and looked around.

"I'll clean the kitchen then," and disappeared before he could protest.

THE DISHES WERE DONE, AND I WAS IN THE MIDST OF WIPING the counters when he came into the room. He tossed my manuscript onto the breakfast bar and straddled a bar stool. I couldn't read the look on his face, but if I were to guess, he didn't like what he read.

"First things first...are you done with this prick?"

"Who? Cesar?"

"Yes, who else would I be talking about?"

"Yes, Elijah. I'm done with Cesar."

He questioned me again with his eyes.

"Okay, so I did see him again...a few days ago. I tried to make him understand how much he hurt me. I think he finally understood it this time. It doesn't really matter if he did or not. I won't see him again."

"Does he know you're writing this book?"

I shrugged. "I don't think so."

"Well, you either need to tell him and get him to sign a release form or change his name to protect his identity, because this is a lawsuit waiting to happen. In fact, it would be easier to change all the names."

"Okay, I'll do that then."

He flipped through the pages again, stroking his chin.

"You hate it, don't you?"

"I don't hate it," he said slowly. "But I don't love it either."

I bristled at the sting of his rejection.

"It's just missing something." He looked at me, and I could tell he was trying to be careful with his words. "What made you abandon the third person narrative?"

"I don't know. I thought the first person would be better for memoirs."

"In most cases, yes. But in your case it just feels a little...contrived."

"Contrived!"

"Don't get upset. You wanted constructive criticism, so here it is."

I folded my arms across my chest--officially on the defensive.

"I think the number one reason why I don't love this is that you're leaving out all the witty little things from your blog, all the things that make you a brilliant writer. I think you've gone too far inside yourself. You've let your self-consciousness get in the way and it's altering the story. It just seems very...careful. Does that make sense to you?"

I took a moment to digest everything he said. It didn't take me long to realize that he was right. I leaned on the countertop. "So what do I do?"

"Do whatever you think is best, but in my opinion you need to stop writing as Yves and start writing as the anonymous blogger who started the Lust Diaries."

"But she's not real. She's just some fragmented part of me."

"Of course she's real, Yves." Elijah frowned. "I would argue that she is more real than the person you present to everyone." He walked around the counter and pulled me into his arms. "Did I hurt your feelings?"

"No, everything you said is true. I know that the reason why I can't write it is because I feel the same way. I guess I just needed to hear it out loud." I looked up at him. "I don't know why I let you talk to me this way, and whenever I'm around you, I feel this uncontrollable urge to tell you everything. It seems like I can't do anything without running it by you first."

He chuckled softly. "Well, I'm flattered. I don't know what I've done to deserve this honor, but I happily accept it." He drew his lips across my cheek and I held my breath, wanting, waiting for him to kiss me.

"So...Julian Webster. Is that the sort of guy you like?"

I rolled my eyes.

"Seriously, is that your type? Tall, brown skin, Boris Kodjoe looking dudes?"

"He's a'ight," I said, giving a one shoulder shrug.

"Seems like a nice guy. You should be with a nice guy."

"You're not a nice guy?"

"Far from it."

"What if I don't want a nice guy?"

"What do you want?"

You, my subconscious whispered...but it could've very easily been my body. Great. And now I was thinking of my body against his body and all of me flushed hot. "Are you worried about the competition?" I asked, trying to lighten the mood.

"Who says I'm worried?"

"You think you have your hooks in that deep, huh?"

"I know I do. You're just too stubborn to admit it."

"I think it's me that has my hooks in you."

"You might be right."

"So...?"

"So?"

"What are we going to do about it?"

"Keep things professional the way we agreed."

I rolled my eyes. "You can't be serious. Can't you feel this?" I asked, gesturing at the minuscule space between our bodies.

"Of course, I do. But it's not smart. Not for me. Not for you. And most certainly not for your career."

"Oh, God. You and this responsibility shit. Do you ever shut up?" I pushed up onto my tiptoes and kissed him--pressed my body against his, leaving no room for the Holy Ghost or anything else between us. I felt him give in to it--felt him give in to me. His hands slowly gathered my dress, scrunching it up around my thighs.

"I never should have kissed you the other night," he muttered. "This is just too way too hard to resist."

It's gonna happen.

My heart skipped crazily in my chest as his hand slipped around to my backside--kneading and caressing, drawing me in closer. His hips did a slow grind, pressing into mine.

Just do it. Just lift me on the countertop and...

But he did the exact opposite. He pulled away so abruptly that I was left leaning into the empty air with my mouth still searching for his. I opened my eyes and glared at him.

"You're a damn tease."

He coughed out a sarcastic laugh. "I'm not teasing you, Yves."

"Riiight. So this isn't the part of the date where you send me home all hot and bothered?"

"Hot and bothered, huh? I thought nothing bothered you."

"It never used to," I mumbled. "So we're still not fucking. What up wit dat?"

"It's unprofessional."

"And if I wasn't writing this book...what then?"

He leaned on the countertop across from me. His eyes traveled the length of my body, undressing me again. "It still wouldn't happen. I told you, Yves. We want different things. That hasn't changed."

I narrowed my eyes at him. "What do you want?"

Elijah sighed and shook his head. "It doesn't matter. You can't give it to me."

"Tell me what it is, and maybe I can." I looked into his eyes. His gaze was so heavy, so smoldering, that it made all the fine hairs on my body stand on end.

"If I were to tell you what I really wanted from you, Yves, you would run away from me. And trust me, it will leave more than four quarter-shaped bruises on your hip."

So he read it. He read the fucking blog post. My cheeks flushed hot at the thought of him reading the intimate thoughts I had about him, but mostly I wanted to know what reading them made him feel. The look in his eyes said more than words probably could. It made that fear thump loudly in the places it shouldn't and triggered arousal when I knew I should want to get away. "Is that why I feel scared around you sometimes?" I asked.

His jaw clenched. "Maybe."

I closed the distance between us, felt his warm, hard dick through the soft denim. "You seem so positive that we're a bad match. Our bodies don't seem to agree."

"Hmm," he grunted, pushing his fingers into my hair. "My body definitely wants your body," he muttered. "It's what I do with it once I have it that should have you worried."

"You can do whatever you want to it."

Elijah shook his head. "Come on," he said, placing a gentle kiss on my forehead. "I'll walk you out."

. . .

A STRANGE FEELING CAME OVER ME IN THE ELEVATOR ON THE way down to the lobby. Something like...yearning or, God forbid, desperation. What the hell was this man doing to me? Whatever it was, I wasn't entirely certain I liked it.

No, that wasn't it.

I didn't want to like it.

Maybe I should listen to his warnings.

"I'll see you later," I muttered as he held the door open for me.

"Hey!" he called out once I was a few paces away. I turned to him, already lost in my own thoughts.

"Don't look so defeated. We're still good friends." He laughed after he said it. Like he knew how lame that sounded before it came out of his mouth.

"I don't need any new friends."

"Don't be like that."

"I don't know how else to be right now."

His face grew serious. "Maybe I can show you better than I can tell you."

"Well, that's what I've been saying all this time," I said, throwing up my hands.

"I know...I just..." He shook his head.

Was he stammering? "You just what?"

"I don't want to make any mistakes that could hurt you."

I threw up my hands again. The more he talked, the more frustrated and confused I became.

Elijah shook his head. "I'll call you," he said and ducked back inside, leaving me alone and confused on the sidewalk.

Mistakes that could hurt me? What the hell was he talking about? And why did these mistakes sound like the kind I love to make?

12

Sometimes, having a cat seemed like a good idea. They were cute and cuddly and they purred when you petted them. Other times, like now, when Maniac was pouncing on my face and yowling to wake me up, it seemed like the stupidest idea ever.

"All right!" I groaned, throwing the covers off.

Half awake, I stumbled into the kitchen to rustle up some grub for her. She followed behind me, yowling endlessly.

"Goddammit, cat!" I cursed. I'd dragged in around one a.m. from an event I was covering for the paper, and I had to be at the bookstore in a couple of hours. She was cutting into some essential sleep, and I wouldn't get it back.

And just my luck, we were out of cat food.

Maniac leaped onto the counter and meowed right in my face. I snarled at her. "You're lucky I love you, cat."

I threw on a pair of shorts and a T-shirt, pulled my hair into a ponytail, and put on some sunglasses to head down to the corner bodega.

"Good morning, little girl," Mrs. McKinney croaked when I stepped out onto the stoop. "Another late night?"

"Something like that."

"I figured. Heard you come in late...alone. Are you going through a dry spell?"

"Haha." I laughed. Damn, I must be off my game. Even Mrs. McKinney noticed. "I'm heading to the bodega. Do you need anything?"

"No. I'm fine," she said and waved me off.

As I walked down to the corner, I tried to remember if any of her kids had visited recently. Did she have any food for herself or her cats? I had to get into her apartment again to make sure she had the things she needed, but for now I would grab some basics and leave them on her doorstep.

"Hey, Yves!" Lana, the bodega owner's daughter, called out from behind the register.

"Morning!" I chirped, sounding brighter than I felt.

"Newport Light 100s, right?"

"Yeah. And a pack of Virginia Slims."

The store had hand baskets. I grabbed one and threw in some essentials: milk, eggs, bread. Some cheese and deli meat. I also grabbed a can of Cafe Bustelo for myself and a few cans of cat food, before I stood behind another customer to pay for my purchases. I was contemplating whether my raw belly could digest a slice of pizza when my phone vibrated in my back pocket. A text from Elijah.

HIM: ARE YOU STILL PISSED OFF AT ME?

Me: Who said I was pissed off?

Him: I don't know...maybe it was that pouty face you had on when you left my

place.

Me: What can I say? I'm not used to being told no.

Him: I know. What are you getting into today?

Me: I have to work at the bookstore...after that, nada. What's up?

Him: Would you be interested in going out to dinner with me?

Me: Are you asking me out on a date?

Him: Maybe...are you accepting?

Me: This seems like a huge change of direction in our "relationship."

Him: Is that a yes or a no?

SMILING TO MYSELF, I LET HIM SWEAT IT OUT A LITTLE WHILE I paid the cashier and opened up my fresh pack of smokes for the walk home.

HIM: HELLO?

Me: It's a yes. What kind of date is this? How should I dress?

Him: I'll help you with that when I get there. See you around 7.

HM. I'VE NEVER HAD A MAN PICK OUT MY CLOTHES BEFORE. That sounded a little weird, but really, all I felt was excited. Elijah wanted to take me to dinner. Did that mean that his no-sex policy was under reconsideration? I hoped so. Either way, it was going to be hard to concentrate on the mind-numbing work to be done at Burke's Books. But somehow I waded through the endless restocking and clueless customers. I also cranked out the three articles I had due for websites that I regularly contribute to.

Thompson came to join me behind the cash wrap. "So the guy that met you here a couple of weeks ago...whatever happened with that?"

"Oh! He was an editor for Leaf Press. Why?"

"He's here again."

"He is? Where?" My heart leaped a little as I looked toward the door.

"There," Thompson said and pointed to the shelves that held "employee picks."

When I saw him, my belly dropped right down into my shoes. Elijah looked even more handsome than he did the last time I saw him, if that was possible. He wore a dark navy suit on his tall, lean frame. The cut was the sort that accentuated an athletic build. I knew he had swimmer's shoulders and runner's thighs, but seeing him in this suit made me want to rip it off and get to what it hinted at underneath. His dirty blond hair was combed away from his face in a way that made his usually angelic features look stark and a bit cruel--especially his smirking mouth. Ay Dios, that mouth was going to be the death of me.

"Hey," I said when he approached the register. "This is a surprise. I thought we were meeting later."

"We were...I just thought I would pick you up here."

I smiled. "Eager to see me?"

He held up his thumb and forefinger and squeezed them to a millimeter apart. "Just a little bit."

"You can cut out early," Thompson volunteered. "It's slow and I can handle things here until Gena gets back from her break."

"Are you sure? I wasn't angling to get off early--"

"Go, Yves. Clearly this man has an evening planned for you that he can't wait to get started."

Elijah coughed out a nervous laugh. "Clearly," he echoed.

"Okay, then." I grabbed my bag and tossed out my lukewarm coffee. "I guess I will see you on Sunday."

"Have fun," Thompson called out to our backs.

Elijah took my laptop bag from me and escorted me to his car. Even in jeans and a T-shirt, he made me feel like a lady.

"So how was your day?"

"Productive, believe it or not. I got a lot of writing done."

"Working on the book you promised me?"

"Some. I worked out some of the notes you left on my manuscript and things are flowing a bit better."

He smiled. "Good, because I'm going to need your full attention tonight."

"Really? That sounds ominous."

He shrugged. "Not ominous, but...let's not discuss this now."

My belly did a lazy flip. What the fuck did that mean? I was still pondering that when we pulled up in front of my place.

"So," I began once we were inside. "If your smart suit is a clue, this place is sort of fancy, right?"

"Sort of. Show me to your closet."

I led him back to my bedroom and into my walk-in closet. Elijah walked in right behind me and was instantly overwhelmed by the amount of clothing.

"It's all organized--well, as organized as it can be in a closet this small. Short dresses here, long dresses here, jeans, slacks, shirts..." I pointed everything out for him, secretly hoping that he would lose interest and instead toss me on the bed and do nasty, dirty things to me. He sifted through the contents of my tightly packed closet.

"What's all this?" he asked as he ran his hand down the sleeve of Julian Webster's Armani Exchange shirt. He'd reached the back of my closet, where all the remnants of my nights of pleasure lived. "Why are there men's clothes in your closet?"

"They're just some things I collected over the years."

"Collected?" he questioned, looking at me.

"Souvenirs, I guess." I shrugged.

He frowned. "You mean to tell me that these clothes belong to the men you've slept with?"

I nodded and then for some strange reason; I felt ashamed. Why I started collecting the shirts and jackets of my one-night stands escaped me, but I knew that it began not long after my breakup with Cesar. Elijah smoothed the flat of his hand over the hangers and as he did, I considered the sheer amount of the clothing again. That was a lot of men in only three years...but why should I be ashamed of that? If I were a man, I would be some kind of stud.

He chose a black dress for me to wear. It just happened to be one of my favorites. It was a strapless, fifties-style "wiggle" dress with little white polka dots. I loved it because it made my waist look tiny and my hips curvy in a way that didn't make me curse my genetics.

"I'll wait in the living room while you get dressed."

"Okay."

This dress called for dramatic hair and makeup. For my hair, I made two big victory rolls in the front and left the back loose and curling. On my eyes I used a dark liner and lots of black mascara and painted my lips red, red, red.

When I emerged from my bedroom an hour later, he greeted me with a slow appreciative smile.

"You look beautiful."

"Thank you," I murmured, feeling bashful. "You never told me where you were taking me."

"This place called The Den Bar & Lounge."

"Never heard of it."

"I know. You have to have a membership to get in. It's one of Philly's best-kept secrets."

"And you're going to share it with me?"

"Of course. Are you ready to go?"

"Yes."

He stood up. "Then let's get out of here." Maniac stretched and made a soft mewing sound. I hadn't even noticed her tucked in next to him. "Your cat's purring nearly put me to sleep."

I smiled. Something about that tugged at my mushy, girly feelings. "Okay," I murmured, extending my hand. "Let's go."

~

THE DEN BAR & LOUNGE WAS A SWANKY ESTABLISHMENT IN the heart of Old City, with a forties, old-school vibe. Flashy, high-end cars pulled up to the curb outside to be parked by valets. The tables inside were filled with Philadelphia's smart, influential, and beautiful people. The booths were deep and dark and upholstered with plush, aubergine crushed velvet. Each table setting was illuminated with soft, flickering candlelight that created a dreamlike glow. I felt like I fit in nicely in my slinky, fifties dress and peep-toe pumps.

Elijah knew the owner, Alexa De Costa. She greeted us at the door and escorted us to a private booth. Alexa was slight and gorgeous in that androgynous, high-fashion model kind of way, with a head full of chocolate brown curls and dark olive brown skin. I couldn't decide if it was a tan or her natural complexion. Her surname implied the latter. She wore a flawless white suit, tailored to fit her frame.

"Eli, it's been a while." She waved over a server who brought over a frosty bottle of champagne. "I was beginning to wonder if I should refund your membership."

"Why would you do that? Is there some sort of clause about inactivity that I don't know about?" he asked.

She smiled. "No, but I was beginning to think that something had gone wrong during your last visit."

"Nothing like that. I've just been busy."

"I can see that," Alexa said and gave me a knowing look. Her eyes were that sort of pale, greenish blue that reminded me of the Caribbean. "And who is this beauty?" she asked.

"This is Yves Santiago."

"Wait...The Yves Santiago? The one that writes entertainment column for the Philadelphian?"

"The very same," I replied, feeling humbled. It always knocked me for a loop when people knew about my infantile writing career.

"I'm a fan."

"You flatter me. Thank you."

"Well, I hope the two of you enjoy yourselves this evening. If there's anything you need, please don't hesitate to ask," she said, giving me a seductive wink.

"We will," Elijah answered.

I watched Alexa move through the crowd, smiling a hello at a few of the patrons and glancing back at me.

"That Alexa is too pretty to be real."

"Is that so?"

"And sexy, don't you think? Skinny, but sexy."

Elijah raised a brow. "I'm more interested in the idea that you find her sexy than anything I might think of her."

"I mean, I recognize a beautiful woman when I see one. I'm not intimidated by that."

He nodded. "Good to know."

"So...are you going to tell me what an exclusive membership to this place buys you?"

"You've really never heard about this place? No secret murmurs in the back rooms of one of those bars you frequent?"

I looked around the room and took in the opulence. "I might be selling myself a little short here, but I don't rub elbows with these kinds of people in the places I frequent."

He smiled. "You'd be surprised."

"Will you quit with all the cryptic talk and tell me what sort of super-secret club this is?"

Elijah leaned in close. "It's a bdsm club," he stage whispered.

"Bdsm?"

"You know...bondage, dominance, sadism, masochism--"

"I know what it is. It's just..." I looked around again. "This looks like a nice high-end restaurant. Where are the whips and chains and all that?"

"That's all in The Cellar."

I literally gulped. "I th--thought The Cellar was just where they kept a really old wine collection and guys smoked cigars."

"There's some of that going on, too."

"But mostly the whips and chains and all that?"

"Mmm hmm," he nodded. "All of that."

"Careful. Your freak flag's showing," I joked, trying to ease the tension.

"Who says I was trying to hide it?" he asked with a raised eyebrow.

I almost laughed again because that had to be a joke, right? But then it hit me. "This is the reason. This is why you're not into casual sex. Why you need a commitment."

"Yes," he answered, like the topic needed no further explanation. "Let's order, okay?"

The Den had a menu full of savory, spicy, and delicious fusion food. A mix of Asian, African, and Indian flavors. Elijah ordered for both of us and ate his fill. I barely made my way through my dinner plate and instead tried to steady my nerves by drinking half the bottle of champagne gifted to us by Alexa. We made idle conversation, none of which I heard, because all I could think about was The Cellar full of kink under my feet. I looked at the gorgeous man seated across from me in his expensive navy-blue suit with his perfectly styled hair, high cheekbones, and straight nose that spoke of good American breeding. Was he really into all this stuff? It didn't add up for me. He seemed so...normal.

"Why?" I blurted, interrupting his one-sided conversation about the state of publishing.

Elijah bisected the last bite of his dinner--a stalling tactic if I ever saw one. "Do I need a reason?"

"Yes, you do!"

"Why?" he asked, turning the question back around on me.

"Because you don't look like the type."

"And how should I look?"

I looked around, hoping to find a perfect example of the idea in my head. Some sinister-looking man or a woman in shiny latex. Of course, I found none. "I don't know. I guess you shouldn't look so..."

"Tame?" he volunteered.

My belly did a nervous flip. He looked anything but tame in that moment. He looked downright feral.

Elijah pulled his napkin out of his lap and wiped his mouth. "I think we should take a trip downstairs. Maybe it will help to dissuade some of those misguided ideas in your head."

"Downstairs?" I squeaked.

He stood and held out his hand. "Don't worry. You don't have to do anything you don't want to do." His mouth quirked into what I used to think was a shy, sexy smile before he added, "This time."

THE BAR AND LOUNGE ITSELF WERE ON STREET LEVEL AND covered about two thousand square feet of dining space with deep, high-back booths skirting small, intimate, round table settings in the center of the room. The restrooms were along the back wall just to the left of the shiny, mirrored bar. To the left of that was a door. It was a seemingly innocuous door, but as we made our way toward it, people emerged with flushed, excited faces. Terrified, but equally curious, I followed Elijah inside with barely a second thought.

We found ourselves at the top of a flight of cement stairs on a dimly lit stairwell. I stood there for a moment contemplating the dangers of navigating hard, unforgiving stairs in six-inch stilettos with half a liter of champagne in my belly.

"This is a fucking lawsuit waiting to happen," I muttered, then grasped the handrail and prayed that I didn't tumble end over end all the way down to the bottom.

"Wait a minute." Elijah stilled me before I could take the first step. He eyed my damn near treacherous heels for a moment, then scooped me into his arms. "Can't have you breaking an ankle on my watch."

I wasn't entirely sure, and I would never admit to this in mixed company, but I may have gasped.

"Well, this is very gallant of you." I'd meant it to sound sarcastic, but instead I sounded like some breathless debutante, because my body was pressed right up against his and the solid muscle of him felt like some thinly veiled threat.

"I've been nothing if not the perfect gentleman with you."

And when he said it, I realized that it was true. He hadn't pushed himself on me in any way. In fact, he had been so careful with me that before he revealed this; I had this strange sense of security with him.

So why should I be afraid now?

I draped my arm around his neck. He responded by cradling me closer, bringing that cherubic mouth of his close to mine. I wanted to kiss him, but before I could lean into it, we had reached the bottom of the stairs and he was setting me down on my feet.

Now we stood outside another door. Big and intricately carved, the dark wood stain gleamed in the dim light. It also had a heavy, ancient looking lock.

"How do we get in?" I asked. Following my journalistic impulses, I pressed my ear against the heavy wood door. I didn't hear much. Just what sounded like someone laughing or maybe weeping and a crack that sounded like leather or--

"From terrified to curious in a matter of seconds."

I shrugged. "I decided when you were carrying me down the stairs that I could trust you." I rattled the door on its hinges and tried to open it. It didn't budge.

He laughed, shaking his head. "Curious little kitty wants to know what's on the other side of the door, huh?"

"M-maybe," I stammered.

He reached into his pocket and produced a long, smooth

leather strap--a key ring. A single key dangled on the tarnished hoop.

"Come, come, little one," he murmured as the lock slid home and the door swung open. "Let me show you what The Cellar is all about."

13

Elijah escorted me through the oak door into a long, dimly lit hallway. Whoever designed this place must've taken on the literal interpretation of a dungeon, but on a more high-end scale. Staggered on my left and right along the walls were openings that yawned like great, empty mouths. The air in the corridor felt charged with tension and electricity. Behind me I heard whispering followed by a loud and decisive crack of leather against skin and the subsequent whimpering of a gagged mouth. I groped blindly behind me for Elijah's hand. He laughed, but readily laced his long fingers through mine.

"Don't worry; I've got you," he whispered into the place behind my ear, his lips softly brushing the lobe.

He pulled me along the corridor, his thumb stroking against mine in a way that was oddly soothing. "This cellar was used to store wine and spirits during the prohibition," he said. "It's rumored that Al Capone had some dealings here in the late twenties."

He meant to calm me with this historical information--mindless chatter to distract me from the pounding of my heart. His voice was exactly what I needed to keep me from bolting.

"How did you find this place?"

"A friend of mine in New York. She knew I would need a place to scratch my itch."

"But, Alexa said you haven't been here in a while."

"I haven't. I just...I need a deeper connection and that's just not the sort of thing you get at a club. No matter how intimate it is."

"Oh. So how long have you been into this?"

"A long time. Probably since I was about his age or younger."

Elijah gestured toward a young man, sleek and hairless as a pre-pubescent boy, who was bound and blindfolded to some sort of hobby horse. His male Dom paced around him, cane in hand, periodically flicking the boy, striping his flanks.

"You're into that?"

"I'm into all of it," he said with a sly grin. "But mostly I'm into that."

He pointed out another couple on our left. In this scene, a dark-haired, female submissive was bound about the waist and breasts by tight interlocking ropes and suspended by one leg from a strong D-ring attached to a ceiling. Her Dom slid in and out of her with slow, deliberate strokes. Her face was contorted with pain or pleasure--I couldn't tell which. I felt Elijah watching me and cleared my throat in an attempt to regain my composure.

"How can...?"

"We do this without getting arrested?" he finished for me.

I nodded. The champagne and the atmosphere had

made me dumb as a box of rocks. I could barely put two words together, let alone form an intelligent question.

"It's easy. This portion of the restaurant is an exclusive club. You pay membership fees to be allowed past that door back there, and you're issued a key. There's no criminal activity going on here. Everything that takes place behind the big oak door is between consenting adults." He turned toward the couple and watched them with what I would swear was longing. "Consent is the key," he murmured.

WE LINGERED NEAR THE SUSPENDED SUBMISSIVE FOR A LONG while. We watched her Dom fuck her. It seemed excruciatingly tender to me. I never knew that it could be like this--so affectionate. When she climaxed, a single tear traced its way across her face and in that moment our eyes connected. She didn't say a word, but it felt like she was speaking to me. That connection with her made me feel a little weird. I was definitely outside my comfort zone. I liked to consider myself uninhibited, but this was something else. Something that I felt was just a little too on the fringe. But before I could protest, Elijah took my hand and pulled me in a different direction.

"Come on," he urged. "I want to show you something else."

We headed back toward the big oak door, and again we encountered the whispering followed by that loud crack of leather. This time, a laugh accompanied the whimpering voice. A throaty, deep laugh that reminded me of butterscotch or good whiskey.

We rounded a corner that opened onto a cavernous room. The walls were earthen, and it smelled wet, like it used to be an underwater well or spring. A crowd of people stood in the room--all facing the center--most of them men, but also a few elegant women with their subs standing quietly and obediently at their sides. All of their eyes were focused on a singular point. Elijah found his way to the center, pulling me behind him.

"I think you may have spoiled this one. It seems she can only respond to your loving touch," a voice mocked from somewhere in the middle of the crowd.

"See how you embarrass me, Naima?" the butterscotch voice implored.

Finally, we made it to the inner circle. Alexa stood in the middle next to what could only be a whipping post--a log with manacles, polished near the bottom by the writhing of bodies, and driven into the smooth cement floor. At Alexa's feet sat a shapely woman. I couldn't see her face, but her skin was a gorgeous, nut brown. The hair on her bowed head was cut short and close to her scalp in natural, soft waves. The smooth line of her back accentuated her full hips and her round, ample ass. She may have been on her knees, but this was a careful pose. She looked like a model posing for a painter or sketch artist.

"You are a disappointment," Alexa murmured to the woman.

The submissive's head dipped even lower. "I'm sorry, mistress," she whispered.

"Not yet, you aren't."

Alexa touched the back of the woman's neck and she stood in one slow, controlled motion. She then gathered the sub's wrists in her hand and led her over to the whipping post. I could see her face now. It was full of angles--high cheekbones, large, liquid-brown eyes that tilted slightly upward, a mouth with a full top lip that gave her a permanent pout. She was gorgeous--like nothing I'd ever seen before.

Alexa latched the woman's hands into the manacles and paced around her for a moment. Someone on the fringe of the circle handed her a whip made of thick, chestnut-brown leather split into three strips. She tested its weight in her hand as she paced. Her brown-eyed beauty trembled as she drew closer. Every muscle in her body twitched and quivered in anticipation.

"What is that?" I asked.

"A three fingered tawse."

His hand slid around my middle, pulling me against him. "She'll start with a few mild slaps to bring the blood to the surface."

"And then?"

"She'll increase the intensity..."

"Until it hurts her?"

"Yes." His free hand drifted down the length of my arm to my wrist and brought it between us, cupping my hand over his fly. He twitched in my palm. "Watch."

The first lash landed on her thighs. Every muscle in her body tensed and she moaned through tightly pursed lips but still didn't drop her eyes. Alexa hit her again and again. But it was just like he said, nothing too hard. I could tell she was moaning in pleasure and not pain.

The woman lifted her head and her eyes met mine again. Those deep, chocolate eyes of hers pulled me in. I felt that internal shift again. I didn't know what it was. We connected just as I had with the woman down the hall. Not on a physical level, but mental...emotional. I felt her desire. I felt her hunger. It echoed the hunger I felt in myself. I felt it in Elijah too. His hand skimmed over my lower belly, over my pelvic bone, and pressed against the apex of my thighs.

He grew full and heavy in my hand. Too much for me to hold.

The bound submissive licked her lips.

When she began to whip Naima in earnest, I had to turn away. I couldn't watch. My knees felt weak. I leaned on Elijah and buried my face in the collar of his shirt, but I still heard it. I heard the stinging smack of the tawse hitting her skin. I heard her whimper, gasp, moan, and cry out.

"There, there, sweetness," Elijah said. "She's not hurt. Not really. Look at her and see. She loves it."

The sound of Naima's moaning increased. I peeked around his collar and I saw Alexa lean in close to slip her hand between Naima's thighs. The whip flicked at her breasts and the look on Naima's face -- God, it was bliss. My entire body clenched at the sight.

I want that...something in me growled. Whoa. Where the fuck did that come from? This wasn't me. It couldn't be.

Could it?

The floor swam under my feet and I gripped his jacket tighter. "Get me out of here."

"It's okay," he cooed, trying to calm me. His voice was soothing, but his hands...his hands were all over me. On my ass, inching up my dress, slipping dangerously close to my hot, slick cunt. I was terrified, confused, and aroused--hopelessly, hopelessly aroused.

"I want to go!" I slipped out of his arms and stumbled toward the back of the room, pushing against a crowd that seemed intent on keeping me in. I felt sick. I thought I might throw up. I could still hear Naima's whimpering moans and Alexa's vicious whipping. And those hands of his...I still felt them on me...caressing me. It felt like I couldn't escape. This was all becoming too surreal--like a scene from some sadistic horror movie.

"Let me go," I moaned. "Stop--stop touching me."

"Shhh," he quieted. His lips against my ear, his arm around my waist. "You're okay." The arm around my waist pulled me closer, so that I was leaning into him. We were in the long hallway again. Doors stretched out into oblivion like a funhouse dungeon.

"I'm sorry. I think I'm drunk or sick. I feel..."

"You feel sick? Here, put your face against the wall for a moment. It's cool and might help you feel a bit better," he said.

We stopped for a moment and I pressed my cheek against the cool, dark stone wall. It did make me feel better. "Thank you," I muttered, though I wasn't sure what I was thanking him for.

"Are you okay?"

I nodded. "That was just...really intense."

"I guess it was intense for you. Watching how you responded to it was..." he let the thought trail off unfinished. "Come on, sweetness. Let's get you home."

Elijah was quiet most of the ride home, and I was thankful for the silence. Now that my heart had stopped trying to escape my rib cage, I felt a little ashamed of my reaction. So he liked to tie girls up and hit them with whippy, hurty things before he fucked them...was that a deal breaker? My knee-jerk response was no, although I had to admit that it scared me. But the fear didn't do what it was supposed to do. Instead, it set off that crazy yearning in me. Like a sort of freedom lay beyond what he had shown me. Freedom that could be mine if only I were brave enough. And more than that, this thing didn't change how I felt about him. I still wanted him--maybe more. That had to mean something. If his kinky secret was a deal breaker, I would've been immediately turned off, right?

He parked two blocks away from my place and walked me to my door. I hoped that meant he would come up, but when we reached my stoop, it was clear that he wouldn't.

"Did you have a nice time?" he asked as he brushed a stray curl away from my face.

These little gestures of affection...they're a sticky web. I like them too much, and I'll find myself caught if I'm not careful.

"Wonderful. How about you? Did you have a good time parading me around like I belong to you?"

"You noticed that?"

I nodded. He blushed.

"You're not offended, are you?"

"No, I liked it. It felt good belonging to someone. Even if it was only for a few hours." I bit my lip, pissed at myself for having let that slip.

"It doesn't have to be that way--"

"Yes, it does," I interrupted. "I'm not a relationship girl."

"No, you're just a girl who is afraid of relationships."

I grabbed a handful of his hair and pulled him close to me. "You think you're so clever," I whispered on his mouth.

"I'm glad you noticed. I work real hard to get you to notice." He drew his lips across mine, kissing me with his breath and nothing more. "I'm sorry to have sprung all of this on you like this. I know it's a lot to handle, but I didn't know how to tell you."

"I was okay until the whipping post. Everything else was really sexy."

He smiled wistfully. "I know it was sexy. I know it turned you on, but that's not why I took you to The Den tonight."

"Why did you take me?"

"I had to. I had to let you know that this isn't something I want to do every now and again. This is me, Yvie. This is the man I am. I can't just fuck you. I can't be your Prince Charming--"

"I don't want you to be--"

"Yes, you do. I see how you look at me. You think I'm your great white hope." He said it in jest, but I could tell he meant it. "Also, I wanted to let you know that it wasn't you. I've wanted you since the moment I laid eyes on you. I just...I can't keep making the same mistakes. I can't get involved with another person who isn't completely into this or isn't able to accept this part of me."

"I accept it."

"Do you? Because accepting it means that you realize that I want to do all those things to you. Everything you saw tonight. Everything and more. I want to do them all to you, Yvie. Do you accept that?"

"I want to."

He smiled. Too many teeth. He looked like a predator. My heart kicked in my chest.

"You're terrified by the thought of it."

"I am terrified by some parts of it--"

"And what would you say if I told you, knowing that it scares you turns me on? "

"I--"

His brow furrowed, and he took on that observant, intense look again. "You're even more afraid now, aren't you?"

There was no point in lying. "What gave me away?"

"These big hazel eyes of yours," he said, and kissed both my eyelids gently.

"So what happens now? You just dump this heavy shit on my doorstep and walk away, huh?"

"Exactly," he said with a laugh. "I have to say that I'm a bit surprised though."

"Really? About what?"

"Your reaction to the whipping. I guess I didn't realize you were so sensitive."

"Who's sensitive? It was that expensive champagne--"

He narrowed his eyes at me. "Seriously? You're blaming your behavior on the alcohol?"

"What do you mean?"

He moved in dangerously close. I pressed my back into the door to keep our bodies from touching. I didn't know why I was running away from him when a moment ago I would've begged him to come to my bed. My reaction was purely instinctual. Something about him made me wary. And the thinly veiled merriment in his eyes told me he was gobbling it up.

"Sometimes our bodies have a way of signaling wants and desires we never knew we had. Sometimes that signal can cause a physical reaction that is so strong that you can't understand or control it. It's perfectly natural. Just as it's natural for you to envision yourself being tied down and fucked or like that woman tonight...naked, shackled to that post, begging for every lash of the whip--"

"No, I would never want a thing like that."

"Oh, you want it. I can see it in your eyes."

"I'm no submissive. I don't want to be abused--"

"Who said anything about abuse? "

"I..." but I'd run out of protests.

Elijah moved in closer. I held my breath. His full lips spread into a feral grin as he cupped my cheek in his hand. He brushed his mouth against mine. His breath puffed against my lips, causing a dull ache of longing between my thighs.

"You would be a joy to break," he whispered. "Just the thought of you wet, sweaty, and quivering at my feet makes me so fucking hot." And then his mouth was on mine. The kiss was all hunger and naked lust. Both hands cradled my skull, held me delicately while he feasted on my mouth. He was so slow and deliberate and so full of intensity that I whimpered each time his tongue passed over mine. This kiss was too damn good. My sex-depraved body felt like it was climbing toward orgasm. He pulled away slowly. Punishing my lips with little nibbles before backing away.

"Good night, Yves."

"Don't go."

His hand gripped my waist, and he appeared to contemplate staying. "I want to break you open, pretty girl." He looked at me, his eyes filled with a look so foreboding and iniquitous that it made me flushed and wet. "But not tonight."

"Wait! " I called out before he could walk away. The things he wanted terrified me, but more than anything I wanted him to come upstairs to my bed and try out all those deviant, filthy things I saw tonight. I wanted him to convince me that it was what I really wanted.

"I've added about twenty thousand words to my manuscript," I finished lamely.

"Really?"

"Yeah, it's not much, but you can come upstairs and read them if you want."

"Cute, but no."

So muthafuckin' sexy. Is he getting sexier? Or is it just that I haven't fucked him yet?

"It was worth a try. I thought you might want to hear me moan for real."

He laughed, his eyes twinkling with amusement. "I do, but you really need some time to process all of this."

"Really? I guess that means that I get to spend the rest of the night masturbating while I think of you."

Elijah stifled a groan. "If you only knew a third of the things I want to do to your mouth when you say filthy things like that."

I grabbed his face in both my hands and kissed him. Turned on every bit of passion I could muster, but he pulled away anyway.

"Don't. I need you."

"You don't need me, Yves. You just need someone." He turned away from me and walked back to his car. "When I'm the one that you need, call me. I'll be waiting," he called back over his shoulder.

And once again I stood on my stoop and watched him walk away.

"Eli!" I called out to his back, stamping my foot.

He turned toward me and laughed. "You really don't get told 'no' much, do you?"

"No, you're the first."

"I like that I'm the first."

"Okay, you won the prize; you get a cookie. Now come upstairs and fuck me."

He laughed again. "No, Yves. I meant what I said. I want you to think about everything you saw tonight and consider what it really means. I know this thing between us is pretty fucking intense, but I can't afford to go into this blindly. I need you to be sure. Think of it this way," he said once he got to his car, "maybe it could be the beginning of something real between you and me."

"Stop trying to make me fall for you," I warned, narrowing my eyes and pointing my finger at him.

"Sorry, I can't do that." He blew me a kiss, slipped into his car, and drove away.

While climbing the steps to my apartment, I tried to figure out what the hell was wrong with me. This man had all but told me he wanted to beat me and make me his slave, and I still wanted to climb him like a tree. What did that say about me? Was I sick? Depraved? And if I was, how much did I care?

When I closed my eyes, I found him there. Burned into the place behind my eyelids like when you looked directly into the sun. That was probably exactly how he wanted it. He wanted me to long for him. I thought about that night at the bar when he said, "If you were mine..." Those words spun in my head. What did that mean? He thought of me as someone that could be his? And what was wrong with me to make me feel like I wanted to be his?

What are you trying to do, Elijah Weinstein?

But I already knew the answer to that. He'd told me tonight. He was trying to make me fall in love.

"Not gonna happen, buddy," I muttered as I dropped off to sleep.

My subconscious must not have gotten the memo, because all my dreams were wet and filled with him filling me in some way with his dick...goddamn you, Elijah Weinstein.

UNTITLED (BECAUSE THE MAN DEFIES ALL DESCRIPTION)

AUGUST 30, 2013

Hands calloused and hardened from rough work. Raw wood, turpentine, sweat--smells so familiar that she would've sworn they were cologne. A mouth that tasted of sofrito, lime, the maltiness of cheap beer. Love that smothered and left her feeling empty and lonely, all at once. Gruff words meant to control her masked as care.
This was manliness.

He challenged all of those ideas. Obliterated them, really.

His hands were soft, but strong and hot against her skin. If warmth had a taste, that was what she tasted when she kissed him. The malt on his tongue tasted sweeter. His mouth never spoke harsh or hurtful words.
If she had to pin him down with one word, it would be careful.

Yes, he was careful with her.

There was an animal in him.

He didn't deny it, but kept it tightly leashed. It bled into everything he did, but was most evident in the way he dressed. His Brooks Brothers suits were tailored to fit. Smart ties and bright pocket squares that complemented each other. Real handmade leather shoes--the kind that need to be polished. The crisp, white dress shirts he wore that were laundered and delivered to his door, clean and stiff with starch.

Those stiff clothes keep his animal in a cage. She wanted to tear them off and let it out.

This man cared about things she never knew were really important and that care translated into his words, and the way he handled her.

God, how he handled her.

This was what her body was made for. The knowledge was so basic. So primal. So true. She was made for him. From the first time he touched her, he'd left his mark on her. She was his.

And the last thing she wanted him to be was...

Careful.

14

"I swear they only make clothes for itty bitty bitches like you," Ava grumbled as she yanked off yet another dress. Like every woman, she had issues with her body image. Her figure was the European idea of perfect, but she longed for the ample ass and shapely thighs stereotypically attributed to Black women. It was understandable that she felt this way, but when I looked at Ava, I only saw my gorgeous friend.

"I am far from itty bitty," I muttered, turning around to look at my ass in the mirror. I had more ass and hips than I did breasts, so shopping was just as difficult for me as it was for her. Somehow, she didn't see it that way.

"I meant short and shapely. I would kill for an ass like that. You should be thankful that you have been blessed with that body."

"I am thankful, and you should be, too. You're tall enough and thin enough to wear all those runway clothes. Here, try this," I suggested handing her a black-and-white print, flair-leg jumpsuit--something I could never wear because, even in five-inch stilettos, I barely reached average height for a woman.

"That's too loose. I'll be swimming in it," she immediately complained.

"Just try it on." I thrust it into her chest and padded bra.

She grumbled but slipped it on, anyway. When she turned to inspect herself in the mirror, a smile spread across her face. "See, bitch? I knew this would look good on me."

I rolled my eyes. "Of course you did."

She gave me her best over-the-shoulder Veronica Lake look.

"Beautiful," I whispered, blowing her a kiss.

"Thank you, love."

"No problem."

"So what's up with that editor and what's going on with your book?"

I had to fight to keep the smile off my lips, but I knew Ava saw it, anyway. Might as well have ticker tape running across my forehead, broadcasting my every thought.

"It's going well." I pulled another dress over my head. "But I still feel a bit unsure about it sometimes."

"What aren't you sure about?"

"Well, I'm just wondering if this is how I want to publish my first book. I always imagined myself as a respected author with a book of brilliantly crafted short stories and poems that sold really well into my old age."

"And who says you can't have that?"

I shrugged. "I don't know."

"No one, but you. This book will make you an author. Respect is something you have to earn no matter what you publish. You know that."

"Yeah, but these are my raunchiest inner thoughts about

the men I fucked. I can't help feeling worried about sharing them with the world."

"True. But they're good, right?"

I grinned. "Elijah seems to think so."

Ava tipped her head to the side and narrowed her eyes. "And what's that silly grin about?"

"What silly grin?"

"The one plastered all over your face, chica. Spill."

I looked at myself in the mirror, smoothing a short, tight dress over my curves. "Well," I said, "he's kinda beautiful. Tall and blonde with green eyes and the sort of mouth that makes me weak at the sight of it."

"Mmm hmm, and what about the dick?" Ava asked, licking her lips.

"Ava!" I exclaimed in mock indignation.

"Don't give me that good girl act. I want the details. My life is sad, empty, and full of bad sex. I need to live vicariously through you."

Part of me wanted to say that my brother was still holding that torch high over his head for her, but I kept that thought to myself. "Well, I hate to disappoint you, but I haven't had sex with him. I mean, we've kissed, and that was..." My mind wandered for a moment, drifting back to when Elijah's scorching lips had me swooning on my stoop. My neck and face flushed with heat. "Yeah," I muttered, "that was...lovely."

"And if the kiss was as good as all that, why don't you have more to report?"

I shrugged as I looked at myself in the mirror. "Well, he wants to keep it professional, which is understandable, but there's this other thing..."

"What?"

"He's--" I bit my tongue. Was this oversharing? It wasn't really my business to tell, but I needed another person's perspective on it. "He's kinky," I blurted.

Ava's head whipped around on her shoulders. "How kinky? Like tie-you-up-and-fuck-you kinky? Bend-over-so-I-can-spank-your-ass kinky? Lead-you-around-on-a-leash kinky? There're all kinds of kinky, honey."

Stunned, I just stared at her and blinked for a moment until the giggles took over. This was not the response I was expecting from my friend. "I'm not sure how kinky, but I'm thinking all the above. Lemme tell you what happened last night."

I told Ava about The Den and even included the bit where he pinned me against the door and nearly made me come just by kissing me. She listened without interrupting, and when I finally paused long enough to let her get a word in, she gave me her honest opinion.

"There's nothing wrong with kinky. A lot of people believe that only people who have been abused or have some sort of mental health issue are into it, but in my experience, that's just not true."

"What's your experience then?"

She shrugged. "It's just a sexual preference. To me it seems no different than being heterosexual or lesbian or bi or gay. It's just the way they like to fuck. The real question is, how do you feel about it?"

"I don't know. I mean...I still want him, but I don't know how I feel about this kinky business."

"Well, you need to figure that out before you get involved. It could end badly if you don't."

After a couple more hours of retail therapy and girl talk, I felt a bit more knowledgeable about what Ava called "the lifestyle." I was still no closer to making a decision, though. She said that it was a myth that everyone into the kinky lifestyle was abused in some way. As much as I hated to consider myself a victim, I had been in an abusive relationship. Did that mean that I shouldn't get involved with Elijah?

I was unloading my shopping bag while pondering these thoughts when my phone rang. Thinking that it was Elijah, I raced to answer it.

"Hello?"

"Uh...Yves...?"

Fuck. This can't be who I think it is.

"Yves? It's Gabby."

Gabby and I hadn't spoken in years. It was safe to say that if you were my best friend, and you fucked my fiancé and had his baby, there was nothing else for us to talk about. I didn't want anything bad to happen to the woman, I just didn't want her to exist in my world. That's why my first inclination was to wish my cell was a rotary phone so that I could slam it down so hard that her ears rang.

"Yves, don't hang up. I know you don't want to talk to me. I just need to..." and then she started sobbing. Sobbing so hard that I was afraid she might hyperventilate. No matter how much bad had passed between me and this woman, I couldn't listen to someone suffer like that and do nothing.

"What is it, Gabby? What's going on?" I asked, but not without some reluctance. The last thing I wanted was to be pulled into more drama.

"He's drinking again."

I sighed heavily. "I can't say I'm surprised--"

"No, no, he was doing really good. He hadn't had a drink in nearly four years."

"Okay, whatever. What does this have to do with me, huh?"

"I don't know...This has never happened before. At least not with me. I thought you might be able to tell me what to do. When he came home last night, he was already drunk. He hit me. He's never hit me before, but he hit me right in front of Yasmin."

"Are you and Yasmin, okay? "

"Yes, we're fine. It's just that he hasn't come back home. Have you seen him? Is he there with you?"

"No. I haven't seen him since last week. What time did he leave last night?"

"I don't know. Late. After midnight. I've called all the hospitals, but he hasn't turned up. I don't know what else to do!" she wailed.

"Well, first you need to calm down."

"Okay." Her sobbing quieted down to a more tolerable decibel.

"Second, you said you called all the hospitals, right?"

"Yes."

"So you know that he's not hurt or worse. Is this your first fight or something?"

"Well, we've had little arguments before, but nothing like this."

Amazing. When Cesar and I were together, we had a huge blowup at least once a week, but with Gabby he was a saint.

"Well, what did you fight about?"

"We fought about the two of you fucking. What else would we fight about?" she spat bitterly.

"He told you about that?"

"Cesar tells me everything. We don't keep secrets from each other. He's been all fucked up since that night."

"And you're blaming that on me?"

"Who else should I blame it on? He broke up with me because he thought he still had a chance with you, and like always, you broke his heart."

"I broke his heart?"

"Come on, Yves. I've known both of you forever. You weren't looking for a boyfriend when you two got together. You never wanted to be his fiancée or even his girlfriend--"

"Wow. I knew there was a reason why we didn't speak anymore. You're delusional."

"And you're spiteful. You should just let him go, Yves. I love him. We have a family."

"I know that, Gabriella. That's exactly what I told him."

"Before or after you fucked him?"

"Does it matter?"

"Of course, it matters! What type of woman are you to lure a man away from his family?"

"I didn't lure him anywhere, Gabby. And I'm not the cause of whatever issues you and Cesar are having."

"That can't be true, because he's drinking again, and he hit me. None of this would've happened if he didn't think he might have a chance with you. He would've never had his heart broken by you again. Did he tell you that we're having another baby?"

"What?"

"Yup. A little boy."

It shouldn't have bothered me, but it did. Why did she get to have his son?

"That's what started all this," Gabby continued. "We found out the baby was a boy and he got all depressed and started thinking about the baby you lost."

"I don't know what to say. He didn't tell me. I'm sorry."

"Yeah, you should be fucking sorry. You fucked all of this up."

This conversation was going nowhere. The bottom line was that Gabby had to make her own mistakes with Cesar. She knew how volatile our relationship had been, and still she chose to get involved with him. Whatever happened to her and her babies was her responsibility, not mine.

"Look. I'm not going there with you. This has nothing to do with me. You should just take care of yourself. Take care of your baby. I'm gonna hang up now."

"Wait, Yves, before you go, can you do something for me?"

"I don't know, Gabby. I really don't want to get involved."

"Please, it's just a small thing."

I clenched my teeth. "Fine, what is it?"

"If Cesar should call you or come by there, will you promise to call me? I just want to know he's okay."

"Oh, come on, Gabby."

"Please, Yves. You didn't see him last night. I'm really afraid he might do something to hurt himself."

She should be more afraid of him hurting her and the baby.

"Whatever. I'll call you if he shows up."

"Thanks, Yves."

"Sure."

I hung up the phone and decided that this was the absolute last time I got involved with Cesar and his shit. He wasn't my problem anymore. I was tired of him cycling in and out of my life. I wished to God he didn't know where I lived, but that couldn't be helped now. If it became a problem, I would just find another place. I needed to sever all ties. This constant state of stasis was exhausting and demotivating. Never moving forward, always looking back. Never gaining enough distance to change and grow and completely leave behind the woman I was when I was with him. If he showed up, I would talk to him about that; he was just going to have to understand that it was time for him to be out of my life. And I would have to do everything I could to make that happen.

15

Two days and still no word from Mr. Weinstein.

Two fucking days.

I thought he would've given in by now. I fantasized about him pounding on my door in the middle of the night. Breaking in. Ravaging me. I wasn't even entirely sure what it meant to be ravaged, but when I played it out in my mind, it seemed amazing. He had to be obsessing over it. Clearly, I was. It affected my mood--got in the way of my writing. I sat at my desk for hours, trying to cement together a bunch of ideas that had been swimming around in my head, but I couldn't focus. All that seemed to come out was poetry or extremely lyrical, stupid, silly prose. Lazy lines of love spilled out across the page. Lazy lines of love about Elijah. Love? That word kept surfacing again and again. In Elijah's language, in my language...over and over, this word, love.

AMOR, AMOR, MI AMOR, HAY MUCHAS COSAS QUE QUIERO DECIR a usted...so many things I want to say to you, but I don't know how. So much gets lost in translation. There's a barrier--language barrier. A barrier of communication. How do I know what language to use if I've never known the right way to communicate it? This thing that you speak of sounds like Greek to me or else some strange Slavic language that my Latin tongue isn't meant to work its way around.

SHIT...THIS READS TOO MUCH LIKE A JOURNAL ENTRY.

Delete.

Restore deleted file.

Save to super-secret-password-protected file buried in C drive.

Sulk.

Pace.

Smoke.

Think...

MORNING PASSED INTO AFTERNOON. THE SKY DARKENED AND A quick downpour cleansed the streets and dropped the temperature to a more bearable eighty-five degrees. It was around this time that I realized I had daydreamed the day away--reliving those moments in The Cellar with Elijah again and again.

I thought about what he said about the ways a body could react, even when the mind was actively resisting. My body was definitely doing that. When I thought about it, my hands went straight between my legs.

It suddenly occurred to me that waiting for Elijah to call me may be the wrong answer. Maybe I needed to call him. Was that weak or needy? I wasn't sure, but I grabbed up my cell and dialed his number before I could talk myself out of it.

"Yves?"

"Elijah..."

"Hey, how are you? "

"I'm okay. Are you busy?"

"Not really. What's up?"

"Nothing. I just wanted to talk to you about what happened the other night."

"Have you thought about it?"

"Yes. And I've come to a decision."

"Well, what is it?"

"It's not something I want to get into over the phone, Eli."

"You're right. I'm gonna be done here in about an hour. Do you want to meet at Fuji for sushi and saké?"

"Okay."

"Good. So, I'll see you at like seven?"

"Seven's great."

"All right. See you then."

I DIDN'T WANT TO WEAR ANYTHING TOO ALLURING OR TOO modest. First, I chose a dress that was conservatively sexy and some demure heels. Then I changed out of that and put on a fitted T-shirt; my favorite ripped jeans, cuffed at the ankle; and a pair of summery sandals. As I looked in the bathroom mirror, I applied light makeup; just big eyes and lip gloss. I didn't need a costume tonight. No cleavage or short skirts to hide behind. I didn't want to distract him from my real purpose. I wanted him to see me--just Yves. Not the sex-in-heels Yves, but the real me--stripped down.

Because naked was what I wanted to be with him. Bared and stripped down to the bone.

As I swept my hair into a messy chignon, I tried to dissect every word of the three-minute conversation. Did he sound strange? Apprehensive? Was that regret I heard in his voice? The conversation was so short that I couldn't be sure.

"Well, here goes," I muttered on my way to the door. Maniac followed me, mewing softly to draw my attention.

"Do I look pretty?" I asked her. She gave me her usual disinterested glare. I checked my hair and makeup in the hall mirror before walking out.

My cell phone rang as I bounded down the stairs of my apartment. It was Elijah. "I'm running out the door right now. I should be there in ten minutes," I said by way of greeting.

"Good, cause I'm here already. I can't wait to see you."

I smiled. "Good. I'm dying to see you, too."

"Am I going to be happy about what you have to say?"

"Yes, I--" The words died on my tongue.

"Yves? Are you all right? "

"Yeah, I just...I might be a few minutes late."

"I thought you said you were on your way out the door. Is something wrong?"

I wanted to answer him, but I was still processing the fact that a very drunk Cesar was swaying on my doorstep.

"Look at you...so pretty," Cesar slurred, one hand reaching out to tug at my belt loop.

"Cesar, what are you doing here?"

"I came to see you, baby. Ain't you happy to see me?"

"Yves," came Elijah's voice over the line. "Did you just say Cesar was there? Talk to me. Is everything all right?"

I wanted to reassure him, but getting Cesar out of my

doorway was more important. "Look. You can't be here. I'm on my way out."

"I just wanna talk to you, corazón."

"We've already said everything that needs to be said. Go home. Your girlfriend is worried about you."

"She can wait. We need to talk."

"Like I said, I don't have time to talk to you. I'm on my way out. Excuse me--"

In all the years I had known Cesar, through all the arguments, all the beatings, I was never afraid of him. Crazy, I know. I just never thought he would intentionally do permanent damage to me. Foolishly, I believed that there was a kernel of love in there that kept him from hurting me so badly that I might end up dead.

The calloused hand he clamped around my neck proved me wrong.

"I said we need to talk," he growled in my ear then dragged me back up the stairs.

I kicked against him and clawed at his fingers, but that only made him grip me more tightly. This wasn't happening. This couldn't be happening. It was broad daylight. People were on the street. Kids were playing on the sidewalk. How could this be happening?

"Come on, now. Don't make a scene," he coaxed, his voice saccharine sweet. His grip on my neck tightened and pinched off my airway.

"Okay!" I said, my voice high and frantic. Fighting against instinct, I forced myself to relax and cooperate. Maybe if I went along with whatever he wanted, he would let me out of this in one piece.

Cesar found his way into my living room and tossed me on the couch. I scrambled to the opposite end in an attempt to get as far away from him as possible.

"Please, Cesar. Don't do this."

"Don't do what? We're just going to talk." His eyes went to my cell phone. Seeing that I was still on a call, he snatched it from my hand. "Called you a bunch of times." He looked at the screen, saw Elijah's name and ended the call. "Guess I know why you didn't answer." He tossed the phone across the room where it immediately began to ring again. Cesar loomed over me, swaying drunkenly.

"What do you want from me?" I asked shakily.

"I want you to listen to me for once. I want you to acknowledge that you weren't the only one hurt by losing CJ. I was hurt, too."

"I never said you weren't--"

"Just shut the fuck up and listen, will you?" He sighed and sat down heavily in the middle of the couch. Too close to me. "Look at what you do to me. You made a mess of me, Yves. Four years sober and one night of you makes a mess of me."

I clenched my teeth, preparing for another one of his drunken rambles where he would paint himself as the victim and me as the huge cunt for expecting him not to treat me like a punching bag.

"Just that little taste of you. It's not enough. It's never enough..." He leaned in close, crowding me against the arm of the couch. "You know...when I'm with her, I'm always thinking of you. When I'm sitting with them, eating dinner or watching TV, I feel like I'm caught up in some alternate reality that I can't get out of. I keep thinking this isn't the life I'm supposed to be living. Do you ever feel like that?"

I was reluctant to answer. I didn't want to give him the wrong impression, but I had to give him something to keep this situation from escalating. "Sometimes we all feel out of place," I responded blandly. "Have you ever thought of leaving?"

"Leaving Gabby? I think of it all the time. I want to start over with you so badly, Yves--"

"I don't mean leaving to be with me. I mean, leaving just to get yourself together."

"You mean be alone?"

"Yeah, don't you think you should?"

"I've never been alone, Yves."

"I was never alone either until we broke up."

"I'm not like you. I can't be alone. When I'm alone...I get myself into trouble."

"Well, it seems to me that you get yourself in trouble either way."

My cell phone vibrated from where he'd thrown it across the room.

"You had a date tonight, didn't you? That's why you don't have time for me. Didn't have time to answer my messages. I heard what you said that night. You know you don't have to be lonely. We could be together. We could be there for each other like it was before. You know I love you."

He pulled me to him and kissed me gently. My belly roiled and pitched, nauseated by the smell of the liquor on his breath and what it meant. I pushed him away.

"Cesar, don't," I begged again. "I did love you, but this is over. We are over. I don't want to try again with you. I want something good and healthy and real--"

Out of nowhere, he slapped me. It came so quickly. He slapped me hard. Hard enough to rock my head back on my shoulders and knock me right off the couch.

"Real?" he bellowed, standing over me. "Are you saying that what we had wasn't real?"

First thought that crossed my mind as I held my face in

my hand was, Fuck you. You're not going to hurt me again. Then I hit him back. I launched myself upward and punched him square in the face. All the anger and so many years of pain bunched up in my fist. Knuckles met flesh. Bone crunched into bone. Blood--his blood--so red. Too bright. This was nothing like the love taps I gave him last time. Last time I was hurt. This time I was just fucking angry.

Cesar wiped his mouth with the back of his hand. When he saw the blood, his anger shifted and morphed into rage.

He hit me again.

This time his hand wasn't open. This time he hit me with a closed fist. Oh my God...I'd forgotten how much that hurt. My skull felt like it had shattered. Like my face was broken into little pieces and scattered on the floor. My vision swam. Bright spots danced across my eyes.

"Motherfucker..." My speech was slurred. I tried to keep him off of me, but he was so strong. So fucking strong. Felt like wrestling a bear.

"See, that was always your problem, Yves."

He slammed me to the floor, and my head cracked against the hardwood. The room swam and whirled, and then his face came into vivid focus.

"You never know when to shut your fucking mouth."

"Fuck you!"

He laughed, and I could hear the madness tickling around the edges of what should be a joyous sound. "This is how it always is with you," he breathed into my face. "It's never good unless we fight. This is how you like it, isn't it?"

"No, you just can't get it up unless you beat the shit out of me first, you sick fuck."

His eyes stretched and danced in his skull. He was wild with rage.

"Are you gonna rape me now?"

Another blinding slap. This time my jaw cracked under the blow.

"I may be a sick fuck," he cursed, leaning in close. "But what does it mean if you like it?"

All of this was so familiar. His hot breath stinking of malt liquor. His unpredictable anger--the beating and then sex, rough and brutal and rarely consensual. He kissed me hard, mashing his mouth into mine, crushing my bruised lips into my teeth.

"Get the fuck off of me," I growled in his face. The breath puffed out my cheeks as I made another effort to push him off me.

"I know you want this. I can feel how hot and wet you are through your jeans." He ground into me for emphasis.

My stomach lurched and threatened to spill out of my mouth. He was right. I hadn't noticed it until he said something, but I was aroused. "Please, get off me." I suddenly felt weak. All the fight had drained out of me to make room for the shame. Hot tears slid down my cheeks.

"Oh, now she gives me tears!" he mocked as he ripped open the button of my jeans. He reached in past my panties, groped me, and showed me his fingers--fingers wet with my arousal. "You may not know what you want, but your pussy does," he said.

I turned my head away, wondering how my body could betray me like that. Was I really that twisted? Was I that fucked up?

"Please, Cesar," I sobbed. "Don't do this."

"Don't do what? Make you love me again? You said that when you fuck all those guys, you can't feel anything. Do you want me to make you feel something, corazón? If I fuck you like I used to fuck you on your mother's living room floor, while everyone was asleep, do you think that you could feel the same love you felt then?"

What was I feeling? Reckless? Hopeless? There was nothing I could do to stop this from happening, but something in me still wanted to fight.

I spat in his face.

God, how many times had I wanted to do that when he was on top of me? It felt so good it was almost worth the next blow he delivered that sent my head reeling. The world narrowed and darkened to a tiny pinhole, and I happily passed out.

16

Lips brushed against my cheek. A familiar voice pleaded, "Yvie. Yvie. Wake up, Yvie."

Was I sleeping? Was all of that a bad dream? I tried to open my eyes. My eyelids felt like lead weights.

"Yvie?"

I tried to open my eyes again. And that's when I felt it. Every bruise, every scratch--layers and layers of pain. My lips were swollen, and when I swiped my tongue across them, I tasted blood and felt raw, split skin. The salty, metallic trickle in the back of my throat probably meant I had a bloody nose. And when I finally opened my eyes, I realized that the right one would only open partially. The left took forever to focus on the face leaning over me.

"Elijah," I groaned and tried to sit up.

"Don't move," he cautioned. "You're pretty banged up. The cops are on their way."

"And Cesar? Where's Cesar?"

"The motherfucker took off."

"What are you doing here?" I asked.

"I could tell by your voice that something wasn't right. He was drunk, Yves. Why'd you let him in here?"

"He just pushed his way in. He's never done anything like that. Not without a reason. I didn't think he would..." I wanted to say that I didn't think he would hurt me, but why would I think that? All this man ever did was hurt me. I closed my eyes. I let the tears fall. I was hurt. Cesar had hurt me again--from the surface of my skin all the way down to my soul.

Sirens sounded, drawing the whole neighborhood out onto their stoops to watch. The police arrested Cesar two blocks from my apartment. They found him sitting on the curb crying; he admitted to it right away and told them he deserved whatever came to him. Gabby arrived just in time to see Cesar being carted off, handcuffed in the back of a squad car. He must have called her in that moment of clarity when he realized he was going to be arrested. Their daughter stared at me with her father's big brown eyes from the backseat of the car while her mother screamed in my face, her swollen belly between us.

"¡Puta! This is all your fault! You did this to us!"

I didn't bother disagreeing with her because she was right. Never mind the fact that she had stolen him from me four years ago. He was her man now. The father of her children. I never should have meddled in that, and for that, I was sorry.

I tried to insist that I was fine and didn't need to go to the emergency room, but after a quick examination, the EMTs carted me off. Elijah followed in his car to the hospital and stood by while they patched me up.

A CT scan verified that I had a concussion. Fifteen stitches mended my scalp where Cesar had slammed me to the floor. Iodine and bandages were applied to my scratches and cuts. The nurse also insisted that Elijah get an X-ray of his hand, which was swollen and bruised from beating on Cesar. His knuckles were scraped raw and the back of his hand was black and blue. If that was how his hand looked, I hated to see Cesar's face.

When the nurse left to get him an ice pack, Elijah finally sat next to the bed and looked at me. He reached out hesitantly to touch my face, fingers tracing the most painful spots--places that I knew were bruised and ugly.

"I look pretty bad, huh?"

Elijah nodded, but didn't speak. His eyes misted over a bit and his Adam's apple bobbed repeatedly as if he were trying to swallow back tears.

"I'm sorry," I whispered.

"Yves, what--?" His voice snagged in his throat, and a tear slipped down his cheek. He brushed it away awkwardly and cast his eyes downward. "What are you apologizing for? You did nothing wrong."

"I pulled you into the middle of my fucked-up existence. I'm sorry for that."

"You didn't pull me into anything. I'm here because I want to be."

The curtain around my hospital bed yanked back with a clattering rattle, and the nurse reentered with two uniformed police officers. "Mr. Weinstein? Ms. Santiago?"

Elijah stood. "Yes?"

"We're going to need to a statement about what happened at your house this evening, Ms. Santiago."

"Can't this wait?"

"It's okay, Elijah. I want to do it now. When I wake up in the morning, I want all of this to be over."

I told them every detail of what happened. Told them how drunk he was and how he slapped me, then punched me, and then wrestled me to the ground. Elijah filled in the portion that happened after Cesar knocked me unconscious. He told it in hitching breaths--his face blotchy and twisted with anger. According to him, he came in before Cesar could rape me. He stopped it before anything happened.

So why did I still feel so violated?

Shortly after we gave our statements, my brother and sister arrived.

"Oh my God, Yves!" Mercedes descended on me, tears forming in her eyes. "Cesar did this to you? Oh, my God."

"What are you guys doing here?"

"It came across the scanner. The guys called me the minute they heard your name and address. What the fuck happened?" Marcelo asked.

"I was heading out my door, and Cesar was waiting for me. He jumped me--"

"I can't believe this. I can't fucking believe this," my brother ground out between clenched teeth. "He's lucky the police already have him, because if they didn't, I would murder him."

"I tried my best to do just that," Elijah muttered from where he stood in the corner.

"Who are you?" Marcelo asked, bristling with barely checked rage and testosterone.

"This is Elijah. He helped me."

Marcelo gave him a tight nod. "Thank you."

Elijah answered my brother's thanks with a nod of his own.

"Could we step outside and talk for a minute so you can tell me your side of what happened?" Marcelo asked him.

"Of course."

They stepped out into the hall, leaving me alone with

my sister. Mercedes was barely holding it together. Her bottom lip quivered as she gingerly touched my bruised face.

"Oh, sissy," she whispered, her voice thick with tears.

I swallowed back my tears and smiled, ignoring the pain. "It's not as bad as it seems. I'll be fine."

Before she could respond, my mother burst in.

"¿Yves, que paso?" she wailed. She came to me, hands fluttering over my body, afraid to touch me. All the color drained from her face. I'd never seen her this scared before.

"Mamí, calm down," I urged. She needed to hear the truth about what happened, but I wanted to do it the right way. It was bad enough she had to see me in the hospital.

"Don't tell me to calm down! Look at your face! Who did this to you? Was this some crazy girlfriend? A wife of one of the men you've slept with?"

That hit me in the gut. Here I was in a hospital bed, beat to shit, and my mother assumed that I'd brought it on myself in some way.

"I told you something like this would happen," she continued. "I told you that you can't keep messing around like that and expect it not to come back on you--"

"Mamí!" Mercedes shouted, silencing her for a moment. "Cesar did this."

"What?" My mother looked from me to Mercedes and back again. "Is that what you're telling people?"

"It's the truth, Mamí. Cesar did this to her," Mercedes said, jumping to my defense before I could open my mouth. "Not some crazy girlfriend or jealous wife. It was Cesar."

"I don't believe it. Why would he do something like this to you? He loves you."

That did it. I couldn't be strong for them. I couldn't

explain it to my mother when she thought I brought all this on myself. This thing happened to me. Cesar hurt me. I didn't need to make her feel better. I needed to take care of myself.

"I need you to leave," I hissed.

"What?"

"I want you to go," I repeated and looked up at her. "Now."

A strange look came over her face, as though she had just realized that I was telling the truth and that she was making a huge mistake. I didn't have it in me to console her. I just wanted her gone.

"Okay," she said quietly and gathered her things. She left without a backward glance, too stubborn to admit she was wrong.

"Can you believe she said that?" Mercedes asked.

"I'm surprised you didn't agree with her."

"What? I never--"

"I think need you to go, too."

"What?" she reached out and touched my arm lightly. "Yves, I'm here for you."

"Are you? If he hadn't put these bruises on me, you would still believe Cesar is the one for me, right?"

"No, Yves. Please--"

"Is everything all right in here?" Elijah asked, stepping back into the room.

"I'm fine. I just want all of them to go."

"Yves! You're being unreasonable!"

"Maybe it's best if we go now," Marcelo suggested, putting his hands on Mercy's shoulders.

"She can't stay here alone."

"She won't be," Elijah said softly and came to stand next to my hospital bed.

"But we're her family. We should be here with her," my sister insisted.

"We can see her tomorrow. Let's give her some space." Marcelo stepped forward and kissed me on the forehead. "I love you, sissy," he whispered. "I'm sorry I didn't see it. I'm sorry I didn't recognize him for who he was. I'm just so, so sorry." He sniffed and gathered up Mercedes before she could say anything else.

"Are you all right?" Elijah asked once they were gone.

"Yeah, I just need to close my eyes for a minute, I think."

"Okay." He sat back down in the chair next to the hospital bed and took my hand. "Close your eyes. I'll be right here."

THEY KEPT ME OVERNIGHT FOR OBSERVATION. ELIJAH LIED AND said he was my fiancé so that the hospital staff would let him stay with me. He helped me out of my bloodstained clothes and into the sterile hospital shower, wincing at the bruises that I could feel blooming on my arms and back. He washed my hair, taking extra care not to wet my stitches. With gentle hands, he lathered every inch of me, and he was so careful and attentive that it made my heart ache.

So this is how it feels to be taken care of?

It seemed ridiculous that I had never experienced this before. Even more ridiculous that I nearly married a man who would never do this for me and made me believe I didn't deserve to be treated this way.

When I was clean, he patted my skin dry with a tiny, rough towel and helped me into the hospital gown. The lights went off on the ward, and we climbed into the narrow bed together. I started to cry and couldn't stop. Elijah held me and tried to reassure me that everything would be okay. I wanted to believe him, but it was hard. Especially when I knew that on some level I wanted it to happen. On some level, my body responded to and needed that sort of violence.

"What if he's broken me, Elijah?"

"We'll find someone to help you fix it."

"I wish it was that easy."

I wanted so badly to be free of Cesar, but now I felt like that would never happen. When I thought about my sex life, I realized that in some way I had acted out that relationship over and over again. And this thing with Elijah, my willingness to be submissive to his dominance, was probably a symptom of that too.

"I don't think I can be fixed."

He didn't respond right away. He just held me tighter. "What would make you say something like that?"

The last thing I wanted to do was to say this out loud, but I felt like I needed to tell someone. I felt like I needed to tell him. "When--when he pushed me to the floor, and we were fighting? There was a moment when I gave in--"

"There's no shame in that, Yvie--"

"I'm not finished. That's not all of it."

"Okay." He gave me another encouraging squeeze. "Tell me all of it."

I closed my eyes and took another deep breath. "He was on top of me. Right in my face. He said something like--this is how it always is with you. You never like it unless we fight. I told him that he was sick and twisted. Told him that beating me up was the only way he could get it up. Then he said, 'I may be sick and twisted, but what does it mean if you like it?"

"Fucking prick," Elijah growled through clenched teeth.

"But he was right! He put his hand on me and--I swear,

in my mind I was angry and scared but...my body...I was...when he put his hand on me I was--"

"Shh..."

"No! I want to know what the fuck that means! How can I get that turned on when he's trying to rape me? Am I that fucked up?"

"No, you're not fucked up. Just confused. I'm sure it wasn't in response to what he was doing to you."

"You're sure? How can you be sure? The last time Cesar and I had sex, I beat the shit out of him. I was so angry that I slapped him and I kept slapping him until it started to feel good. I kept slapping him until the slapping turned into fucking."

Elijah made a noncommittal noise and grew quiet. I didn't know how to interpret his silence. Was he shocked by what I told him? Repulsed?

"So what is it that you're saying to me, Yves? What are you asking me?"

"Do you think what he did to me changed me somehow? Distorted how I think about sex?"

"I think what he did to you changed you in a lot of ways. Sex is only one of them."

"So now I'm some sort of deviant that can only get off if she's being smacked around? That's crazy."

"You're jumping to conclusions, and for the record, it's not so crazy. More than one person in this bed is into that. I'm more concerned about what this is doing to you emotionally. That nurse gave me the number for a rape counselor--"

"I wasn't raped."

"It was close enough. I think you should talk to someone, Yves."

"You think I'm really fucked up, don't you?"

"That's not what I'm saying."

"So why are you bringing up the rape counselor?"

"Yvie, look at me."

"No." I buried my face in his chest. He cuffed me under the chin, tipping my head back so that he could look in my eyes.

"I just suggested the rape counselor because I think it would be good to talk to someone about it. Someone who can help you sort through all of this."

"I don't want to sort through it. I want to forget it. I want to forget him. Erase him. I wish he was never part of my life."

"I understand that. But maybe you need to talk about it so that you can forget."

"No fucking way." I turned away from him in a huff. Elijah pulled me against him, tucked my body into the curve of his.

"All things have their purpose. No matter how fucked up your relationship with Cesar was, it had a purpose. Yes, it changed you, but some of that change was for the better. You're stronger for all that has happened between you and Cesar. At least you have that foundation to draw from when you're working on the other not-so-good stuff."

"It's the not-so-good stuff that I'm worried about."

He kissed my temple. "Don't worry," he said softly. "Just sleep. I'll do the worrying for you if you want, but for now, just sleep, okay? I'll be right here. I won't let anything happen to you."

His words seemed to have a deeper meaning, one that I didn't want to acknowledge right now. I just wanted to lay there, listen to Elijah's soft breathing, and enjoy the feel of his arms around me. I was safe and warm in his arms, but I knew I didn't belong there.

Elijah said that everything had its purpose. I guess that

meant that somewhere in this, there was a lesson to be learned. What had I learned? What had this beating taught me?

This lesson was no different from the one I learned four years ago. I learned that a broken heart would only heal when it was ready, and nothing could speed up that process. I learned that my self-worth was tangled up in my relationship with Cesar and that in a lot of ways I believed that because I failed at that, I would fail at everything.

I didn't need a degree in psychology to know that when something was broken or torn over and over, there was always some sort of evidence of the trauma. Bones sprouted strange calcium deposits; torn muscles and tendons grew sinewy, tough scar tissue. I knew that when these bruises healed, it would still hurt way down deep, as if the wound was new and nothing but time would heal that. A shrink would tell me I shouldn't be in a relationship and that, along with everything else, was something I already knew.

These hard lessons were firmly implanted in my psyche--lessons I couldn't forget. But I would try tonight. Tomorrow I could face reality. Tonight I would let him hold me.

17

I expected to see Elijah when I woke up in the morning, but instead I woke to Mercedes, who was sitting in the chair next to my bed, reading a magazine.

"Hey." She greeted me with a small smile.

"Hey." Guilt about the way I'd spoken to her yesterday swamped me. I pushed myself up in the hospital bed, groaning when my head swam. Pain thudded into the place behind my swollen eye.

"Do you need me to call the nurse?" she asked, preparing to launch from her seat.

"No, just give me a minute." I closed my eyes, took a few deep breaths, and waited for the worst of the pain to pass. Whatever they had given me before they put the stitches in had worn off. I could feel the skin pulling in an unnatural way against my scalp. I wondered if I would have a visible scar. "Where's Elijah?" I asked once the pain and nausea began to subside.

"He had to go to work, but he said he'd be back at lunchtime. He also brought your laptop and a couple of books from your apartment." She pointed to the table where my laptop and journal were stacked, along with a few writing craft books I didn't recognize--gifts from him.

"What about Maniac?"

"He said your next door neighbor has her. Mrs. Mackenzie or something? He took care of everything. Seems like a nice guy."

"Don't go getting your hopes up. He's my editor and a friend. That's it."

"I wasn't implying that--never mind," she said with a dismissive wave. "I can't seem to say anything right."

"Sorry," I said, shaking my head. "I don't mean to snap at you. It's just...when Mamí came in and said all those things--"

"I know. I can't believe she came at you like that, but she was blindsided, Yves. She didn't know he was like this. None of us knew."

"I get that, but it sounded like she was blaming me."

"I wasn't blaming you!" My mother stepped into the room from the hallway. Evidently, she'd been listening in on every word.

"That's strange. I'm not sure if what you said to me could be taken any other way."

"Like your sister said, I was blindsided. None of it made any sense! It still doesn't. But you have to believe me, if I had known that he had this in him, I would've never--" She shook her head, trying and failing to ward off her tears. "I'm sorry that you had to go through that, chiquita."

There were things I wanted to say...things I should've said a long time ago to defend myself, to help them understand everything better, but I realized that I'd have to do that another time. My mother had just apologized, and it felt good to have her on my side for once.

"I'm sorry I didn't tell you. I guess I didn't know how. I'd spent so much time lying and covering everything up. Trying to make things perfect. It was hard to admit that my relationship with Cesar wasn't what it seemed."

"I guess that's what's so hard for me. You two always seemed so happy. Even when you called off the wedding, it seemed more like cold feet than something like this."

"I know."

"So, this isn't the first time he's hurt you?"

I took a deep breath, and instantly a lump swelled in my throat. "No, he was abusive the whole time we were together," I stammered. My voice sounded tight and small. "Verbally and physically."

"And the baby?"

I could only nod. It was still too painful to say the words out loud. I looked at my mother. The corners of her mouth pulled down, and a frown creased her smooth brow.

"How could you go back to him after that?" Mercedes asked.

I shrugged. "I loved him. I thought I could help him."

My mother was quiet and thoughtful for a moment. "I wish you had told me. I thought it was just the cheating. I even thought you were a bit of a hypocrite. You were so flirty with the boys, chiquita. I thought it was something the two of you could work through." Her gaze dropped to her lap. She pulled at the wad of tissues in her hands. "I feel horrible for those things I said to you back then."

"You didn't know. I didn't want any of you to worry about me."

"Oh, Yves," she cooed and leaned in to brush my hair away from my bruised face. "Yves, why do you think you have to be so strong all the time?"

I shook my head. "I just do. I won't be like that again. I

can't trust anyone or let them get close to me like that. It's just too painful."

"Oh, no." My mother pushed me away. "Don't use this as an excuse for why you shouldn't trust or fall in love again," she said, shaking her head. She looked into my eyes. "It's okay if you feel something, Yves. You're a woman. You're human. It's not weak to admit it. It's not weak to give in to it. Of course, there are risks. There's risk in everything we do, but that doesn't stop you from living right?"

"No," I muttered, shaking my head.

"Well, it shouldn't stop you from loving either."

I narrowed my eyes at her. "How d'you get to be so wise?"

My mother gave me a smug smile. "By reading your blog."

"I don't think I've ever said anything like that."

"You did in your own way." My mother reached for my hand and gave it a gentle squeeze. "I trust and believe that you will eventually find true love."

God...I hoped I would, too.

After another head CT and a really disgusting lunch of foods in various stages of mushiness, I was granted release. Collectively, my family decided that I should go home with Mercy. It was the best place to recover. My sister was eager to take care of me, so I might as well let her. They were finalizing my paperwork when I got a call on my cell. I smiled as I brought the phone to my ear.

"Hey, bruiser," Elijah teased as soon as I brought the phone to my ear.

"Hey, I missed you this morning."

"I'm sorry I had to leave before you woke up. My boss called me in early."

"No problem. I totally understand. I'm glad you called,

because it looks like I'm going home. Well, they're releasing me from the hospital, but I'm going home with my sister."

"Oh...well, when are they discharging you?"

"Right now. I'm just waiting for them to bring me the discharge papers."

"Oh..." he said again. "How long do you think you'll stay at your sister's?"

"I'm not sure. At least until my face heals."

"Right. Of course," he said. "But we'll talk, right?"

"Yeah, sure," I answered. "I'll work on my book while I'm out there and call you to let you know my progress."

"Well, that's great, but I wasn't talking about the book."

"I know," I said softly.

"Yves...I'm not trying to pressure you. I just want to know that you still want this. That you still want me."

"I want to want it, Elijah."

He chuckled. "Well, that's a new one."

"I just feel really broken right now, and I think I should deal with that before I think about what's happening between you and me."

"I understand."

"I'm sorry--"

"Will you stop apologizing? You've done nothing wrong." He sighed. "I guess, I'll wait to hear from you."

"I'll call you."

"Take care of yourself, Yvie."

"You, too."

SOMETIMES I FEEL LIKE I'M FULL OF SCARS.

hidden beneath my brown skin
is the evidence

of abuse of the worst kind
emotional cuts and slashes
against my soul and psyche.
Once an open wound
healed over with time.
Scars
raised like braille.
Slashes
left to remind
my heart...
so eager to love
that love is not always kind.
Not always giving
not always true
left there
to remind my heart
to be wary
of you.

THREE DAYS AT MY SISTER'S AND I WAS BEGINNING TO FEEL something like my normal self. I still didn't have the courage to look in the mirror. Honestly, I didn't need to see my reflection to see the damage Cesar had done. I felt it in every bone, every cell of my being. Part of me felt relieved and vindicated now that this was all out. I didn't have to tell them what he had done to me; they could see the evidence on my face. But I felt guilty and even a little sad. Cesar had a dysfunctional family. My family wouldn't be there for him after what he'd done. He was alone in this. He was alone in that jail cell with no one to visit him or even care whether he lived or died. I never wanted that for him. I hoped Gabby would go to him, but that seemed unlikely. Besides, that wasn't the love he wanted. He wanted my love. He wanted the love of my family. And now, because of what he'd done, he would never get it. Even though I knew he should take full responsibility for what he did to me, the guilt of that was heavy. I didn't know what to do with that guilt, so I wrote it all down.

This would be the last time I visited this time in my life...the last time I thought of him. I allowed myself to think about the good times, because Mamí was right--things were good between us once. Things were sweet. Our future held a shining promise. A promise of a baby boy I never met, but whose face I still see clearly in my mind's eye. I wrote it all down and when I reached the end of that story, I moved on to the next and the next until I realized that I was writing the book that Elijah wanted me to write.

Elijah...At some point I had to deal with this thing between us. I still wasn't ready, so I avoided his calls. He continued to call, of course; he filled my voicemail with heartrending messages. All this love around me, coming at me from all sides, and I just wanted to hide...bury my head in my words, the one thing that had never abandoned or hurt me.

After six hours of sitting hunched over my laptop at Mercy's kitchen table writing, I stood up, stretched, walked into the living room, and plopped on the couch. My sister's house was home-catalog perfect. How she managed to keep white couches clean with two little ones, I would never know. Back in the sunny, sage-green kitchen, I heard my phone ring again.

"Damn, Yves. Who keeps calling you?" Mercedes asked as she picked it up. "Elijah...looks like he's left you a bunch of messages too. You never did explain who he was to you," she said while walking into the living room with my phone in her hand.

"He's the editor from Leaf Press. The one who got in contact with me about writing the book." I took the phone from her and it vibrated again, alerting me to yet another voicemail.

"Why are you dodging his phone calls? Did you miss a deadline or something?"

"No, I just don't want to talk to him."

Mercedes frowned and crossed her arms over her chest. She looked just like Mamí when she made that face. "You slept with him, didn't you?"

"I wish it was that easy."

"What's that mean?"

"It means that he is the only man I haven't slept with in the last three months. In fact, I think we may even be...friends."

Mercy laughed. "You? Friends with a guy? I don't believe it." She sat next to me on the couch. "So how did you get stuck in this friend zone? Is there something wrong with him?"

"No, that's the thing. He is absolutely perfect. I mean, you met him."

She nodded. "So why aren't you sleeping with him?"

"Well, at first I didn't sleep with him because I thought it would be bad business. You know, shitting where you eat sort of thing. But then on the Fourth of July, he met me in a bar and we talked. I told him about Cesar and practically everything about my life. I'm still confused as to why I did something like that with a total stranger, but he sat and listened. He walked me back to my place. I invited him up and he said no. He gave me some line about wanting me for my mind, not what's between my legs."

"Do you believe him?"

I shrugged my shoulders. "He seems to be sincere, which frustrates me to no end," I said, rolling my eyes.

"Well, he sounds like a nice guy. A real gentleman."

"He is. It's me. There are just some things wrong with me that I think would make a relationship with him...difficult," I said with a shrug.

Mercedes reached for me and pulled me in for a cuddle. We were never the type of sisters that cuddled before this whole thing. I mean, we loved one another, we just weren't super affectionate. I have to admit that the cuddling was a little off-putting at first, but now I went into it willingly. Apparently, we were a couple of natural cuddlers. And it didn't hurt that Mercedes had that mothering gene that instantly calmed and soothed whoever was in her arms.

"You know I love you, sissy," she said softly.

"I know."

"And I want you to be happy."

I hesitated before answering. I wasn't sure where this conversation was headed. "Of course, you do. I want you to be happy, too."

"Okay, I'm going to ask you something, and I don't want you to get offended," she said, then began to play with my hair like she did when she was a little kid.

"All right..."

"This Elijah...he sounds pretty perfect. He seems to know you and understand you. He came to your rescue and sat with you while you were in the hospital...what's the real reason why you ain't more than friends?"

There were so many reasons. His kink. His need for a committed relationship. My aversion to monogamy and how I didn't want to give up my entire self to be with a man.

"It's complicated," I responded.

"Hm," she grunted. "I hear what you're saying, but there is nothing complicated about the way your face lit up when you were talking to him on the phone before we left the hospital."

I pulled away from my sister. "Are you seriously pushing me toward another relationship when the bruises from my last one are still fresh on my face?"

"Come on, Yves. You can't use Cesar as an excuse not to get into another relationship."

"I don't know. An abusive ex seems like a pretty solid reason why I should be wary of men for a while."

"True. But you don't seem particularly wary of Elijah."

I narrowed my eyes at her. "What makes you think that he's any different than all the other guys I slept with?"

"You did. It's in the way you were when he was around. And it's in the way he cares for you. I think there is a lot more than friendship between the two of you. You should call him."

I sucked my teeth and sunk deeper into the couch cushions. "I told you. It's complicated."

"What's complicated?" she asked. "The man nearly broke his hand defending you."

"I know, but the fact that he had to defend me is the number one reason why we shouldn't get involved."

"So you're giving up on love? You're just gonna let Cesar win?"

"I didn't say that I was going to give up. I just don't think this is the right time--"

"There is no right time."

A strained cry came from the baby monitor, interrupting us. My niece Sacha was waking up from her nap.

Mercedes stood up. "Call him, Yves," she ordered and tossed my phone onto the couch before leaving the room.

I don't know what kept me from dialing his number. Pride? Shame? Fear? Some combination of the three that rendered me inactive? Whatever it was, dinnertime rolled around, and I still hadn't found the nerve to call him. What would I say anyway? Thank you? I'm sorry? More than that, I was afraid of the things he might have to say now that he'd had some time to think. Maybe he thought I was too damaged or too much trouble. Maybe all of this made him realize that he wanted nothing to do with me.

After dinner we sat out on the back deck and watched the sun go down. The girls were playing in the yard and Mercedes and Desmond sat arm in arm on the swing, cuddling and necking like people in love do. The whole scene was idyllic and domestic, and part of me yearned for something like this.

If I tilted my head and squinted, I could almost see myself in this life. But like ghosting in my peripheral vision, thoughts of Cesar and what happened to my son marred the picture.

God, I had to quit doing that.

Mercedes was right. If I gave up on love because of what happened with him, he won. I might as well have stayed in the relationship. I deserved better than that. I deserved more.

18

I didn't intend to press charges against Cesar, but the severity of the crime and the fact that he was already on probation took that choice out of my hands. The more I thought about it, the more I realized it was the right thing to do. Cesar needed to accept responsibility for what he had done and facing the legal repercussions would be a good first step. This meant I had to make a written complaint.

Mercedes drove me back into the city.

"It'll be quick," she said as she parked in the lot of my local precinct. "You just need to tell them what happened again, sign the stupid paper, and get out of there."

Telling them what happened was no less difficult the second time around. My bruises were still dark, ugly, and tender. I hid behind big sunglasses, but they asked me to take them off so they could take more pictures.

The police officer said that there was a slight chance that Cesar might decide to press charges against Elijah for the beating he gave him, but he thought it unlikely. He advised me to get a restraining order, but I knew that a restraining order was only a piece of paper. It couldn't stop him from doing anything. It wouldn't stop him from drinking, and it wouldn't stop him from hurting me again. But what would? I had to know.

"I need to talk to him," I said to Mercedes the moment we left the station.

"What?" she asked, incredulous. "He beat you, Yves. Put you in the hospital for the second time. What could you possibly have to say to him?"

I shrugged. "I can't explain it to you. I just need to see him."

My sister frowned. "¿Qué te pasa? Are you still in love with him?"

"No! It's nothing like that. I just need him to see me. To see my face. He needs to see what he's done. It won't be real to him if he doesn't."

"What makes you think seeing you this time will affect him differently? He's hurt you before--"

"I know. But this is different, Mercedes. You just have to trust me."

Mercedes shook her head. "And what are you going to say to him?"

I shrugged again. "I don't know. I just know he has to see what he did to me. I can't let him delude himself into believing that he didn't hurt me or that I brought this on myself. He needs to see this."

"Is that even something that can happen? I'm sure there are rules about victims of inmates visiting them in jail."

"There are, but I just put in that formal complaint. It will probably take weeks for all of that to be entered into the system. If there is a chance I can get in to see him, I want to do it."

She stared at me for a long time, hazel eyes scanning my

face and the bruises that discolored it. After a moment, she nodded. "Okay."

THEY HAD TAKEN CESAR TO A FACILITY OUT IN CHESTER, Pennsylvania. Apparently that was where they sent inmates with substance abuse problems. He had only been drunk to my knowledge, but obviously the urinalysis had revealed something else. My stomach was a mess of nerves that didn't improve on the drive out there. By the time we arrived, I felt like I would vomit or cry or maybe both.

"Do you want me to go in with you?"

I glanced over at my sister. She looked pale and fearful. Mercedes may have grown up in South Philly, but she was definitely more sheltered and less streetwise than me and Marcelo. That wasn't necessarily a bad thing. If I could avoid exposing her to the dirtiness of life, I would.

"No." I unbuckled my safety belt and pulled off my jewelry. "I'll be okay."

"Okay. I'm going to find a coffee shop or something. Just call me when you're done."

I nodded and got out.

My knees barely supported my body on the walk across the lot. I'd dreamed of visiting Cesar in jail numerous times, but it still felt surreal to actually do it. I knew the procedure well enough from friends who had visited their loved ones in jail. Leave your cell phone and your bag in the car. Bring your wallet or ID, but don't bring any money. I'd done all of that, so I passed through security easily enough, though being groped by a corrections officer was something I never hoped to do again.

In the movies they brought you to a room with a glass partition and you spoke to the inmate through a two-way telephone. Instead, the other visitors and I were escorted to a room filled with round tables where the inmates already waited. I spotted Cesar immediately. He stood in line with the other inmates in his orange jumpsuit--the uniform they gave the newbies until they were placed permanently. He had his head down, but even with a layer of scruff and no haircut, I recognized him.

Once I was sitting at the table, I spread my fingers out on the linoleum top. My palms were slick and sweaty. A spike of fear wet my armpits and made them itch. So strange to be feeling that after all these years. He'd hurt me so many times, but it took this to make me afraid of him.

Some sort of buzzer sounded and the doors opened with a heavy click, letting the inmates in. All around me I heard the warm greetings of loved ones.

"Yves...What are you doing here?" he asked softly.

"I needed to see you." I swallowed hard and pulled off my sunglasses.

Cesar drew in a sharp, startled breath.

I don't know what I expected him to say or do. I just held his gaze and waited. The swelling had gone down around my left eye, but the lid and surrounding area was a blue-black and the white of my eye was darkened by a blood clot. A rainbow of colors decorated the rest of the left side of my face. My lips were healing, but still split and sore. I was a fucking mess, and I wanted him to take it all in. After a moment, his knees gave out under him and he collapsed into the plastic chair opposite me.

"I did this to you?"

"Yes," I said with a nod. "You did this to me."

His hand reached for mine tentatively. I pulled it away and forced it into my lap.

"Yves, I'm so sorry..."

"You know, you've said that before and you've hurt me again."

"I know."

"You can't keep doing this to me. I can't allow you to keep doing this to me."

"I know," he said again.

"Everybody knows now. Mamí, Marcelo, Mercedes...they all know."

"And they all hate me now?" His mouth flattened into a thin line, but he didn't look up at me. His posture, his voice, all of it spoke of remorse, but he wouldn't look at me.

"It doesn't matter how they feel. I just couldn't keep it from them anymore. I couldn't keep your secrets anymore, Cesar."

"You never should've had to."

I licked my lips. "Look at me, Cesar."

Reluctantly, he raised his head, and his gaze met mine.

"I pressed charges against you, Cesar. Not because I want to punish you, but because I think that it's what you need to get well. I think you need to stay in here for a while--"

"What? Yves, you don't know what you're saying. I can't stay here. I'll die in here."

"No, you think I don't know what I'm saying, but I know better than anyone what you need, Cesar. You're an alcoholic, a rage-aholic, and I don't know what else. You're a danger to yourself and others. You need to stay in here until you get yourself together."

"And how am I supposed to do that around these criminals, huh? How am I supposed to do that if I have a criminal record?"

I slid away from the table. "I don't know. But I'm going to do everything in my power to keep you here long enough for that to happen."

"Yves--" He grabbed my hand.

"No touching," the guard bellowed, and he released it instantly. I felt a pang of guilt at that momentary insight of what his life would be for however long he would in there. No one would touch him or speak to him with love or concern. He might even be forced to defend himself. The guilt was nearly enough to change my mind, but then I thought about his fist slamming into my face over and over again and that burned away any sympathy I may have had left for him.

"Listen. You have to go back and tell them that this was just a misunderstanding--"

"It's too late for all that, and I know it's not the right thing to do. You belong in here, Cesar."

"No...please, Yves. I'll do anything. I'll go to rehab. I'll move out of state if you want me to. Don't leave me in here."

I pushed away from the table and stood. "Take care of yourself," I said. "Get well." Then I turned and walked out of there with no intention of ever seeing or speaking to him again.

I made my way through the jail and back to the parking lot, waiting, anticipating some sort of breakdown. I waited for the tears, the screams, the agony of realizing what I'd done and how much it would affect him. I waited for the Berlin Wall of feelings to topple down on me. I waited...but felt nothing. Nothing but free. All of our secrets were out in the open. I'd broken his heart, broken it for real this time. Things between us had met an irreparable end, and goddamn it if life didn't go on. The sun sank down hot and bright on the horizon. Evening traffic swelled. Kids played in schoolyards, and life went the fuck on.

And now, so could I.

THE CITY FELT LOUD AND CROWDED AFTER SO MUCH TIME IN the suburbs. As much as I hated to admit it, I kinda missed the quiet, green streets of Langhorne. Staying with Mercedes had given me time to focus on my writing. The words had poured out of me during my stay, and it felt so weird after struggling with them for so long. When I started this thing, I was afraid I didn't have enough in me to write a book. But in three weeks, eighty thousand words of my story had spilled out on the page. Now I just had to find out if they were worth reading. My face was healed and my book was written. It was time for me to go home.

The weather was nice, and everyone was outside, sitting on their stoops, drinking beer, barbecuing. Usually this sort of thing would make me happy, but after the incident with Cesar, I worried my neighbors might whisper behind my back and pity me. I walked with my head down until I reached my front door. After a quick trip upstairs to drop off my bags, I went to collect my cat.

Mrs. McKinney usually greeted me with a grunt and a nod; today she gave me a grim smile and patted me on the shoulder with a "Hey there, girl."

"Hey, Mrs. Mac. I'm just here to collect my cat."

"Of course! She's in the kitchen." She ushered me inside.

I could count on one hand the number of times Mrs. McKinney had actually invited me into her house, and I had basically bullied my way in all of those times. To be standing in her kitchen while she fussed around felt strange and endearing.

Maniac mewed soundlessly and padded over to me. I smiled and scooped her up. I had to admit that I wondered if she would even recognize or want me.

"She was no bother at all," Mrs. McKinney said. "So sweet and quiet. I think she may have taken a liking to my tomcat Leonidas," she said pointed to the window ledge Maniac had just leaped from. A huge tabby cat with a fluffy, white mane was stretched out there now. I smiled to myself. My girl had good taste.

"Thank you so much for taking care of her."

The old woman dismissed me with a wave. "That nice young man left plenty of money and cat food. Like I said, it was no bother at all."

"Thank you, anyway."

Mrs. McKinney paused for a long moment, her hands still clutching the bag of cat food and Maniac's bowls. "I was the one to call the police."

"Thank you." I wanted to say more, but what more could be said? I was thankful that she had called. I couldn't imagine what would have happened if she hadn't. "You wanna go outside for a smoke?"

She nodded.

"Okay, lemme put Maniac inside and make a phone call. I'll be right out."

I expected my living room to still be trashed from my struggle with Cesar, but it was spotless now. Elijah must have straightened up when he came to pick up my laptop. The fact that he would even think to do something like that made me giddy in a way I would never admit in mixed company. Regrettably, I never worked up the courage to call him while I was at my sister's, but I had every intention of rectifying that right now. I still wasn't sure what I would say to him when he answered, but I knew I had to talk to him--had to see him. Hopefully, he wouldn't be too pissed to answer my call. The phone only rang twice before he picked up.

"Yves? "

I smiled at the eagerness in his voice. "Yeah, hey."

"Hey, baby. How are you?"

My whole body reacted to him calling me baby. Would hearing his voice always do these strange things to me? I had to get these stupid, girly feelings in check. "Good. I'm back in the city."

"I'm on my way," he said and hung up so abruptly I couldn't say okay or goodbye.

I joined Mrs. McKinney on the stoop. We smoked quietly, and I wondered how this thing would go. My mind tumbled endlessly over what I would say to him when I finally got him alone. I knew I had to finally be real and honest with him and tell him all the feelings that I'd tried to keep to myself. I did want this something with him. And while I was at it, I had to admit that it was more than something...more than infatuation or lust. It may be love, but I couldn't be sure. It had been so long since I'd felt anything remotely close to this. The thought of it scared me, but I was willing to try. I was willing to try with him.

19

Elijah's Benz rounded the corner about a half hour later. He parked a little ways up the block, hopped out, and jogged toward where Mrs. McKinney and I sat. I stubbed out my cigarette and stood up.

"Ah," Mrs. McKinney said knowingly when she saw him. "This one stuck."

I rolled my eyes, but couldn't say she was wrong. A confusion of emotions rioted through my body. I was scared and happy--happy to see him, scared to say everything I wanted to say. Part of me wanted to skip all of that and jump into his arms. Kiss him. Tell him with my body that he was what I wanted. Instead, I smiled and said, "Hey," as he approached.

"Hey," he said and smiled back before he kissed me on the cheek. "Good afternoon, Mrs. McKinney."

"Yeah, it is pretty good. And it's probably about to get a lot better for you," she said with a knowing waggle of her brows.

Elijah laughed. I could only groan. The old bitty had a talent for making me feel uncomfortable.

"Let's go up. Little pitchers have big ears," I said, jerking my thumb in Mrs. McKinney's direction. She sucked her teeth and shooed us away.

Maniac went right to Elijah and mewed to be picked up once we reached the top of the stairs. He reached down and gathered her into his big hands, but his eyes were on me.

"What?" I asked self-consciously.

"Come here. Let me look at you," he said gently.

I knew he wanted to inspect me, to see if there were any lingering scars or damage. I pushed my hair out of my face and stepped closer. Elijah curled the purring Maniac to his chest with one hand and cradled my face with the other. My bruises had healed, but there were still some yellow and green ones that were so deep, they'd literally bruised the bone. He stroked his thumb over those lingering discolorations and kissed them gently.

"How are you?" he asked, his eyes scanning my face.

I knew his question had a deeper meaning than concern for my surface wounds. "I'm good. Not so broken."

He gave me a small smile. "Good."

"You wanna..." I gestured toward the living room. He nodded and followed me to the couch. "I finished writing the book," I said as we entered the room and sat down.

His eyes stretched wide with surprise. "Is that it?"

"Yep." I hefted the ream of paper held together by rubber bands into my hands and placed it in his lap.

"Lust Diaries: the stories of Yves Santiago, self-proclaimed slut," he read with a smile. "Congratulations, Yves Santiago. You completed a book."

"Thank you. Do you think the title is too much? Too...on the nose?"

"No. I think it's perfect. So why did you decide against using a pseudonym or publishing it anonymously?"

I shrugged. "Everyone knows everything now. I see no point in hiding. It's nothing like my blog. I decided that I wanted to keep writing there...it's my diary. I'm not ready to give it up. Besides, this is a true memoir with all the ouchy, shameful parts included."

Elijah nodded. "Good." He set the sheaf of papers back on the table and shifted on the couch, turning toward me. Maniac was still cradled against his arm, and he petted her absently. God. I was so nervous. My mind raced to fill in the awkward silence. I shifted and twitched on my couch cushion.

"I've been thinking about what happened that day," he said finally. "It's all I think about, actually."

"Me too." I turned toward him. "I never thanked you for what you did. I can't imagine what would've happened if you didn't come to my rescue."

"You don't need to thank me, Yves. I wish I had done more, which is kinda what I want to talk to you about."

"Okay."

He took a deep breath and leaned in. He spoke again softly, as if he was afraid his words might hurt me. "Seeing you like that, broken and bruised by that man's hands, it made me ask myself a lot of questions."

"Questions like what?"

"Like...what makes me think I will be any good for you? As much as I want you, I know I shouldn't take this any further because the way I want you could hurt you more than either of us knows."

"So what are you saying?"

"That I don't think we should see each other romantically. I think me and my...proclivities are no good for you and will only traumatize you further."

"Who said I needed you to make that decision for me?"

"Yves, you know I'm not right for you. I'm all fucked up--"

I laughed. "Is that what you're worried about? In case you haven't noticed, I'm pretty fucked up, too. Don't two negatives make a positive?"

"It's not that simple." He shook his head.

I moved closer and curled myself into the empty space between us. "It seems pretty simple to me. I want you. You want me. Let's be fucked up together."

An involuntary laugh spilled from his lips before he set them in a grim line again. "You can't understand how much I want you. I want to claim you. Devour you. Consume you. These are not things I can do by half. Do you understand that? I will destroy you, Yves. And I'll love every minute of it."

I knew his confession should scare me, but it didn't. Instead, it sounded like the sweetest words I'd ever heard. I wanted to be his to claim, devour, consume, destroy. Just the thought of it made my skin flush. Heat prickled and spread from the places his lips brushed when he kissed me earlier.

"I want all of that," I breathed.

He groaned. "Somehow you've gotten it into your head that I'm a fairytale prince. I'm not."

"What if I don't care?"

"If you thought about it logically, removing all lust and emotion, you would care. We shouldn't be together, Yves."

Tears burned in the corners of my eyes. I blinked them back, as surprised at their presence as I was at this situation. This was not what I had expected to happen. He should be kissing me right now. Tearing my clothes off. This felt like we were breaking up before we ever began.

"So that's it? I don't get a say in this? You're making the decision for me? I could've sworn I was woman enough to do that for myself."

"Not about this. You don't know me. You don't know what I'm capable of."

"You'd never hurt me."

"How can you possibly know that? You've only had a glimpse of who you think I am. You don't know me."

"I know I want you."

"You've wanted lots of men."

It was a low blow. I could see that he regretted the words the moment they came out of his mouth, but he didn't bother to take them back. And why should he? The words should've hurt me, but they didn't. They didn't hurt because they were true.

"Is that what this is about? Those other men that I've wanted? Those other men that I've had? That's too fucking easy." I stood up from the couch and went straight into my bedroom and into my closet.

"Yves?" he called after me.

Wordlessly, I turned on the light, found the clothes of those anonymous men, and took them down, hangers and all.

"What are you doing?"

"Something I should've done months ago." I stalked out the door, went down the steps, and dumped the clothes on the curb. Mrs. McKinney was still sitting out there, smoking her Virginia Slims and eavesdropping on our conversation, no doubt. Her eyes grew big when I dumped the heap of expensive clothes on the curb. I didn't care. I had no idea what I was doing, but I knew I had to do something to make him see that I wanted this.

It took me two trips to get them all. Elijah stood by and watched me, speechless. When I came back into the apartment, I calmly closed the door, took his hand, and led him back to the bedroom again.

"Yves, I--"

I quieted his protests with a finger to his lips and took off his shirt. With it bundled in my hands, I walked into the closet, found a stray hanger, and hung it up in the now hugely empty space.

I felt like a lunatic making this grand gesture. Did this sort of thing even work? Those traitorous tears closed up my throat again, making it impossible to speak. I fought them back. Falling apart was the last thing I wanted to do right now. Tears would only remind him of my fragility. I wanted to show him my strength.

Elijah stood in the doorway of my closet, now shirtless as well as speechless. When he looked like he might say something, I launched myself at him and kissed him. I kissed and kissed him until all he could do was surrender--and then launch an attack of his own.

His hands pushed into my hair. His mouth on mine lost all hesitancy. "Okay," he said when our lips parted enough to take a breath. He said it as if I had asked him a question. His answer was to toss me onto the bed.

I ripped my yellow sundress over my head and wiggled out of my underwear. Elijah stood at the edge of the bed, blond hair disheveled, tugging off his belt and unzipping his fly. His eyes gobbled up my nakedness, dragged from my face to the place between my legs. My hand followed the path his gaze took and skimmed over my clit.

"You have condoms?" he asked.

"You didn't bring any?"

"No. I came over to end it with you. I had no idea this would happen."

I nodded and crawled across the bed to my night table drawer. His hand came down on my upturned ass. I yipped and glanced over my shoulder at him. He had the sexiest crooked grin on his face. I wiggled my bottom and that earned me another smack and a quick nip in the place just under my right ass cheek.

"This ass is just as amazing as I thought it would be."

I smiled and turned toward him, condom in hand. "You really would've quit seeing me?"

He sighed. "I was gonna try. It would've been really hard. But I was gonna try."

His fly was splayed open, a hint of his black boxer briefs peeking through the V-shaped gap. I reached for them, pulled them down until his dick leaped free. I caught its warm, ridged length in my hand and brought him to my mouth.

"What about now?" I asked and gave him a long, luscious lick. "Still wanna end it?"

His hand fisted in my hair. I opened my mouth and he thrust deep.

"Not a fucking chance."

I surrendered to him. Let him have his way with my mouth until he yanked me off his dick and demanded, "Put on the condom. I need to be inside of you, sweetness."

Fuck yes. Finally.

I tore the condom wrapper with my teeth and used my mouth to roll it down his length.

"Jesus," he said and pulled away from me. "Lay back. Spread your legs for me."

Eager as ever, I did what he asked. I lay back against my rumpled bedclothes and let my knees fall apart. He stood there for a long moment, seemingly transfixed. He stared for so long I began to feel self-conscious again. I tried to remember the last time I'd done any sort of maintenance down there. It'd been a while, at least since before the thing with Cesar.

"What? " I asked, fighting the urge to close my legs.

"You're fucking beautiful."

He leaned over me and kissed his way down to my pubic bone, his head angling toward the thighs he now held apart with his big hands. Once he was there, one broad lick brought my hips right off the mattress. "Squirmy little thing. Next time I'll have to tie you down," he whispered.

I thought about how it would feel to be bound down. His mouth on me. Completely at his mercy. My pleasure his to give or withhold. I thought about that submissive and her Dom, how she was tied up and suspended, tears streaking her makeup. Could I be her? Could that be us?

"Hmm," he hummed. "You like the idea of being tied up, don't you?" He kissed his way back up my body until he covered me completely. "Too bad I don't have any rope right now. But I've been told that I have big hands." He grabbed both my wrists and pinned them high over my head. The other hand slipped down between us to grab hold of his dick; he began to circle my throbbing clit with the tip.

"Tease," I whispered.

He smiled against my mouth, the edge of his teeth against my lips. "You think this is teasing?"

"Why else would you spend so much time right there when you know where I want you?"

"Maybe I'm trying to be gentle."

"Did I ask you to be?"

Elijah reared back to look at me. The summer afternoon light caught in his eyes as they scanned my face. His brow crinkled into a contemplative frown.

"Do you realize what you're asking for?"

"Yes," I answered without hesitation.

He grunted and shook his head. "You still have the bruises he left on your body."

"You're not him."

"And if I told you that seeing them made me want to cover them with my own?"

"I'd beg you to do it."

He regarded me for a long moment. Then with a quick nod, he flipped me onto my belly. The sudden motion forced a startled whoop from my lungs, followed by an uncontrollable giggle. The two fingers he plunged into my pussy changed that giggle to a moan. I arched my back, wanting those fingers deeper. Before I even thought about it, or even realized what he was about to do, his hand came down on the round of my ass. I whooped again and cast an accusing look at him over my shoulder. The eyes I met were wild with raw lust and some other emotion I couldn't put my finger on. That look made me lose my train of thought; it wiped my mind clean of whatever sassy comeback I could come up with and replaced it with an urge, an inclination that was beginning to feel familiar to me.

"What's your favorite flower?" he asked.

I frowned. "Stargazer lilies."

He smoothed a hand over the roundness of my bottom and leveled another smack to the sensitive skin between ass and thigh. "Lily. That's your safe word. Do you know what a safe word is?"

My head bobbed up and down, and I answered with a raspy, "Yes."

"Good. I want you to use it if you feel like I'm going too far."

"Okay."

"Spread your knees."

I braced myself on all fours, spreading my knees wide. He smacked my inner thighs, urging them wider.

"Just breathe and relax," he urged. "If you tense up, it's only going to hurt more."

I nodded and let my head hang loosely between my shoulders, forcing my body to relax. Every muscle in my body quivered with the anticipation of the next blow, but it never came. I turned to look at him again. His jaw was clenched and his entire body was tense, waiting. He needed something more from me. I turned to him, reached for him.

"Eli," I breathed across his lips, my eyes closed tight against the words in my mouth. "You don't scare me. Knowing that you're holding back or that you're afraid to show me who you are does." I tugged at the too-long hair at the nape of his neck. "Show me."

I could feel that anxiety building in him, begging to be spilled out, but still, he managed to hold back.

"Yves," he whispered. The sound of his voice was nearly unrecognizable. It was the sound of gravel and broken glass, his insatiable being rubbing against worn thin self-control. "I hope you don't think this just a game, because--"

"I know it's not a game," I answered quickly, trying to reassure him. "I want you. I want this. Show me," I said and rolled onto all fours again.

He didn't have to dig deep for it. It had been dancing under the surface of his skin since the moment we met. With a hungry little grunt, he yanked my hips back, angled my ass high, and brought his hand down, unchecked. The sound rang in the quiet room followed by my closed mouth scream. A twinge of panic prickled my skin. Instinct took over. Before I could resist, he grabbed both my hands by the wrists and secured them in a vise-like grip behind my back.

"Don't move," he growled. The tone of his voice struck something in me, and my body responded before my mind had a chance to protest. He spun me around, repositioned me so that I was over his lap, and angled my ass higher and spread my legs apart a bit. He swept my hair off of my neck and back so that it puddled on the bed, and then traced the line of my spine with his fingertips. Every muscle in my body tensed in anticipation of the next blow, but once again, the blow didn't come right away. He caressed my backside and squeezed like he was testing it for ripeness, as if it were fruit. He did that for so long that when the next blow landed, it caught me completely off guard.

"Jesus Christ!" I screeched.

He must have been holding back before. Now I felt the full weight of his large hand as he delivered an intense volley of blows. I squirmed and wiggled in his grasp, but all my cries of "no" and "stop" fell on deaf ears. Fresh tears sprung in my eyes. The blows landed with startling accuracy, striking the backs of my legs, my ass, and the inside of my thighs until it felt like every nerve in my body was concentrated in the screaming, trembling flesh of my backside.

He paused for a moment to let me catch my breath. His lips and breath kissed over my inflamed skin, and he fingered my sex with a slight, delicate touch. I moaned. It was so loud that it startled me. I couldn't believe that the sound came from me. I had never heard myself sound like that before. He spread my legs wider, exposing my sex. It felt swollen and heavy. Hot tears streaked across my face.

"God, why the fuck am I letting you do this to me?" I whimpered.

His answer was a low, dark chuckle, and I knew he was going to hit me again. My mind screamed stop, but my body wanted it more than anything I'd wanted in a long, long while.

He pinched the welts his hand had raised on my skin,

sending another delicious shiver of pain through my body. How could it hurt and feel so good all at once?

I heard him draw in a deep breath, and then he delivered a blow straight across my pussy. I moaned, and I lifted my ass higher. He struck me again. The pressure of an orgasm bloomed and spread into my lower belly. Every cell in my body reached toward it, aching for release. The next blow landed flush against my pussy. I writhed and came violently, sobbing and shuddering--my body a confused tangle of nerves. The evidence of my release trickled down the inside of my thighs. He let up then and turned me over onto my back.

I felt vulnerable and exposed. The sheets were like sandpaper against my flaming ass and thighs. I closed my eyes in an attempt to quiet the trembling in my body, the rapid beating of my heart, and my ragged breathing. His lips brushed across my skin, kissing me with his breath and the very tip of his tongue. My thighs and belly quivered violently. I tried to stop it, but there was no controlling it. I could only lay there and quake like a virgin. He leaned over me. His warm, bronze skin smelled like summer. The Star of David around his neck dangled in my face, tickling my cheek.

"Yves, open your eyes."

I lost myself in his when I did. My breath snagged in my throat. Tears streamed down my cheeks. I didn't know why I was still crying. He must have forced some sort of release in me.

"Did I hurt you?" he asked softly.

I shook my head no, even though my legs and ass were still stinging from the impact of his hand. It didn't hurt the way I'd expected it to. I felt open--stripped bare. When he kissed me, that helplessness, that weakness that always sparked fear in me overwhelmed me. I bit my lip to stifle it down as he made slow, wet kisses down my neck, between my breasts, and over my belly. His mouth closed over my pussy; his tongue suckled gently. I kept my eyes wide open, watched him as he parted my lips with his fingers so that nothing kept his mouth and tongue away from my clit. He paused to take a breath and our eyes met. The ominous intent that I saw there startled me. He gave my clit a quick pinch; it sent a shiver down my spine that ended with a little trickle that he eagerly lapped up.

"That's a good girl," he murmured and did it again and again. He fucked me with his tongue, until I begged, "Make love to me, please, please, oh, God." But he only teased me more. He pinned me to the mattress with one of his strong hands while he pulled another orgasm from me with his fingers and his mouth.

He prowled up my body, marking me with wet kisses on the way to my mouth. "I want to get into that place inside of you where no one has ever been," he whispered against my lips. "Will you let me in, Yvie?" he pleaded. "Will you let me inside?"

"Yes," I said, panting deliriously, barely aware of what I agreed to. "Please."

In one swift movement, he thrusts deep--filling me completely. I cried out against the unexpected bite of pain that mingled with my pleasure. He moaned and melted against me, weak from that first delicious moment of our bodies coming together. I whimpered like some soft, stupid girl. I couldn't help myself. It felt good--he felt good. More than good--he felt right. His mouth covered mine and his hips pressed deeper. I shuddered and tipped my hips up to him, already so close to coming again that I couldn't keep still.

He hooked my knees over his shoulders and thrust again. My God, I couldn't remember the last time I was filled so sweetly. Every inch of him fit every inch of me. I didn't even have to work for it. The orgasm just snuck up on me in delicious, spasmodic waves. I'd never been fucked like this. Never.

"Yes," he whispered with a grin. "You are my perfect little slut."

He said some other words, but all I heard was him claiming me. I pulled him closer, but I still didn't feel close enough. The skin we were in felt like a needless barrier. Watch yourself, Yves, the logical side of me cautioned as he bore down and fucked me hard, his dick coaxing me toward another orgasm. But I didn't want to listen to logic. For once, I wanted to follow my heart. I didn't know if he was the one. Nor could I pretend that he possessed some magic to convert me or change me from a tragically flawed woman into someone who could love and be worthy of love. All I knew was that he felt right. So I closed my eyes and then...I just gave in.

NEXT IN SERIES

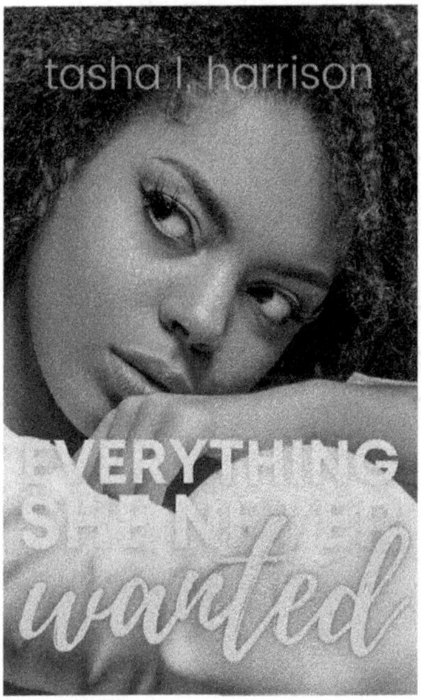

"I am the first to admit that I have special talent for falling for the wrong guy."

But Elijah Weinstein is wrong for Yves in all the right ways. The kinky, pretty boy and his filthy, delicious mouth has burrowed his way under her skin and she isn't sure how can or if she wants to get him out.

And he believes in her talents and supports her dreams… seems a little too good to be true.

When they begin to explore her submissive and kinky tendencies, their feelings for each other become more intense, she fears that she is falling into old patterns, losing herself in him.

Elijah keeps pushing her boundaries, making her want and feel things she doesn't feel ready for, but when they come right up to his limits will he be brave enough to let her in?

CW: Dubious consent

EXCERPT

CHAPTER ONE

I came to the meeting at Leaf Press dressed for murder. Black pencil skirt, black pinstriped shirt, glossy black pumps, sheer black stockings with a Cuban heel. To quote the greatest rapper alive--all black everything. Even my hair, parted in the middle and straight enough to cut a bitch, looked darker than its usual brown. I might be overreacting, but this armor felt very necessary. My suit was the embodiment of the woman who wrote The Lust Diaries--assertive, professional, and sexy. I must have nailed it, because the look Elijah gave me when I entered the conference room said that he approved.

Many cigarettes were consumed and much sleep was lost in preparation for my meeting with the acquisitions team. As the acquiring editor, Elijah knew all the details of my contract. We had debated discussing it, but decided it would be best to keep our professional careers out of the bedroom. Or rather, he decided it would be best. I hated that he wouldn't talk shop with me now that we were fucking. When I got especially petulant about it, he reminded me that I wrote an amazing book. A book a step beyond my

Lust Diaries blog that revealed a more intimate layer of myself. He reminded me that I deserved a chance to see it published, and he refused to do anything to jeopardize that. When he put it like that, how could I disagree? But it was also a good reason for me to be armed and prepared to fight for my interests. There was no room for error. This blog was my life's blood, and I wanted to get it right the first time.

"Ms. Santiago," he said, greeting me with a warm smile.

"Mr. Weinstein," I answered evenly. I had to bite my cheek to keep from grinning. Pretending not to be intimate felt like drawn-out foreplay, the intensity of which was heightened by the fact that I wore his bruises and a rug burn under my clothes. Elijah had paid me an early morning visit, even though we'd agreed it was probably best if I slept at my place last night. Not that I slept much. Apparently he hadn't either, because he banged down my door at six-thirty in the morning and fucked me into a screaming orgasm right there on my hall steps.

After introducing me around, Elijah guided me to the nearest empty seat. His hand slid over my bottom discreetly before I sat down, waking the bruises I had acquired in our early morning tussle. That was bold. We'd agreed to be careful, and that groping hand on my ass was anything but. Was it the skirt? My ass did look amazing in it. He wasn't used to seeing me all buttoned up and professional. Clearly, this was something I needed to do more often.

"Hello, Ms. Santiago. May I call you Yves?" Helena, the woman Elijah had introduced as editor-in-chief, greeted me. Not pronounced Hel-lay-nuh but Hell-in-uh like hell in a handbasket, hell in a black Gucci suit, hell in six-inch Gucci heels. Her legs were long, firm, and coltish--runner's legs. They were gorgeous, and she knew it. She sat at the head of the table with her legs angled toward Elijah. He told me she'd been trying to seduce him with those getaway sticks since the day he'd started working at Leaf Press. A lesser man would've fallen prey to her charms long ago. I knew he never would. Elijah was an ass man. I had the marks to prove it.

"Of course...as long as I can call you Helena."

"Yes, please do. It's so wonderful to finally meet you, Yves."

"Thank you. It's wonderful to meet all of you as well," I said, acknowledging the rest of the table with a nod and a smile.

"You have written an amazing book," she said with measured praise.

"I'm glad you think so, but it's still so hard to believe that any of this is happening."

Helena smiled. "Understandable. Especially considering the fact that you had such a modest readership. We would never have known who you were if it weren't for Mr. Weinstein. I guess we can credit him with discovering you early on."

Even a socially illiterate person could feel the shade she threw with that comment. She thought she was doing me a favor.

"I was searching for ways to monetize my blog before Mr. Weinstein got in contact with me, but he should be credited with encouraging me to do so."

"Oh, we definitely acknowledge his diligence in pursuing you." She smiled. "I'm sure this will be a mutually beneficial relationship."

"I certainly hope so. I may not have thought of publishing my blog as a book before, but I do know what I'm worth."

The EIC's mouth twisted into a smirk. "Good to know.

Maybe we should go ahead and review the contract?" She lifted a questioning eyebrow at Elijah and he pushed the contract in front of me.

"This is a pretty standard contract for first-time authors," he explained. "I've tabbed the pages that require your signature. You are more than welcome to take the contract with you and review it with a lawyer."

"That won't be necessary. I've read several contracts." I picked up the ream of paper. It was thick enough to be a short novel all on its own. I tried not to let that intimidate me as I scanned the portions on the grant of rights and searched for the ever-tricky non-compete clause. I found no major issues. Standard author representation, warranties, and indemnification of the publisher were sited. I had three months from the date of this contract to complete the edits. Barring any major issues, when the flowers bloomed, Lust Diaries would be hitting stores. It seemed too poetic to be real. A little shiver of excitement rushed through me. I stifled it down, making a professional mask of my face. "This all seems to be in order," I murmured. "Except for one thing."

"What's that?" Helena asked.

"I'd like to have it written in that I own the Lust Diaries brand. That it will be considered separate from the copyright you hold on this book. I would also like final approval of the book cover."

The room fell quiet. Elijah looked stunned. I hadn't discussed this with him, and now he was blindsided by my request.

"Ms. Santiago...this is a very uncharacteristic," Helena said, an irritable edge to her voice.

"I understand, but this book is an extension of a brand that has taken me years to create. I want to make sure that it remains true to that. Also, I want to ensure that I am the sole owner of that brand."

Helena glared at Elijah, but he didn't notice because he was too busy glaring at me.

"Leaf Press is not prepared to--"

"Save whatever legal mumbo jumbo you're about to feed me. I want to retain the trademark licensing. I refuse to wake up one morning to discover that my book has been made into some lukewarm cable TV show that will offend everyone in the free world and die in three seasons. I won't sign the contract without this addendum. It's too important to me."

The editor-in-chief tapped her ink pen on the table and regarded me with intense scrutiny. I met her gaze with a boldness I didn't really feel. I'd practiced these words in my bathroom mirror before I left, but it was entirely different to say them to her face. Rejection was what I expected. Condescension. I had deeper arguments if she chose that route, though I hoped she didn't. This was not the time to be weak or ingratiating. This was my livelihood.

"We will do all that we can to make sure your requests are met." Helena stood and extended her hand to me. "Welcome to Leaf Press. We are honored to include you amongst our illustrious authorship."

I shook her hand and smiled. "Thank you," I said. Though I knew she didn't mean a word of that.

She stepped around me and exited the room on a gust of agitated wind.

"Yves, can I see you in my office?" Elijah asked.

"Of course." I smirked, though a tiny sliver of fear snaked through me. He was pissed and I would catch all of that the moment we were alone.

Elijah led me out of the conference room on the main

floor of the building, across the lobby to the stairs. His office was two flights up and at the end of a short hallway. The walls were frosted glass and didn't offer much privacy, but the moment we were inside with the door closed, he rounded on me and hauled me into his arms. I suppressed a surprised giggle and returned his hug. I'd expected a completely different reaction.

"I really want to be upset with you, but I have to admit...I'm extremely turned on by what just happened in that conference room."

"What? Me protecting my interests?"

"Yes. Did you know you were going to do this all along, or did you decide it this morning?"

"I've been thinking about this all along."

"It was smart and bold, and I'm ashamed of how much I underestimated you. But aren't you concerned? Everything is up in the air now. It really could go either way."

"I think it'll go my way."

"You don't know that. You could lose this contract. I really wish we could've discussed this first."

I rolled my eyes. "This was your rule, Elijah."

"Yes, it was my rule and probably not the smartest thing I've ever done," he said ruefully. His full lips stretched into a slow smile. "I really loved the way you handled her, though."

"Who Hell-in-uh?" I asked, drawing out the pronunciation of her name. "I had to let her know she couldn't kick me around. Women like that need boundaries."

"They do, huh? What about you? What do women like you need?"

"To never be caged in."

"Really?"

"Yup. I'd just gnaw myself free, anyway."

He grunted, then kissed me. I gave a surprised

complaint, concerned about the red lipstick I had meticulously applied, but he didn't give a damn about my lipstick. His hand slid up my back to cradle my neck and the other palmed my ass, pulling me flush against him. I sighed, parting my lips to accept his tongue. God, would I ever get used to kissing this mouth? His mouth had claimed mine so many times, but it still caught me off guard. How his tongue slid over mine. How his hand gripped my ass so that I felt each individual finger imprinting my flesh. He owned me. With his kiss and his touch, he owned me.

"Can you go out for lunch?" I asked, when he finally pulled away long enough for me to catch my breath.

"Can't."

"Bad form, sir. I feel like I never see you anymore."

"I feel the same way. Which is why I broke down your door this morning." He pulled away a bit to survey what damage he'd done to my makeup with the kiss. He smoothed the smudged edges with his thumb. It must not have been too bad.

"Let's go out to celebrate."

"Where?"

"The Den."

A tiny shiver rushed through me. More than a month had passed since he took me to the swanky lounge that doubled as a BDSM bar. When I asked, he couldn't rightly say what kept him away. Maybe it was an innate need to keep me to himself with things being so new between us.

"I want you all dolled up."

I grinned. "I'm gonna get all dolled up to watch a bunch of perverts flog and fuck each other?"

"We're gonna do more than watch."

My smile faltered a little, but I swallowed down that fear,

gripped his arm, and pulled him closer. When my mouth aligned with his ear I whispered. "I'm ready for more."

He growled deep in his chest and sought my mouth for another kiss.

"When?" I asked.

"Tonight."

AFTER A FEW MORE LINGERING KISSES, I LEFT ELIJAH TO HEAD back home. I was dazed and feeling unsure of the ballsy move I'd made in the conference room earlier but still proud of myself for asking for what I wanted. All they could do was say no.

"Ms. Santiago! Can I see you for a moment, please?" a voice called out to me, just as I reached the elevator.

I'd never met her before today, but I was already oddly familiar with the crisp, abrupt tones of Helena Davidson's voice. As much as I wanted to avoid her, I knew it wouldn't be proper, so I took a deep breath, turned around, and headed back to her office. With clenched teeth, I rapped twice on the frosted glass of the slightly ajar door. Ambient music filled the space beyond, and I could see Helena at her desk.

"Come in, Yves."

I pushed the door open and stepped inside.

"Have a seat," she murmured and gestured toward the chair opposite her desk.

I lowered myself into the chair. "Is there something more you need from me?"

Helena held up a finger and continued to read the document in front of her for what felt like an eternity. I understood what was happening here. She felt disrespected by my demands during the contract negotiation and was paying me back for that. It still pissed me off.

After a few moments, she set aside the manuscript and took off her glasses. "So..." She angled her legs under the glass desk to create an enticing view. The woman did have great legs. "You gave us a run for our money this morning? Was it always your intention to make those demands?"

I shrugged my shoulders. "Of course. I did a bit of my own research. Investigated the careers of a few bloggers who came by their book deals the same way. I wanted to make sure I didn't make the same mistakes."

Helena nodded. "Smart. Reckless, but smart. And did you discuss this with Elijah prior to the meeting?"

"No. Believe it or not, I have friends in the publishing business to advise me. I didn't tell Elijah because he works for you. Not me."

"Are you fucking him?"

I smirked. "So now we get to the real reason why you called me in here." The question hung between us, tainting the air along with Helena's underlying reason for pulling me in here: she wanted him. And if her reaction to me was any indication, he had exactly zero interest in her.

"If you're fucking him," she continued. "I have to inform you that this company has very strict policies on fraternization between authors and editors. This sort of transference is common between authors and editors of the opposite sex, but is strongly discouraged as it can muddy the waters in the relationship with our authors. If you are fucking him, you would be reassigned to another editor and he would be fired."

"I'll keep that in mind." I stood and smoothed my pencil skirt over my hips. "Are we done?"

The corners of her mouth pulled down, as though the

words on her tongue were so vile she couldn't stand the taste of them. Surprisingly, she managed to swallow them back. I gave her a curt nod and then turned to leave her office.

"One thing you might also want to consider," she said as my hand closed around the doorknob. "An accusation of preferential treatment based on a sexual relationship with your editor could be damaging to your career. All those feminist ideals would tank at a hint of a rumor about your involvement with Elijah. No self-respecting feminist would take you seriously after that. I mean, the man is beautiful, but is he worth ruining everything you've worked for?"

She was baiting me. Digging around in my psyche trying to find my hot button and goddamn if she hadn't hit it. Even knowing this, it took everything in me not to round on her and unleash every expletive I knew in both the English and Spanish languages. Instead, I nodded stiffly and said, "You have a good afternoon, Helena," and left, barely resisting the urge to slam her office door so hard that it shattered.

I should've seen this coming. Should have recognized it in every cutting look Helena cast my way during the meeting. It still made me furious. How dare she threaten me! But even knowing that her threats came from jealousy, her parting words nagged at me as I made my way back to the elevators. Had I fucked my way into this book deal? It was true that Elijah found and read my blog in totality before we ever met. But had our instant attraction improved my chances somehow?

No. That couldn't be true. Elijah had been nothing but honest and transparent with me.

I hated that a single vindictive word from his jealous boss could put the thought in my head so easily. It didn't escape me that the if the thought was so easily planted in mine, just a hint of a rumor would get potential readers there just as easily. I refused to let my first book--the compilation of every experience, everything that made me the woman I am--to be discredited by something as simple and private as who I chose to sleep with. Nor would I let it push us apart.

"Fuck," I cursed under my breath. Elijah and I needed to talk about this. Hopefully, he could come up with a solution that would keep us together and keep Helena off of his back.

Get Your Copy Here

ABOUT THE AUTHOR

Often accused of navigating life without a filter, Tasha L. Harrison has branded herself as the author who writes what she likes to call, filthy women's fiction that make you feel all the feels. Her Black and interracial erotica and erotic romance has brazen heroines and heroes that struggle to tolerate all of their back sassing while trying to get them in the sack.

Tasha lives in South Carolina with her husband and two not so smallish men. When she's not writing filth she's pretending to be a photographer or riding around with the top down on her Jeep Wrangler.

She's also a freelance editor.

CPSIA information can be obtained
at www.ICGtesting.com
Printed in the USA
LVHW010948151021
700535LV00019B/1520

9 798709 936195